Strength of an Eagle

LIN WEICH

Copyright © 2012 by Strength of an Eagle
Second Edition – November 2012

ISBN
978-1-77097-385-5 (Paperback)
978-1-77097-386-2 (eBook)

All rights reserved.

No part of this publication may be reproduced in any form, or by any means, electronic or mechanical, including photocopying, recording, or any information browsing, storage, or retrieval system, without permission in writing from the publisher.

Published by:

FriesenPress
Suite 300 – 852 Fort Street
Victoria, BC, Canada V8W 1H8

www.friesenpress.com

Distributed to the trade by The Ingram Book Company

Acknowledgements

First and foremost, I must thank Keith Rowsell for telling so many stories aboard the *Anvil Cove*. His tales of smugglers and adventurers, his vast knowledge of the west coast of Haida Gwaii and keen sense of humor influenced the writing of this book.

Many others have given their support and encouragement as I embarked upon this journey of discovery. Thank you to my family, friends and strangers who have offered advice, clarified facts, read and reread parts of this book.

Although I drew inspiration from life, *Strength of an Eagle* is completely fictional. Any resemblance to actual facts and incidents is coincidental.

Chapter One

"Well, I'm game," she called to Connor as she jumped up from the grass. "Let's go."

Connor didn't need a second invitation. He quickly rose and followed Maya up the path. *Finally, success! She wants to be alone with me. I'll show her a good time. Have to take it easy, better not spook her.*

They toiled on for half an hour, chatting affably. As they climbed higher, the trail meandered through tough grasses and then through prickly stunted spruce.

"Whoa," exclaimed Maya getting sweaty from the exertion. "Are we getting close?"

"Wait till you see the view from the cliff face. It will be well worth this climb," Connor said.

As they crossed a small creek bed, Connor casually took Maya's hand to help her over a rough patch of shale. Maya let him continue to hold her hand. He was nice, and the mood was light and friendly.

Reaching the top of the trail, they ventured out on the cliff face. The view was spectacular. Miles and miles of breaking surf glinted in the brilliant sunshine. In the distance small rocky islands were silhouetted against the sky. The endless seascape seemed to stretch past the horizon. It felt as though they were alone in the world.

When they stood close to the edge of the cliff, they could see the entrance to the cove clearly but the tiny beach where they had landed was hidden from view by the overhanging rock. They listened to the waves crashing and gulls screeching as they soared above the cliff. Connor reached out to enclose Maya in a quick embrace.

Maya pulled away, sensing the clasp was more than friendly.

"Come on, don't worry—the others are way down the trail. We won't be disturbed," Connor said, holding her tighter. She pushed at his arms, shifting backwards trying to get out of his clasp.

"Connor," she laughed nervously, "I'm sorry, I'm just not interested."

"The hell you aren't, you little cock teaser! You've been leading me on ever since you boarded the *Ainslie*," he hissed.

"No, no I haven't. I wasn't leading you on. I was just being friendly. Besides you're my boss. It wouldn't be right."

"Right, I am your boss and what I say goes. Listen, bitch, women don't say no to Connor. Be nice, you'll like it," he growled.

He grabbed at the waist of her flimsy shorts. An angry scowl crossed his face as he felt her resistance.

Fear shot through her body. There was no way she could match his strength. There was no point in screaming. The rest of the group was well out of range; but scream she did.

"Bitch," roared Connor. "Shut up, bitch."

Again she pushed at his arms desperately trying to make her escape.

A murderous look stormed across his face. Grabbing her arm, Connor spun her around towards the sea. One strong shove and she was over.

****

That stupid bitch. Look what she made me do. Connor began to panic, realising what had just happened. He edged closer to the cliff face and peered over. He could see no movement other than the swells of the surf and the heaving bull kelp rising and falling in the waves. He couldn't hear anything except the crashing waves against the rocks below and the squawking seagulls. Where was she? He sank to his knees and watched the swirling mess of breaking waves and pulsating kelp. He remained motionless, anchored to the spot searching the pitching swells. *What the hell just happened? How did it get to this?*

****

"Hey, Connor. You two coming?" Jake was standing at the edge of the clearing staring at Connor. "Come on, man, we gotta get back to the *Ainslie*. The tide's almost ready to turn. You said we only had a little while if we wanted to get through that pass tonight."

Slowly, Connor got up from his knees and turned towards Jake.

"Hey, what's wrong with you?" Jake asked. Looking around, he said, "Where's Maya?"

His face ashen, Connor motioned to Jake to come quickly.

"Jake … she fell backwards over the edge. I can't see her …One minute we were looking at the view and the next she lost her balance and fell."

Jake rushed towards the cliff and joined Connor in his desperate scanning of the waters below. Maya was nowhere to be seen.

Connor turned to Jake and said, "God help us—she won't last long in there. Come on." They ran towards the forest trail. It would take at least an hour to make their way back to the landing spot. Finding it impossible to make good time, they struggled, slipping and sliding, down the steep, winding path.

Fifty meters down the trail, Sue, Rachel, and Don were relaxing in the clearing. They looked up startled as the two men came crashing into sight.

"Maya fell over the cliff!" Connor rasped in a hoarse voice. "Let's go. We have to see if she made it to shore."

"What? What did you say? Maya fell?" Don struggled to take in what Connor had said.

"Oh my God. She's dead. That's too far to fall," Sue declared.

Don reached out to Rachel as her face blanched. Shock and disbelief etched on her pale face.

"Come on. There's no time for this. There's always a chance. We can't waste time. Let's get down there." he said forcefully.

Frantically, the group made their way back down the overgrown trail. As they entered the surrounding forest near the beach, they once again had to crawl over the moss-covered nursery logs. Their feet squelched through the boggy undergrowth. The return trip was slower than any one of them wanted it to be. Panic and haste made them clumsy in the wet, slippery environment.

Finally, they reached the small, sandy beach where two double and two single kayaks rested on the sedge grass. Grabbing their discarded equipment from the driftwood log, Sue and Jake threw on their lifejackets and quickly put their kayak in the water. Rachel and Don scraped the bottom of the heavy double in their effort to launch quickly. Connor jumped into the single and paddled out to the edge of the small bay. Only Maya's boat remained nestled in the grass.

Rounding the point, Connor aimed his boat directly into the tumbling surf just below the cliff face. The couples were anxious to join in the search but a stiff wind had come up. Conditions were not good for the inexperienced kayakers in the clumsy doubles. Besides, Connor knew that he couldn't risk one of them finding her alive. Maya had to disappear without a trace.

"Stay back, for God's sake. It's too dangerous. Raft up. I don't need to rescue you guys as well. I'm going in," Connor yelled to his clients.

The couples held back at the mouth of the bay. Water churned around submerged rocks, lifting and dragging at the bull kelp. They struggled to maintain their positions in the turbulent water.

"Maya! Maya!" Calls echoed off the rocky shoreline. Nosing the kayak as close as possible to the barnacle-covered rocks, Connor peered into crevices and searched the jagged landscape for any evidence of Maya. Nothing. He scanned the seething ocean terrified he would find her alive.

After searching for well over thirty minutes, Connor was forced to give up. "There's no sign of her!" he called to the waiting kayakers. "We're wasting time. It's impossible to search in this much surf. We'll have to call the Coast Guard and report her missing. Turn and head straight for that outcropping of rock. The *Ainslie* should be waiting for us just off the point."

The group reluctantly turned their kayaks in the direction of the *Ainslie*. The wind caught them as they ventured out into the unprotected water. Waves crashed over the bows of the doubles. Rachel glanced fearfully at Don but he was intent on making ground and was oblivious to her discomfort. With heads bent to deflect the increasing winds, the group dug their paddles into the foaming sea. They faced a gruelling slog back to the vessel.

Connor sped ahead leaving the other two kayaks in his wake. Adrenaline and fear drove him towards the *Ainslie*.

As he reached the swim platform, he shouted, "Herb! Herb! Get your ass out here. We have an emergency! Maya's gone over the cliff."

Hearing Connor's yell, Herb bolted up to the deck and onto the platform where he grabbed the front of Connor's kayak. He rotated it sideways and held it steady as Connor climbed out and stood shaking on the deck. One look told Herb how serious the situation was. His friend and employer's face was stern and hard as he threw his paddle down on the deck and got out of his spray skirt.

"What? What happened out there? What are you on about?"

Connor quickly gave Herb the bare facts and told him what their next moves should be. It was imperative that they get the Zodiac ready and return to the cove for another search. Kayaks had been useless in the rising surf, but they would do better in the more rigid rubber boat with a 150 Mercury engine powering it.

As the double kayaks drew alongside the vessel, both men helped the couples get out of the boats and up on deck. Jake and Don's faces were grey with concern. The girls were barely keeping it together. Wind and waves had chilled them to the bone. Shock was beginning to take its toll on everyone. As Rachel took off her life jacket, she began to sob uncontrollably. Compassionately, Sue gathered the sobbing woman in a sisterly embrace. They stood immobilized beside the wheelhouse.

Connor gave rapid directions. "We'll have to go back out there in the Zodiac. You guys will be okay on the *Ainslie*. It's well anchored and can easily ride out this wind. Just don't touch any of the controls. The radio is there if you have to use it. Follow the directions posted above it. There's no need to get concerned unless we're gone more than four hours."

"No worries," Jake assured him. "I handled a boat before when I was a teenager. It's not going anywhere."

With pale drawn faces, the clients simply stared at Connor and Herb as the men prepped the Zodiac for the search. The guys threw a searchlight, an extra life jacket, blankets, and spare clothes into the rubber skiff.

Herb leapt into the small boat and then held it steady for Connor to get in. The motor roared to life and the Zodiac took off into the gathering dusk. Back on deck, the worn-out kayakers automatically turned, gathered up the discarded equipment, and numbly put it away.

After changing into dry clothes, the group huddled together in the galley to wait for Connor and Herb to return. It was unbelievable how quickly events had turned around. Tension was etched on their faces. This morning they had been excitedly watching a colony of sea lions and now they anxiously hoped against hope that the cheerful, confident guide, Maya, would be found alive and uninjured.

"We're in for a long wait," Don said. "We may as well get some food going. Where's the damn coffee kept?"

"I feel more like a whiskey, but we'd better keep a level head," muttered Jake.

"Here, give me that," Rachel said, grabbing the coffee pot out of Don's hand. "I'll heat up some leftover chowder and make some more bannock. It'll give me something to do, other than just wait."

The somber group picked at the food that Rachel prepared and then sat drinking coffee. No one felt much like talking, and when someone did, the short conversation always centered on Maya.

****

It was next to impossible to talk over the roar of the outboard, but as they slowed down and chugged around the edges of the rocky cove, Connor told Herb his version of what had happened.

"I don't know what came over me. I didn't really shove her. She more or less pushed away from me. Standing too close to the edge, I guess. Result's the same … she went over. My fault. I shouldn't have grabbed at her in the first place."

"No, Connor, it's not your fault. It was an accident."

"Maybe. But if she's alive, she might be looking to get even. What if she decides to ruin our only chance to make a profit? Or … what if she's *dead*? No one could fall from that height and survive—unless they were extremely lucky."

"No matter. Best we keep looking. Have to find her if we can. You'll have to deal with the results later."

Herb shone the searchlight on a spot in the distance that suddenly caught his attention.

"What's that, over there, snagged on the log?"

They motored over in the direction that was illuminated by Herb's searchlight. The light-coloured object turned out to be a plastic milk jug. They continued their fruitless search around the entire perimeter of the cove. As the surf became increasingly dangerous, the men decided to return to the *Ainslie*.

"Con, what about her kayak? Should we leave it where it is or drag it with us?"

"Let's leave it. It'll just bounce around too much in these waves and make it harder to get back to the boat."

The Zodiac rose and fell heavily in each breaching wave. Finally, they nosed up against the *Ainslie's* swim grid. After tying the Zodiac to the railing, the exhausted men hauled themselves aboard.

"No, no luck. Not a sign," replied Herb, as the anxious couples questioned them. "We'll look again in the morning. It's useless to look any more tonight."

"Well, shouldn't we call the Coast Guard?" demanded Rachel.

"No point," Connor said. "They can't get here before light. We'll take one more look tomorrow morning. You have to realise … there's very little chance we'll find her alive. Those rocks, that height—no one, *no one* could make it."

Connor sat down at the galley table. "Give me some of that," he said gesturing towards the pot simmering on the stove. Rachel filled two bowls with chowder and placed one of them in front of him. She offered the other to Herb but he waved it away, reaching for the whiskey instead.

"Sorry, can't eat," he muttered. "This is God awful." He slammed the bottle down on the table and reached for a glass. "What in hell are we going to do?"

One by one, each member of the group drowned their anxiety in booze. As the liquor took effect, they began to cope in their own way. Rachel and Don drifted off to bed with their arms around each other.

Sue and Jake, used to solving their own dilemmas, desperately fired off seemingly useless suggestions.

"Let's call for a chopper to search. Go on deck and keep watch. Use the bullhorn or signal with the ship's whistle in case she is swimming in the surf. Move the *Ainslie* closer to the bay."

"For Christ sake, shut up! You don't know squat. The choppers around here are not equipped to fly at night. Besides, searchers couldn't see anyone in these rough seas. The *Ainslie* is too big a vessel to get any closer to those rocks. Maya's probably dead, either from the fall or from exposure. Give over. We're doing all that we can do at the moment," Connor told them rudely.

"What an ass," Jake said to Sue as they took leave of Connor and Herb. "We can't even make a suggestion. He's not the only one with experience."

Herb sat with Connor for a few more minutes. When Connor slumped over the table, his head resting on his arms, the first mate grabbed the bottle and left the galley. There was nothing he could do for his boss at the moment. He disappeared into his quarters leaving the morose man to his thoughts. Not bothering to switch on his light, he climbed into his bunk and lay wide awake. Though he hoped things might look better in the daylight, he doubted it was possible.

Shortly before four in the morning, he heard Connor make his way up towards the wheelhouse.

Connor didn't go into the wheelhouse. Instead, he wrapped himself in his raingear and spent the rest of the night staring at the silhouettes of the islands between the *Ainslie* and Pantal Island.

Chapter Two

Maya anxiously scanned the cliff's rugged silhouette outlined against the sky. She thought she saw one, maybe two heads peering over, then nothing. She couldn't be sure. Carefully inching over towards a thicker mass of kelp, she bobbed in the wave action. Her clumsy, water sandals dragged at her feet, but she couldn't risk kicking the Tevas off, as she might need them later. The kelp churned in the surf. Salty water splashed over her, stinging her eyes. Cold water numbed her hands and feet causing her breath to come in short, hard gasps. A band of hot searing pain wrapped itself around her temples. Realizing the frigid water was beginning to take effect on her, she knew she had to get out of it or risk becoming hypothermic.

As the ocean's icy grip became intolerable; she started hand over hand through the kelp towards a rocky ledge. The slippery kelp leaves slapped at her face and were often dragged out of her reach by the tossing waves. Reaching the rocky shore, she looked for a place to get out. Grasping the slimy rock seemed all but impossible. She desperately felt around with her numb fingers and seized on a substantial crevice. Using this purchase, she hauled herself up out of the sea; pausing only long enough to listen for sounds of the others approaching.

Hearing nothing, she sloshed over the seaweed-strewn rocks to the sandy beach.

Maya's brain was whirling with panicked and somewhat irrational thoughts. *I've got to hide, if Connor finds me, he won't let me go. The others can't help. They don't know what happened. He'll say I fell, that I've drowned in the surf. Besides, he'll get to me first. He knows where to look.* As she passed her kayak, she quickly yanked her paddling jacket and her water bottle from under the front deck cord. Then, with another furtive glance around the beach and in the direction of the trail, she made a dash for the cove's second beach. Reaching the tide pools, she turned and headed to the end of the beach. Once there, she waded back into the churning sea to get around the far point.

Shivering and shaking, Maya crouched down behind some driftwood that had piled at the high tide line. As she peeled off her wet clothes, she was dismayed to notice a large amount of blood trickling down her right leg. She realized she must have injured herself getting out on the rocks. After hastily pulling on her paddling jacket to protect her still shivering body, she used some of the fresh water in her water bottle to wash off the blood. The water revealed a jagged cut about six inches long and at least half an inch deep. She dried her leg carefully with her T-shirt. She knew that she probably needed stitches to close the gash properly, but given the circumstances, that seemed a highly unlikely possibility. It was the least of her worries. If she could get back to her boat, she might be able to use the butterfly bandages from her first aid kit to bring the edges of the wound together. The bandages, along with liberal amounts of antibiotic cream, would have to be enough to fix her up. These days, even the ocean waters around these remote parts were contaminated to a certain degree.

Wringing out as much water as she could from her sodden clothing, she spread her clothes over the logs to dry in the brisk breeze. She cautiously stretched out in the warm sun, sheltered from view and the wind by the huge driftwood logs. Lying on her left side, she felt the air drying her cut. She couldn't hear any voices or movement other than the waves. Shock and the sun's gradual warming of her body lulled her into a dreamy state. Occasionally, she started at a sound, but soon found herself drifting off again.

As evening fell, she woke to waves lapping near her feet. Quickly retrieving her clothes from the logs, she hurriedly dressed. Memories came flooding back as she pulled on her pants that were stiff from the salty water. Would he be looking for her? Would everyone be frantically scouring the beaches, or would they have given up and returned to the *Ainslie*? *Should she have called out to the couples?* She wondered. *No, Connor would just wait until he got her alone and try again to kill her.*

The weather was becoming more and more uncertain. If the conditions in this sheltered cove were this rough, outside on the open sea they would have definitely deteriorated. She knew no one would search in kayaks after nightfall. Thankfully, the *Ainslie* was too large to get into the small bay.

Slowly she picked her way over the rocky beach and into the sedge grasses. Her cut had opened up again, and blood seeped down her leg. Pausing to check for pit lamps, flashlights, or any other signs of searchers, she ventured out onto the sandy landing spot. Her kayak was still there tied to the overhanging branches. She would have to carry it over to the second beach. Her footprints would blend in with those left by the group today; however she realized that drag marks in the sand from the kayak's hull would give her away.

After emptying her personal things from the cockpit and the emergency dry bag from the back hatch, and retrieving her life jacket and paddle from where she had tossed them that afternoon, she raced back with the gear over to the rocky beach. Returning once again to the landing area, she hoisted the single kayak onto her shoulder and trudged over the grass. Reaching the other side, she hastily reloaded her kayak, grabbed the paddle, and with one last look back at Pantal Island, launched the narrow craft into the darkness.

Maya's eyes scanned the dark water for rocks, logs, and other obstacles she knew must be there. Although the moon was quite full, the water absorbed most of its glow. The wave action was strong. She tried to find the easiest path through the small offshore islands that dotted this side of Pantal Island.

Straining to see water-soaked logs and hidden rocks was proving to be very stressful. She was tiring rapidly, as the current kept pushing her back towards her departure point. She gradually began making some progress only to end up in a tangled mess of floating kelp. This was becoming a futile and dangerous task.

Maya struggled on for just under an hour until she came to a small bay. Judging from the moonlit skyline, there appeared to be some fairly large trees on this island. They might provide shelter and screening from Connor if he searched this side of the island. Digging her paddle into the rough surf, she rounded a point of land and found herself near the jagged shoreline.

Bracing her paddle on a rocky ledge and behind her cockpit, she leaned back. She placed her hands on the paddle shaft, put one foot on the shore, and heaved herself out of the kayak. Balancing on the hard slippery surfaces, Maya floated her kayak over the barnacled rocks. As soon as she was on the rocky beach, she carefully hauled the kayak out of the sea and hid it behind the pile of driftwood to her left. Since it was too dark to see properly, she took a chance and tied it securely to the heaviest log she could find. Then, grabbing her paddle, dry bag, and water bottle, she cautiously made her way into the rainforest. Roots and forest litter made for hard going. Her leg ached and her cut began bleeding again.

Once she was about five hundred feet into the trees, she stopped and dropped to the ground. She was hungry now and her water was running low. Feeling around inside her dry bag, she found one of the granola bars that she'd stowed earlier and slowly began eating it. She had to make her stash of emergency food last for a while. Her knowledge of food that could be harvested in this area was limited to what she had read and things Connor had spoken about on the tour. She remembered seeing rosehips and salal berries yesterday on the way up the trail, and she was well aware that clams, crabs, and oysters could be harvested provided you knew where to find them. She also knew that seaweeds and sea lettuce were okay to eat in small quantities. She wasn't much of a fisherman, but there was a line and hook in the emergency daypack.

For right now, she decided, she was managing. The granola bars would provide paddling energy. In the morning, she would need to get fresh water, although that might prove to be a challenge in these tiny islands.

Most of these coastal islands were no more than an outcropping of rocks that were covered at high tide. Little or no fresh water existed. Even on this larger island, Maya couldn't hear any sounds of a creek rushing towards the ocean.

She felt the blood hardening on her leg and remembered her nasty gash. She knew it was essential to get some antibiotic ointment on it soon, before the wound turned septic. The first aid kit yielded antiseptic wipes, antibiotic cream, and several large butterfly bandages. Darkness made it impossible to see if she had cleaned the wound enough, but hoping for the best, she patched up her leg as best she could.

Searching again in the bag, Maya came up with a solar blanket package. Ripping open the tiny pack, she shook out the silver material and laid it down on the damp ground. Using her life jacket as a pillow and her paddling jacket as cover, she got as comfortable as possible. Morning was still a few hours away. She couldn't do much until she had enough light to read the trip chart and find her way out of the hopeless maze of islands.

Small rustling sounds came from the underbrush beside her. The scrabbling was probably mice or some other small rodent—nothing to worry about, she told herself. Larger animals would not be on these tiny islands since food sources were so limited; it wouldn't be worth their while to swim over from the bigger land masses.

She dozed fitfully. Her leg was aching. The paddling jacket barely covered her torso, leaving much of her legs exposed to the night air. Remembering the unisex clothing she had stashed for emergencies, she once again searched through the dry bag. As soon as she had pulled the baggy grey sweat suit over her other clothes, she felt better. Still, the scrabbling noises continued to come from the bush. She covered her face with the paddling jacket.

As she drifted off into a light sleep, her thoughts were of Chad. He would have laughed at her being scared of small noises in the dark. He would have wrapped his arms around her to keep her warm and safe. Shock and exhaustion began to take their toll. Maya cried softly and curled up in a fetal position.

Maya wondered how she had landed herself in such a mess. The tour had started out so well.

****

Connor sat leaning against the wheelhouse, wrapped in his raingear. He too was reflecting on what initially had promised to be a great tour and on the events that had led to his predicament.

Chapter Three

Connor, a short, overly muscled man with a clean-shaven head, was readying the boat for his new clients. His father had retired several years ago, leaving Connor his successful kayaking business and the mother ship. The *Ainslie* was a sixty-eight-foot wooden vessel that had plied the waters of the Canadian coast in the early 1800s bringing supplies to the scattered settlements. Connor's parents had bought and lovingly restored the vessel. Needing to finance their marine lifestyle, they had outfitted it as a mother ship and began offering supported sea kayaking tours. With freshly painted surfaces, gleaming wood, polished brass fittings, and refinished decks, the *Ainslie* was certainly comfortable and sea worthy.

Connor's parents had enjoyed the ocean life and had encouraged him to become a skilled kayaking guide and expedition leader. Though he was thrilled with it at first, he had been doing tours for years now, and life was becoming somewhat humdrum. This trip might be different though—at least he hoped so.

He had met Maya, a slender and petite, dark-haired girl in the Sea Dog Pub the night before. As they chatted, he learned that the slight waitress was a sea kayaking guide looking for a guiding job. She was eager to gain more experience on Canada's west coast. Most of her guiding had been with a company operating out of the Gulf Islands.

Since she was unfamiliar with the tides, currents, and weather conditions found on this wilder section of the coast, Connor was reluctant to take her on. Besides, he and Herb, his first mate could easily handle the workload of the upcoming trip since there would be only four clients. With the economy taking such a downturn, hardly anyone was booking wilderness tours. But Maya was persuasive and when she offered to guide in exchange for only bed, board, and experience as payment, Connor saw no harm in letting her come along—only benefits. Maya was one very attractive woman.

****

While finishing his final preparations for the trip, Connor stared at the way Maya's cut-off shorts emphasized her behind. Reluctantly, he tore his gaze away and greeted the first of the two couples.

"Welcome aboard, welcome aboard!" called Connor.

Head to toe, the couple was outfitted in expensive but practical active wear. *They must own shares in Eddie Bauer and Mountain Equipment gear,* he thought.

Jake climbed nimbly aboard and held out his hand to Connor. "Nice looking boat," he commented. "Looks very seaworthy. This is my wife, Sue."

Sue grinned. "Hello," she said as she effortlessly tossed their gear to Jake. "Here, Jake, grab these bags while I get the rest."

They seemed to have an easy partnership that told of several years of cooperation. Connor was pleased to see their gear was neatly contained in several waterproof dry bags. Since space was at a premium on the *Ainslie*, clients had to stow all their personal gear in their cabins leaving the common storage areas for group supplies and kayaking equipment.

Less ebullient than Connor, but with a confident smile, Maya led the couple, Sue and Jake, below deck to a small cabin.

"Hope you'll be comfortable. This is the bigger cabin and it's right next door to the washroom," Maya said.

"This will be just fine. This mother ship tour is a first for us. We're more used to camping and roughing it in isolated locations. Coming home to a warm bed and prepared meals will be definitely a luxury for us," Jake explained.

"All right, I'll let you get squared away and see you up on deck." Maya turned and walked out of the cabin, leaving the couple to settle into their quarters.

Glancing around the well-appointed space, Sue and Jake saw it was decorated with pictures of various kinds of sea birds. The double bunk, covered with a homemade quilt, fit neatly into the small space. A tiny porthole, high up on the wall, let in light and provided some ventilation. After sliding their soft-sided bags under the bunk, they returned to the deck eager to explore more of the boat.

Just as they surfaced, they heard Connor welcoming a second couple. Rachel and Don, in their late forties, beamed with enthusiasm. Hailing from New York, this was going to be their first kayaking experience.

While Don was jovial and confident, Rachel seemed to be very shy and retiring. It was also Rachel's first time on a boat smaller than a ferry. Enchanted by the efficient use of space, she couldn't stop exclaiming over every little detail of the boat, including their compact cabin located opposite Sue and Jake's.

Accommodations were tight. Herb, who was both the cook and the first mate, had his quarters beside the galley. They consisted of a bed and chair shielded by a curtain. His personal belongings were stored underneath his double bunk.

Connor, as usual, would be sleeping on the fold-down bunk in the wheelhouse. This suited him fine as it gave him space away from his clients as well as easy access to the boat's controls.

Maya was left with one of the single bunks in the bow of the boat. Her cabin held three single bunks, but she was lucky and had it all to herself, as there were only the two couples on board this time.

A small bathroom with a marine toilet, a sink, and a tiny shower was conveniently located between the two guest cabins. A combined living and dining area was pleasantly decorated with green leather seats surrounding a large table with room for eight. This common area was cosy and warm with pictures of the ship's earlier history, lots of polished wood and brass fittings. Up on deck, the wheelhouse with its ample seating often became the most popular area of the boat. The guests enjoyed chatting with the captain while he steered the refurbished craft along the coastline. Of course the *Ainslie*'s deck was available to everyone except in the worst weather.

Anxious to get his tour underway, Connor gathered everyone on the back deck for the mandatory safety briefing. Rachel's eyebrows raised in concern when he explained what to do in the case of "man overboard."

"Keep your eye on the person, and throw whatever you can overboard to mark the location. Do not lose sight of the person. Scream, yell and bang on the wheelhouse and railings until you get attention from someone else on board."

Don squeezed Rachel's shoulders, and she relaxed slightly. After the safety talk, Connor introduced Maya as his newest guide and Herb as his cook and first mate. He then outlined the route that would take them into the far reaches of the remote west coast islands.

"We'll be out of radio contact for part of our voyage and beyond the quick reach of Coast Guard vessels in the unlikely event of evacuation. Once you've all signed the waivers, we'll be off."

With the necessaries done, Connor smiled and gave orders for Maya and Herb to cast off. He climbed into the wheelhouse and started the engines. It was a beautiful, sunny day with calm seas. Everyone settled down to watch the *Ainslie's* passage out of the harbour and through the narrow channel.

From his position in the wheelhouse, Connor appreciated Maya's efficient movements and great legs as he watched her performed the deck chores. He wondered why someone who looked like she did was travelling alone. He smiled as he imagined enjoying a body like hers.

Jake and Sue sat in the wheelhouse admiring the skill Connor exhibited as he navigated the narrow channel.

"My dad loved to sail," said Jake. "We had a small sloop that we used off the East Coast for a while. Sure brings back those childhood memories." He then sat lost in thought, gazing out at the passing shoreline.

As they cruised, the weather-beaten cottages with their wooden docks jutting out into the channel became fewer and more scattered. Civilization gave way to wilderness. Occasionally a bear or some deer could be seen foraging on the deserted beaches. Birds, in particular eagles, were everywhere. At the end of the channel, Connor swung right and carried on up the coast. The journey had begun.

After a couple of hours of smooth motoring, Connor steered the *Ainslie* into a cove and dropped the anchor. Everyone assembled in the dining area, and Connor and his guests enjoyed the salmon chowder, crusty bread, and salad that Herb had prepared for lunch while the guests had been cruising along enjoying the scenery.

"Wonderful meal Herb," exclaimed Sue using a wedge of bread to mop up the last of her chowder. "Love this chowder. Is there nutmeg in this?"

Herb smiled. It pleased him that the guests often raved about his simple but tasty food.

"No, it's not nutmeg. I added a dash of cinnamon. I've got some recipes run off that I can give you at the end of the tour but truthfully I usually make it up as I go along."

After the meal, everyone followed Maya and Connor to a narrow swimming platform at the stern of the boat. The small deck was just a few inches above the water line, providing clients easy access to their assigned kayak.

"Hang on a minute. Got to get some footage of this," Jake said as he took out his digital camera adjusting it to video mode.

Herb, using a pulley system, swung each kayak down from the top of the wheelhouse roof. Connor caught the boats and then held them steady in the water at the edge of the swim platform so the clients could get in. Sitting on the metal deck, each guest swung their legs into the kayak's cockpit and shifted their bottoms onto the seat. Connor had to reach over to adjust the foot paddles that were attached to the rudder system in the stern of a double kayak. The kayakers were then shown how to attach spray skirts to the coamings around the cockpits.

"Here Jake," called Herb. "Don't forget this." He passed Jake's pelican case down to him. "Put it under the bungees in front of you and fasten that camera strap to the clip in your life jacket's pocket. It's a long way to the bottom."

Handing everyone a double-bladed kayak paddle, Connor launched each boat towards Maya, who was waiting in her own single kayak a short distance from the *Ainslie*. There were a couple of shrieks from Rachel as she got used to the tipsiness and the kayak's low center of gravity, but other than that, the guests were able to get into their kayaks without incident.

As Maya gathered her group of newbies around her and gave them basic paddling instructions, she felt a deep sense of satisfaction. This was what she did well. She would give these clients the best time of their lives. They would learn to love the silent passage of the kayaks in the water, the wonderful ocean life visible around the rocks and shoreline, the ability to sneak up quietly on marine animals like seals and otters, and the overall peace of being one with the coastal world.

After a few tentative strokes, the group was ready.

Sue began to relax, as she became accustomed to the rhythm needed to paddle a double kayak efficiently. As a clinical psychologist she was used to helping others but sometimes had difficulty calming her own anxieties. She and Jake embraced an active lifestyle. They relished new challenges. Ocean kayaking was very different than anything she had done before but she could already see that this was something she would enjoy.

The group headed into a picturesque cove and spent the next hour drifting around the shoreline admiring the abundance of intertidal life. Gazing down into the clear water, they discovered sea stars, anemones, and urchins. Several species of crab could be seen scuttling on the sandy bottom. Blue mussels clung to the exposed rock, and the pungent odour of seaweed rose up as they neared the shore.

Landing the fiberglass kayaks carefully on the small, sandy beach proved to be a little challenging, but the guests managed to master the art of exiting the crafts with only Don getting his feet wet.

"Damn, trust me to be the only one to get wet. Lucky I have water shoes on." Don laughed as he shook the water out of his shoes. "Hey Rach, how cool was that? The sea is so clear I could practically count the barnacles on the rocks."

Rachel gazed up at her husband, thankful to see he was finally starting to relax and enjoy this holiday. It had been a long winter in New York, fraught with business worries, a health scare and to top it all off their teenage son was striving for independence.

"Yeah, so neat." She turned to Connor. "Connor, what were those greenish creatures with lots of petal-like arms?"

"They're sea anemones," he said. "Did you notice the purple spiny sea urchins? Tons of those around this area," Connor told her. "Sea stars and sea otters just love those urchins. You won't see many sea otters around here, though. They are starting to make a comeback after being decimated in the early days, but they haven't reached this far down the coast yet. You might see an occasional river otter later when we paddle close to the shore. If you're interested, there are several books on the plant and animal life found in these parts, on the shelf in the *Ainslie's* galley."

He called over to the group. "Anyone ready for a snack?"

Granola bars and tea were a welcome treat as the clients rested on low, grey driftwood logs. Every once in a while laughter erupted as the group of paddlers chatted and got to know one another. Connor glanced over at Maya.

"The guests seem quite happy. How are you doing?"

"Fine, just fine. I really enjoy listening to you describe the marine life. Did you take courses in marine biology or have you just picked up your knowledge as you've gone along?"

"Self-taught and I learned a lot from my father. My dad knew more than most professors and never shut up about the 'wonders of the ocean world'." Connor replied. "What's your background?"

"Oh, I've had some biology courses at university but there is nothing like seeing the real thing. You have an excellent way of giving information without sounding like a teacher," Maya said and smiled. She did enjoy listening to this man and appreciated his friendly way with his clients.

"Everyone rested up?" Connor asked.

"Yup, I'm ready," called Don.

"I will be as soon as I nip behind those rocks and go intertidal," laughed Sue, referring to the outdoor facilities. She and Rachel quickly disappeared around the nearest point. They chatted companionably as they returned to the beached kayaks.

After another hour spent practising paddling strokes and exploring the next small bay, it was time for the group to rejoin the mother ship. Day one had proven to be a steep learning curve for some, but most of the guests felt the satisfaction that comes from trying and accomplishing something new.

Maya went to bed later that night feeling lighter and more alive than she had in a long time. A beautiful sunny day and enthusiastic clients had worked their magic. This job sure trumped slinging pints at the *Sea Dog*. Everyone there had been friendly enough but she was used to being active and in the outdoors. She still had some savings left so it didn't matter if there was no money coming in for a while. She lived frugally and had no intention of returning to school anytime soon. She drifted off to sleep reminiscing about her life with Chad.

One of their last jobs before his accident had been at a wildlife refuge on Salter after that horrific oil spill off the coast. They had spent many days washing seabirds, ducks and eagles with dish detergent. Those birds that were strong enough had survived and were released back into their environment. They had had little money but working at outdoor jobs that they truly enjoyed and rescuing wildlife was beyond price.

Yes, she was turning a corner. The grey fog that had enveloped her since Chad died seemed to lift a little at the edges. He would be happy to know she was returning to her passion, once again sharing her love of kayaking.

Chapter Four

Morning came early for Maya. Part of her duties included helping Herb prepare breakfast. As she chopped apples, oranges, and nectarines for the fruit salad, and then beat eggs and milk for scrambled eggs, she casually listened to the conversation between the guests who were sipping coffee at the polished galley table.

"How'd you sleep last night?" Rachel asked Sue and Jake. "I don't remember much after my head touched the pillow! Must be all that exercise and salt air."

"Best night's sleep in ages," agreed Jake. "I found the waves slapping the side of the boat a little disconcerting but after a while I didn't notice the sound. Warm and toasty too."

Don smiled. "Just don't get too used to the luxury. You'll never go back to those camping trips you guys were telling us about. I wonder what's on today's agenda. Yesterday was great. I'm ready for more of the same."

It seemed as though they had enjoyed yesterday's outing and were eagerly anticipating today's adventures. While the others delighted in her excitement, Rachel went on and on about her newly-discovered love for kayaking. She loved gliding through the calm seas and appreciated the wonderful views of the underwater scenery.

Maya was pleased as she recognized Rachel's sense of accomplishment. Today promised to be even better; the weather was wonderful, a slight breeze rippled the ocean's surface, and the sun was shining.

After breakfast, the group got ready for the day's paddling. Getting into the kayaks today was much quicker. Rachel and Don even managed to put on their spray skirts without assistance. Sue and Jake, having made such good progress yesterday, were confident as they climbed into the double kayak. Everyone was in his or her boat and on the water within the hour. Connor, who was a passionate kayaker, had decided to go along as well. Herb, who also had his captain's papers, was quite capable of bringing the *Ainslie* to the next rendezvous point.

Setting out like ducklings following their mother, the group, with Connor in the lead, made their way around the far reaches of the bay and along the coastline. Maya kayaked casually behind the group making sure that everyone was safe and at ease.

After an hour and a half of steady paddling, just as muscles were beginning to fatigue, Connor guided them towards a small cove. A pristine, sandy beach lay at the north end of it. Directing the group's attention to the rocks guarding the entrance and causing waves to break onto the sandy shore, Connor called out, "Time to practice surf landings!"

"Everyone get closer to me and raft up," encouraged Maya. With kayaks nestled in beside each other and paddlers holding on to their neighbour's coaming, the clients listened as Maya instructed them on the fine art of surf landings. "Wait until you feel the lift of the wave, then paddle like mad. Ease up as the wave crests and gently sets you on the sand. Rudders up, and make sure your camera is in its pelican case!"

A shiver of excitement ran through the clients. They were ready and anxious. One by one, the kayaks made successful landings, and then the tired group helped each other haul their kayaks up the beach and out of the reach of the tide.

A few minutes later, to their great relief, the hungry couples heard, "Lunch is ready." Connor had spread out a buffet of pita bread, sliced cucumbers, tomatoes, cheese, and a variety of condiments on a large driftwood log. Maya had helped Connor by cutting up a ripe pineapple for dessert, which she set beside the two thermoses that held tea and coffee.

"We sure aren't gonna starve on this trip," Jake said appreciatively.

"Food tastes so much better out here. Isn't it amazing how they can keep everything so fresh?" added Sue. "I can't believe they can get everything into those small hatches. Those soft-sided insulated packs sure help. Maybe we should pick up some for ourselves. Would sure beat using those cumbersome barrels in the canoe."

The group filled their pita breads and settled down to enjoy the food. Maya and Connor, sitting a short distance away from their charges, chatted comfortably while they ate.

"What's on for this afternoon?" Maya asked Connor. "Everyone seems quite capable, and I think they're having a good time. You read your clients well. I notice how you are giving Sue and Jake more leeway and keeping a closer eye on Rachel and Don. Their skills are a little weaker but they are learning fast. Ever had any trouble with clients not following orders?"

"Not really. Most people realize I mean business. What I say goes. I remember the time I had to put a towline on a guy to keep him in the group. After half an hour, he was so embarrassed he was ready to stay close. Not many people give me trouble, not even women." He chuckled to himself. Maya certainly seemed friendly and hopefully she was already falling for his charms.

Connor got up and moved closer to the clients who were beginning to doze in the sun.

"The tide's rising, but I thought we'd check out an area further up the line. It's pretty good for birding. Could see some oyster catchers on the outer rocks and there is always a good chance of spotting eagles," he said beginning to gather up the remains of the picnic lunch.

Maya flashed a smile at Connor.

"Jake will take a dozen more pictures, I imagine. Lucky he's using a digital camera. Perhaps he'll entertain us tonight with a slide show on his laptop."

After lunch, leaving the beach was a little tricky, but everyone finally managed to tug, lift, and push the kayaks down to the water's edge. The doubles were heavy, but with all six of them working together, they made quick work of it.

With a last glance at the beach to ensure no garbage was left, Maya jumped into her single.

"All set," she called. Connor was still leading this excursion, so she resumed her position at the back of the group.

As the afternoon passed peacefully, the group spotted several kinds of birds. Red-billed oyster catchers scurried over the outer rocks calling to each other in their peculiar pitch. Once the clients got used to spotting the eagles' white heads, they easily saw several of the birds perching in the treetops.

Don noted that the food supply must be plentiful in this area as the trees were filled with "golf balls." Maya laughed. The distinctive white heads of mature eagles certainly seemed to resemble golf balls. It was a little harder to spot the immature birds. Twice, the paddlers startled flocks of black-rock terns and were treated to the alternating display of black and white as they whirled away in their flight pattern. Connor eagerly shared his knowledge of the birds, hoping to impress Maya as well as the couples.

All too soon for everyone, they arrived back at the *Ainslie*. Once again, they boarded, lifted the kayaks, shucked the spray skirts, and took off their lifejackets. Rachel and Don sniffed the air appreciatively as the wonderful odour from supper cooking drifted up from the galley. Sue and Jake paused to thank both Maya and Connor for the fun-filled paddle.

****

After supper, Connor joined the guests, who were drinking beer and wine on the forward deck.

"Hey you guys, how do you like our Canadian beer? It's a little stronger than your beer in the States. The one you're trying now is from a microbrewery in Vancouver."

"Not half bad," agreed Jake. "Personally I prefer a darker brew but this one is pretty smooth."

"Can't stand beer," said Sue joining in the conversation. "Just you keep the wine flowing and I'll be happy."

Maya, sitting beside her kayak, repacked her guide dry bag for the next day. Connor's company supplied just the basics: area charts, a first aid kit, flares, a rudder repair kit, and a handheld two-way radio. She added a unisex set of spare clothes, a fire starting kit, an emergency solar blanket, a knife, granola bars, tea, and some dried protein mix she had found in the galley. Though the *Ainslie* was usually within the range of Connor's two-way radio whenever they were kayaking, Maya always liked to be prepared in case a client capsized and needed warming up quickly. Besides, tomorrow they were going through the narrow channel between the main island and a series of smaller outer islands. Since the *Ainslie* would have to detour and meet the kayakers at the end of the channel, they could be out of contact with the larger vessel. In several places, they would need a reasonable tide to avoid hauling the kayaks over partially submerged rocks. If they had to portage, a client could easily slip and fall into the cold water. Maya wasn't overly concerned. Connor knew the waters and he would be leading the group again tomorrow.

Connor noticed Maya working on her kit and came over to join her. She could smell the beer on his breath as he leaned over her shoulder.

"Here," he said, passing her a beer.

"Thanks. I don't drink much, but a beer would be great." Maya smiled. They sat affably in the growing dusk. As the night grew colder and darker, one by one the other couples retired to their cabins leaving Connor and Maya alone on the deck.

Connor, feeling the liquor, slid closer to Maya.

"Come and get to know your boss better," he teased. "Anyone special in your life? Any boyfriends I should be wary of?"

Maya glanced at Connor surprised at the personal questions, but he appeared genuinely interested and friendly.

"Was, but it's a long story. Best left for another day."

"Hmm, a woman of mystery. As for me, my life is an open book. A woman in every port and no one to tie me down," Connor laughed.

Not wanting to alienate him, Maya yawned and stretched her arms. "I better get to bed. Tomorrow seems like it might be a bit of a difficult paddle through the narrows, and I want to be up for it."

Quickly she made her way down to use the head and then to her bunk in the bow. She made sure the latch was fastened on the narrow door. Damn, she thought. She wanted no complications and she was definitely not interested in Connor.

Chapter Five

The shrill of her alarm clock roused Maya from her bunk. After quickly making use of the little bathroom, she knocked on the couples' cabin doors.

"Up you get, everyone," she called.

Don grumbled to himself, "Five-thirty in the morning is a hell of a time to get up." He knew, however, that if they were to catch the rising tide, it was essential to be on the water by 6:30.

"Hey, love, time to open those baby blues," he coaxed Rachel, giving her a kiss on the tip of her nose. Rachel reached up to embrace her husband.

"No, no time for that, you little mink. Best we get a move on before everyone wants into the bathroom," said Don.

Maya dressed swiftly in her usual quick-dry outfit. Though she had a choice between beige or light green colours, her basics did not change. Polyester shirts and pants that could be converted to shorts were practical and could be washed and dried easily. If she ended up having to rescue someone, she wasn't faced with hours in damp, cotton clothing before she could change.

A quiet bunch, enjoying a breakfast of coffee and hot cereal, listened as Connor and Maya went over the day's itinerary. Since they were in for a long paddle, Sue forced the oatmeal down. She hated oatmeal, but it had staying power, and right now lunch seemed like a distant possibility.

Layered clothing was a must for today. The morning was foggy, and the forecast called for clearing skies and warmer temperatures after ten. Maya warned everyone to be sure to bring along a pair of Tevas, rubber boots, or shoes that could get wet as there was a strong possibility of having to line the kayaks. Maya explained that although a kayak can float in much shallower water than a canoe or similar boat, today's passage might be even too shallow for a kayak with its paddlers inside. They might have to attach a rope to the front and rear carrying toggles on the kayaks. The paddlers would then wade through the water or walk on the shore, floating the boats through the shallow areas. Lining kayaks in this fashion would be challenging work on seaweed-covered rocks.

After filling water bottles, climbing into spray skirts, and donning their life jackets, the group made their way down to the swim platform to get into the kayaks. One by one, the flotilla of sleek crafts headed out into the misty morning.

"Keep each other in sight," called Maya. "Remember, we only go as fast as the slowest person!"

The kayakers slid into the silent fog and discovered it was eerie paddling on the ocean's smooth, shrouded surface. A splash sounded from the left, giving everyone a start. Laughter erupted as a curious seal poked his head up to see what had disturbed his peaceful bay. Fog clung damply to the silent paddlers as they made their way cautiously into a narrow channel.

After an hour, the fog started to rise, giving evidence to the shadowy shapes of the rocky shoreline. The sharp, pungent, almost bitter aroma of the kelp and salt water was becoming familiar to the kayakers. Quiet conversation drifted between the couples in the doubles. Maya paddled alongside, keeping a watchful eye on Sue and Jake, who often overestimated their abilities. Rachel and Don travelled beside Connor.

"Look, look," whispered Maya as she spotted three raccoons on the beach. "A mum and her babies."

The raccoons were tipping over beach stones in search of crabs. The mother raccoon hissed a warning to the little ones, and they scampered off ghostlike into the mist.

"Coons aren't native to these parts," said Connor. "Someone introduced them twenty years ago, and they're decimating the seabird population. Seabirds nest on very shallow ledges and provide a buffet of eggs for these invaders."

Hearing this, Maya felt sad as she wondered at the stupidity of some people. Everything had its place in this magnificent environment. Why disturb the natural order?

The current became a lot stronger, and soon their kayaks were drifting along with very little effort. All they had to do was keep a look out for submerged rocks and patches of drifting bull kelp. The channel was widening, and a few sandy beaches could be seen now that the fog had lifted.

"Time for a break," hollered Connor heading his kayak into a small bay.

The group beached their boats and climbed out to stretch their legs. Soon everyone was enjoying coffee and some of Herb's famous chocolate cookies. Rachel sank gratefully down onto the sand. Her muscles were beginning to tire, and she needed this rest. She was glad she was in a double with Don; he was a strong, tireless paddler and could easily compensate for her weaker skills.

After the brief rest, they climbed back into their kayaks. It was the day to see wildlife. Just as they rounded another point, they spotted a small group of deer grazing on seaweed below the high tide line. Connor explained that even when fully grown, the deer here were small, the size of a very large dog. Their meagre diet of sedge grasses and kelp kept them fed, but the vegetation was low in nutritional value for deer.

The very next beach had a small creek bubbling down to the water's edge. Connor held up his arm and pointed. "There … there's a bear over beside that log."

Sure enough, a black bear was foraging for shellfish at the mouth of the creek.

"Neat thing about the black bears here on the coast is how well they have adapted to the food sources available to them," Connor told them. "Their jaws are much bigger than mainland bears and are particularly good for crushing shells to get at the meat inside. We see them searching for crabs, clams and mussels on the beaches all the time. Watch how his huge claws flip the beach rocks. That guy is one big eating machine."

By now, the clients were thrilled at all the wildlife. Eagles were becoming as common as crows, and deer seemed to be everywhere.

At the next creek site, Connor carefully scoured the area for bear signs. Finding none, he decided it would be a perfect spot for lunch and perhaps even an outdoor shower. The *Ainslie* was a well-equipped vessel, but showers had to be limited since it was necessary to conserve fresh water in these parts. In order to replenish the fresh water supply, Connor would have to call in at a fishing lodge or refill by siphoning from a mountain stream that tumbled down into the ocean. Everyone would welcome a chance to freshen up.

"It's a little early for lunch, but let's beach anyway. I know of a waterfall up this creek and we can have a dip," said Connor. "Anyway, we'll have to wait for the tide to start back up if we're to get through the next section."

Maya and Connor helped the guests drag the doubles far enough up the beach so they wouldn't float away with the incoming tide. Using a rope through the lift handles, they fastened the kayaks to an overhanging branch.

"Since Maya hasn't been here before, I'll take the girls up to the waterfall first and we guys will go later," Connor called to the group.

With that, Maya, Sue, and Rachel eagerly followed Connor into the bush and up the steep trail. It was tough going through the rainforest. Huge nursery logs had to be crossed, and the mossy surfaces soaked the women as they moved up the trail. After fifteen minutes of sweaty climbing, they came to a rocky bank and gazed down into a pool under the waterfall. Climbing down carefully, the women perched on a small ledge.

"Wow, that looks so good—but cold!" exclaimed Maya. "Thanks, Connor, we can take it from here. See you back on the beach in a while."

Connor waved, then turned and started to make his way back to join the men. Just out of sight, he stopped and retraced his steps. He was rewarded with the sight of three naked women jumping into the pool.

Shrieks and laughter erupted as the women enjoyed the water.

Desire ignited in him as his eyes riveted to the pale bodies of the women floating in the clear, dark water.

Reluctantly Connor tore himself away and started back down towards the beach.

Rachel looked at the other women and chuckled. "No one will believe I went swimming in a mountain pool. It was freezing at first but now I'm getting used to it."

"This is one of the prettiest places I've ever been in. Just look at those ferns growing right down into the spray area," Sue declared. "Reminds me of Costa Rica."

Rachel looked wistful. "Wow, Sue, sounds like you have travelled a lot. How about you, Maya, have you been anywhere as exotic as Costa Rica?"

"Chad and I went to Belize during the off season two years ago. It was fabulous," answered Maya.

"Oh, who's Chad…the significant other?" asked Rachel. Then she caught the sad look in Maya's eyes. "Sorry, didn't mean to pry."

"That's all right Rachel. I'm starting to get over it. Chad died last summer in an accident. His truck skidded off the road when he tried to avoid a deer. He was coming back with the supplies. We were working for an outfit based in the Gulf Islands. I seem to feel a bit better each day. For a long time I thought I'd never work as a guide again but I missed it. I feel most alive when I'm on the water. I just love exposing people to kayaking experiences."

Sue looked at Maya. "I'm glad you are adjusting. It will help to keep busy and to begin to enjoy life. You are young and although you don't want to hear this, there will be someone else. He will never take Chad's place, but if you're lucky you'll find love again."

"Thanks, Sue. You seem to know just what to say," Maya murmured.

Sue grinned. "I sure hope so. I'm a shrink in real life."

The women laughed and the mood was instantly lifted. Splashing and gliding they relished the silky feel of the cold water. They frolicked in the pool like sea nymphs with their long hair drifting around their naked bodies. Arms and legs made lazy patterns in the crystal clear water.

****

Refreshed, Maya, Sue, and Rachel passed Connor, Don, and Jake, who were on their way up to the falls.

"Keep going. It's well worth it," exclaimed Sue.

"We'll get lunch ready, so don't take all day if you want to eat. We're starving. No guarantee there'll be any leftovers," called Maya as the women disappeared through the trees.

A flashback to Maya's cream-coloured skin drifted into Connor's mind. She sure was a nice-looking girl. It looked as though she liked him as well. *Hey, what's not to like?* He thought, laughing to himself.

Back on the beach, the women found a huge piece of driftwood and set the food out on its rough surface. Herb certainly had packed them a fine feast. Lunch today was hard-boiled eggs, raw vegetables already cut up, bagels with smoked-salmon cream cheese, orange and apple slices, and cowboy cookies.

"Leave any for us?" asked Jake. The men came into view, slipping and sliding down the trail to the beach.

"Don't have to break your necks. There's a lot left," laughed Maya.

After lunch, full and sleepy from their delicious meal, the group stretched out for a short siesta sheltered from the sun by a pile of driftwood logs.

After about half an hour, Connor became anxious to get going.

"Let's go out around the next group of islands. We still have to wait on the incoming tide to get through the next part of the channel. It'll be a little adventurous, but you're all seasoned kayakers now," Connor said. "There's a great beach where we might find Japanese fishing floats if we're lucky."

"Are you sure we're ready for this?" Rachel nervously asked Jake.

"Sure, Connor is the expert. He wouldn't suggest it if he felt we couldn't do it. Besides, we're practically pros now. Relax; I'm in the back paddling and steering. All you have to do is paddle and look pretty," he said smiling at his wife and giving her a pat on her behind.

Paddling conditions were a little rough. Jagged rocks jutted out from the shore and partially submerged rocks were exposed as waves washed over them. They had to be careful not to get too close to the wave action around the protruding rocks. There was always the danger of the kayaks being sucked in under the rocky edges when the waves receded.

Three quarters of an hour later, they found the beach Connor had talked about. It directly faced the ocean currents from Japan.

"Be careful as we go around this section, and make a sharp turn in towards the sandy beach," instructed Connor.

Sue and Jake had difficulty turning their boat in the confined space and scraped the fibreglass side. Eventually, everyone landed on the sandy beach and hauled themselves out of the kayaks.

"Just drag the boats up a ways. We won't be here that long, and the tide's coming in," Connor told the couples.

The next hour was spent combing through a variety of beach debris. It was amazing to see how much garbage littered the beach. Lots of plastic, mostly water bottles with Asian lettering, lay jammed under logs and up by the high tide line. A large section of useable green rope caught Jake's eye, and he spent the next while unravelling it from where it had drifted up into some low hanging brush. Over and over again, the group came across different kinds of footwear including sandals, flip-flops, and sneakers.

"Hey, have you noticed all these sneakers are the right foot ones?" Rachel observed.

Connor laughed. "Yup, some beaches have mostly right sneakers, and some have lefts. No one's sure why. I think it has a lot to do with the shape of the sole and the direction of the currents."

"What's this?" asked Rachel, holding up a small glass object shaped like a rolling pin without the ends.

"Wow, are you ever lucky! That's the kind of Japanese float that they used to connect two sections of the fishing net together. You don't find those very often. Mostly, people just find belly buttons which are pieces of the larger floats. Once in a while small, intact balls can get trapped in the dried sea grass. The Japanese don't use glass balls as much anymore because plastic floats are cheaper by far. Winter storms usually bring the floats in, and by this time of the summer, most of the beaches have already been picked over. Glass balls with rare colours such as light purples, reds, and deeper blues have been drifting on the currents for years."

Rachel was thrilled, and the others set out beach combing with renewed enthusiasm.

Don called to Connor. "Do you think this might work if we put in some new batteries?"

Connor laughed as he saw Don was holding out an old fish finder. The terminals were corroded from the salt water.

"It's amazing what junk you can find," Maya chuckled.

The beachcombers scattered along the sandy beach. Each person was intent on finding the next glass ball or some other unique item. Slowly they searched under driftwood and in the debris-filled seaweed that marked the tide line.

Maya searched along the edge of the sea grasses just above the line of shells, seaweed, and driftwood that denoted the highest tide. She found an Asian whiskey bottle and a small, bluish glass float deeply etched from its encounters with rocks and sand. The whiskey bottle still held some pale amber liquid. Only Jake was bold enough to sample it, declaring it to be nectar of the gods.

Glancing at the water line, Maya noticed the tide had risen considerably. Small waves broke on the beach and the ocean seemed less calm.

"Should get going, I guess," suggested Maya. "The tide's definitely turned, and the wind seems to be picking up a bit."

Back on the water, Connor led the party around the rest of the small outcropping of rocks and towards the passage between the mainland and outer islands. The channel had narrowed considerably, and the water was getting very shallow.

"Damn," exclaimed Connor as he felt barnacled rocks scrape at the bottom of his kayak. He headed over towards the mainland shore. "Might be time to get our feet wet. We'll have to line the kayaks over this section," he warned. "Grab your bowlines from under the front deck bungees."

Maya showed everyone how to attach the lines to the lift toggles in the front of the kayaks.

"Those rocks will be slippery with all the seaweed and slime," Connor cautioned. "Go slow, and keep those boats off the barnacles!"

One by one, the clients slowly lined their kayaks through the shallow passage. The icy water froze their feet. Soon, numbness made it difficult to feel the ocean floor. It was extremely uncomfortable wading in the frigid water. Just at the last of the ordeal, Rachel slipped and ended up waist deep in the channel. Tears rose quickly. She was already at the end of her tether. With chattering teeth, she climbed up the bank hollering to Don to toss her dry bag that held her spare clothes. Abandoning any modesty, she quickly stripped down to bare skin and struggled to pull dry clothing over her shaking body.

Once the channel deepened, they clambered back into their kayaks and quickly made their way to a sheltered bay. Gathering the kayaks side by side in rafting position, Maya passed around the thermos of hot coffee and more of Herb's cowboy cookies.

As the air, confined by the spray skirt, warmed, Rachel stopped shivering and gradually began to relax and see the funny side of things.

"Your wife has some shimmy shake, Don," Jake joked. "You should hire her out for the next bachelor party."

Rachel grinned. "I've never been so cold and I've never cared less about being modest."

The group all chuckled and Rachel's mood greatly improved.

Soon the couples were chatting about their latest adventure and a few more jokes were tossed around about Rachel's impromptu strip show.

"Look over there!" Connor said, interrupting the conversation.

The *Ainslie* could be seen chugging into the next bay. With tired muscles, the paddlers dug deep and crossed over to the larger boat. Herb was smiling and waving a bottle of rum.

****

The evening passed pleasantly. Herb had roasted large pieces of halibut, salmon, and red snapper in the propane-fuelled oven. He served the fish with wild rice and a crisp salad, and then followed it with a fruit cobbler for dessert.

"If you ever get tired of the life on the *Ainslie,* come see me in New York," Don teased. "I could easily set you up in the restaurant business. Man, you can cook. New Yorkers would pay major bucks for this rustic kind of fare."

"Ha," laughed Herb. "I have a very limited repertoire. Each tour, I cook the same things. I know what you can do on a galley stove. Don't put me in a normal kitchen."

"All the same, keep my offer in mind. We could make a fortune!"

Maya paused from washing the dishes and looked up at Herb.

"You'd make some lucky girl a great husband. A man who can cook is a great find." She smiled as she teased this quiet, good humoured man.

Connor's head jerked up from his meal. He was not keen on Maya's flirting. If she was going to do any flirting, it should be with him.

Sue noticed his reaction with some interest. She had suspicions that Connor might be interested in Maya. Problem was that with her training, she could also see some controlling tendencies in his behaviour. Connor was most comfortable when he was in the lead. He enjoyed being the center of attention and often steered the conversation to a subject that he knew well.

"Let's go up on deck and take advantage of this lovely evening," Sue said.

The tired group took their coffees out on deck. It was a clear, moonlit night with the emerging stars appearing to be close enough to touch.

"Fabulous evening following a fabulous day," murmured Rachel.

"Come look over here," said Connor.

Everyone crossed over the deck and stood leaning over the railing. Hundreds of moon jellies were floating on the current past the boat. The transparent white globes undulated as they glided past, their internal organs glowing eerily as their mantles pulsed. A steady stream of the delicate creatures passed silently by, dancing to unheard music in the moonlight.

Chapter Six

Everyone was up early the next morning, impatient for the day's adventures. After a delicious breakfast of fruit salad and baked apple pancakes, the group set off to explore the bay where they had anchored the previous evening.

Although the tide was rising, there was still plenty of marine life visible on the exposed rock surfaces and in crevasses. The couples kayaked slowly beside the rock faces and in and out of the entrances to small creeks. Connor had not joined the group, preferring to have some time away from his guests. Maya paddled by herself while keeping a close eye on her charges.

The paddlers looked up as quiet laughter came from Jake and Sue's boat.

Sue beckoned to them. "Come over here, you guys," Sue said, signalling "shhh" with her finger.

Paddling as silently as they could, Maya, Rachel, and Don joined the other couple. They soon saw what had caused Sue's excitement. Their double kayak was surrounded by a group of harbour seals intent on chasing some fish. Round and round the seals swirled, totally oblivious to their human audience. Occasionally, a seal would flip and dive deep into the depths of the water and emerge with a fish wiggling in its mouth.

Suddenly, the seals noticed the kayaks. Instead of being afraid, they became curious. One by one, they took turns surfacing nearer and nearer to the small boats. The playful seals frolicked around the kayaks, showing their soft grey underbellies as they rolled in the ocean. The air was alive with the *pffft* sound as the seals exhaled. Inquisitive black eyes peered at the humans, and whiskers flared.

Don felt a nudge on the bottom of his boat. As Rachel and he looked down into the depths, they saw a young seal nuzzling at the rudder.

"Go away! We're not your mother," chuckled Rachel.

Don reluctantly put his paddle in the water and disturbed the curious young pup. He didn't want to end up in the ocean because it had become too friendly.

After returning to the *Ainslie*, the couples were treated to a lunch of spinach salad, thick grilled cheese sandwiches, and hot coffee. Over lunch, Connor detailed the afternoon's paddle. They were going to make a long crossing over to Sontoo Island. Then, they would explore Tapla Bay with its beautiful waterfalls and meandering creeks. It was a lengthy paddle, but they should return by suppertime.

Rachel was nervous as they began the long crossing, a short while later. The mainland seemed so very far away. "What if a whale surfaces near us? What will we do?"

Connor didn't laugh. This was a common concern among inexperienced paddlers. He knew that the likelihood of a whale surfacing among a group of kayakers was minimal. Whales are smart creatures and usually keep a safe distance away from anything unfamiliar. Still, he could understand this fear in new paddlers, as most whales were much bigger than a kayak.

"No worries, Rachel," he assured her. "Any travelling whale will give us a wide berth, and those that are feeding are usually only interested in their next meal. If we do happen across any whales or porpoises, we'll raft up together and wait for them to leave the area. A raft of five or six kayaks is much easier for the mammal to see and avoid."

"Have you ever seen any whales up close?" Sue wanted to know.

"On our tours in the Johnston Straits, whales—especially orcas—are pretty common sightings. Here, not so much. The humpback migration route is further out to sea and orcas like other areas better. Once in a while, a lone whale will use this passage."

Again, Maya found herself impressed by Connor's skills with his clients. From what she had experienced so far, she thought his operation was well run. Aside from his seeming to be a little too interested in her, things were working out well. She was sure she could be friendly but keep her distance as well.

For a while, everyone paddled along glancing furtively into the sea. They soon forgot about any possibility of whales and other creatures lurking beneath them as they paddled steadily across to Sontoo Island. Reaching their destination, the group turned north and followed the shoreline for a while.

"See that point about one o'clock? That's Tapla Bay. Half an hour more and we'll be there," Connor said.

Entering the bay, the paddlers were cast into a waterfall-filled oasis. As the water tumbled down steep cliffs into the small bay, the sounds of dozens of falls enveloped the paddlers.

As they paddled in and out of the spray, rainbows could be seen arching in the sunlight. Jake paused and waited for Maya to cross in front of one of the waterfalls. Her bright red kayak formed a perfect focal point for his next shot. The slim guide smiled and waited while he took several pictures. Later that evening, when Jake took a few moments to show everyone the images on his laptop, the waterfall pictures would prove to be some of the best he'd ever taken.

Connor again felt his gut twist. Maya was certainly popular. He wouldn't mind a little more of her attention.

"Let's head up this creek mouth," said Connor. "Keep really quiet and look around you. The creek's pretty shallow, so you won't be able to use your rudder."

As they got closer to the creek mouth, they suddenly noticed eagles everywhere. Perched in the trees hanging over the creek, the vast number of these regal birds seemed to be silently waiting. The occasional eagle would lift off and glide over the creek. Then as the kayakers peered down into the dark, clear water, they saw a few salmon swimming towards the entrance to the creek. Shadowy shapes lurked off to the side. As the shapes rolled, the soft grey speckled bellies of harbour seals were revealed. The seals were waiting too.

"My God, look at them all," Don exclaimed. "There are seals everywhere. Eagles too."

Connor laughed. "Yeah, the salmon run in this stream is just beginning. They have to run the gauntlet. Usually, there are a few bears around as well. Not many salmon yet, so they're probably waiting until it's worthwhile."

As Connor suggested that they venture further upstream, Rachel laughed nervously and scanned the bushes for bears. The kayakers paddled silently, single file behind Connor, keeping well away from the banks of the creek. Rounding a bend in the creek, the quiet group surprised a juvenile black bear, making it dash into the undergrowth.

The sizeable creek narrowed, and they turned back, paddling past the waiting seals and eagles.

"It's amazing that any salmon make it upstream to spawn. This is nature at its fiercest," observed Jake. "Hand me my camera case, Sue. Batteries are shot."

That evening, as the tired guests relaxed with either a cold beer or a glass of wine, Maya surprised everyone by pulling out her tin whistle. The sleek, thin pipe was a perfect musical instrument to take travelling, using up very little room in her dry bag. The old-time Irish pipe had belonged to her grandmother, who had taught Maya the basics of playing it. As Maya played, it was easy to recognise her talent. She didn't know how to read music, but she had discovered she could play any tune if she had heard it before.

Jake then demonstrated how to create a beat with two spoons, and soon the entire cabin was filled with the sounds of people playing the spoons and singing along to Maya's tin whistle.

Chapter Seven

The next morning, everyone sleepily drank coffee and ate Herb's orange and cranberry muffins. Jake munched his muffin thinking it was way too early to get up. However, he knew the ebb tide was at 6:30 and it was at least an hour's paddle to the Narrows.

The Narrows were well known as a very special passage between two large islands. At ebb tide, an amazing variety and quantity of sea life were visible in the shallow waters. In this particular area, the currents were extremely rich in nutrients, enabling the marine life to flourish on the plentiful food. There was an abundance of marine species, including moon snails, sea stars, anemones, crabs, jellyfish, sea cucumbers, urchins, and sea slugs. Many varieties of plants such as seaweeds, kelps, and sea grasses were also evident in the clear sea.

The group eagerly paddled the three kilometres to the entrance of the Narrows. Once there, they spent over an hour floating silently and gazing into the shallows, mesmerized by what they saw.

Jake was in his element taking picture after picture of this magnificent underwater scenery. To do this, he had to hang over the side and immerse his waterproof camera. Connor had explained that no one was allowed to get out of his or her kayak and walk on the sea bottom, as it would cause irreparable damage to the delicate ecosystem.

As the tide rose, the underwater scenery disappeared. Exhilarated, they returned to the *Ainslie* for brunch and a nap.

After about an hour, Connor called, "Grab your swimsuits and join me on the swim platform!"

Everyone gathered around Connor as he detailed their next outing.

"There's a really shallow area in this bay where we can practice assisted and self-rescues. Now, no one *has* to do this, but I strongly recommend you try it if you're planning on doing more kayaking on your own, later on. You never know when you might be called upon to rescue someone. I know you and Sue are up for some more instruction, Jake. Don and Rachel, are you willing to give it a go?"

Don knew this would be too much for Rachel. She had done so well up to now and he was reluctant to push her further. "Not for us, Connor. But we'd like to watch you guys."

"Maya, are you comfortable leading this, or should I?" Connor asked.

Maya thought for a moment but quickly realised that Connor wanted to show off his skills.

"You lead, and I'll help in any way that I can. I've done rescues, but I'm not sure on the instructing. I'd like to watch you first."

The group made their way over to the shallow section of the bay. The area had a sandy bottom and was surrounded by smooth, rocky ledges reaching out into the sea. Waves gently washed over the scooped out rocks. As the sun shone, it warmed the water held within the rocks.

"Oh, it's like a bath tub. Come and sit over here," Rachel encouraged Don.

He joined her sitting in the lukewarm water. They had a perfect view of the rescue lessons now underway in front of them.

Jake and Sue were eager pupils and picked up the techniques quickly. Used to working together as a team, it was not difficult for them to perform the assisted rescues. At first, Sue had some difficulty tipping herself out of the kayak, but after a couple of attempts, she managed to get up enough courage to roll out. It took them a little more time to learn the self-rescue.

"We're always together, so we'll probably never use self-rescue anyway," Jake said, frustrated at their lack of progress in mastering this skill.

Sue just smiled and shrugged her shoulders, knowing that her husband was always very competitive.

"Anyone else for a lesson?" Connor called out to Rachel and Don.

Seeing no takers, he decided to show off a little. Pulling out into deeper water, he hip checked and Eskimo rolled his single kayak. Coming around to face Maya, he asked, "Ever done that? Takes a bit of strength and a lot of know how."

"Actually, I have. This fellow and I used to have contests to see who could roll the most in one go. You up for it?"

Connor couldn't believe this slip of a girl could even roll once. "Fifty bucks says you can only do one. One clean one, that is."

"You're on. You go first."

Connor smiled. "No, ladies first."

Maya executed a perfect double roll. Connor was up next, and try as he might, he managed to do only one complete roll.

"Wow, girl, you're good!" he admitted.

"I have a trick, and my size sure helps. You've got a lot more to roll," she joked.

Connor shook his head ruefully. He was impressed and more than a little intrigued by this woman.

****

Supper that evening was one of Herb's famous chowders. He had managed to catch a small salmon while he was waiting for the group to return to the boat. That salmon, leftover crab and a piece of halibut from the freezer had been simmered with loads of butter, creamy evaporated milk, onions, potatoes, and his secret spices. Fry bread, done in a cast iron skillet on the stove, completed the calorie-loaded meal.

"Great," "fab," and "wonderful," could be heard as everyone gratefully dug into the delicious chowder. No one had to worry about gaining weight with the energy they were expending, paddling all day. As the wine flowed, they eagerly discussed the next day's plans.

"The weather forecast is calling for a frontal system to move in over the next couple of days, bringing increased winds and maybe some rain," Connor said. "But we should have plenty of time to run up to the tip of Pantal Island before it gets too rough. The view from the cliffs is phenomenal, and the island's a good example of the coastal rainforest ecosystem. There's a sea lion colony off the far side and, if we're lucky, we could see puffins on the water." He turned to Maya and asked, "Do you want to go to the colony, if the weather holds?"

Maya nodded enthusiastically, as she was looking forward to seeing the sea lions.

"The *Ainslie* could drop us off just the other side of the colony and start back down towards our present position," he added.

After finalizing the next day's plan, Connor and Herb entertained their guests with stories of lost and found adventurers in this area.

"I have a story of a bank robber who may have got away with over four hundred thousand dollars," said Connor. He then fascinated his audience with a story of a bank robber who had escaped from the RCMP by vanishing into the wilderness. Later, it was discovered that he had left in a dilapidated canoe, from a remote native village, never to be seen again. The canoe had been found over a year later, washed up on a remote island.

However, it was the story of the abandoned camp in the middle of nowhere that really caught their interest. Herb settled down at the table and began his tale.

"As the story goes, a guide searching for new locations for his kayaking company's tours came across a completely set up campsite. When he landed on an island in the middle of one of the most isolated areas of the coast, he discovered a ripped tent with two sleeping bags inside. Logs were set up as seating around a stone, cold fire pit, and a blackened cooking pot and several empty Canadian beer bottles lay strewn around. Beside the tent was a small, red cooler containing a carton of milk. The milk's expiry date had passed by two weeks. He also found a package of hot dog buns. There was no boat, clothing, or any identification at the site.

"He called out repeatedly and waited for a couple of hours, but no one came. After a brief search of the island yielded no evidence of what had happened to the campers, the guide continued on his way. When he returned to the site on his way back, everything was still the way he had discovered it.

"After he returned to civilization, he reported his findings to the RCMP. Coast Guard Search and Rescue investigated but nothing came up. There were no records of a boat in distress, overdue vessels, or similar marine concerns. No missing-person reports had been filed with the police. A search team, sent to the site, thoroughly combed the small island with no results.

"After the story hit the newspapers, two young men came forward to reveal they had camped on the island, got drunk, and left the next day without bothering to take their stuff. They had been too lazy to pack up their gear, preferring to buy more when they wanted to go camping again."

"My God. How bloody stupid of those kids. Of course it didn't occur to them that anyone might come across their garbage and think the worst. They just didn't think." Jake shook his head in wonder over the young men's stupidity and wastefulness. "Imagine how much money the search and rescue guys spent looking for victims."

Not to be outdone by such a gripping story, Connor decided to change the mood. "Let's get some fresh air. Better yet let's go for a swim," invited Connor.

"What? It's dark out," Rachel voiced her concern.

"Best time if you want to see something really special," Connor replied.

Maya knew what he was referring to. She glanced at Herb who nodded.

"Yes, let's go swimming. Come on, ladies, you'll love this," coaxed Herb. "Last one on deck gets thrown in."

There was a mad dash to get changed and everyone gathered on the swim platform. The guests watched as one by one Connor, Herb and then Maya dove off the platform and into the dark water. Their bodies cast sparkling paths through the depths.

"Wow. That is so neat. What causes the water to go like that?" Sue asked.

"Bioluminescence," Maya explained. "Microscopic organisms in the water give off light when disturbed. You can see it best when you move the seawater on a dark night. If you don't feel like swimming just sit on the edge of the platform and swish your feet around."

Jake and Don joined the swimmers but Rachel and Sue were content to dangle their feet. Connor swam closer to Maya.

"You sure look good. Just like a mermaid," he murmured quietly so the others wouldn't hear.

Maya smiled and swam playfully away. Connor's advances were getting more direct, but she didn't want to alienate her employer.

Herb, sensing Maya's discomfort, called to the swimmers, "Who wants some of my special coffee? I can promise that you have never tasted anything like it."

With that for encouragement, everyone climbed back on board and went to change.

As they were heading to the galley, Herb pulled Connor aside.

"Hey, man, you're coming on pretty strong to Maya. Is she your next conquest?"

"Sure thing. She's the next notch on my belt. Won't be any trouble. She's into me. If not, she'll regret it," Connor answered. His eyes took on a hard glint. No one ever denied Connor.

"Hey, Maya's a nice kid. Not many around like her. Best you treat her right, she's worth it," advised Herb.

The stories, wine, swimming and special coffees were having the usual effect on the group. Sue, Jake, Don, and Rachel soon drifted off to their cabins leaving Herb, Connor, and Maya listening to the radio chatter. Suddenly, an offshore wind picked up and started to move the boat. The anchor chain scraped on the sea bottom as the bow shifted.

"Maya, come help me check the anchor chain and make sure that kayaks are securely fastened in their cradles," Connor ordered.

"Okay, Captain!" Maya smiled and left the cabin, relieved to get some fresh air. A cool breeze met them as they climbed the stairs to the deck. She helped Connor reset the anchor and made sure the kayaks were tightly lashed to their cradles.

"Do you think we're in for a blow tonight?" she asked as she joined him at the railing.

"Not too bad. Winds are supposed to pick up but it is pretty sheltered in this bay. Have you had a good day?"

"Really good. You're a good captain and I'm enjoying being on the tour," answered Maya.

"Come sit a spell," suggested Connor indicating the small ledge overlooking the stern. "My ex used to love sitting out here at night watching the sky and listening to the waves crash on the shore."

Maya sat and patiently listened while Connor told her about his ex-girlfriend who had left him for some other man.

"It'll never happen again. If any other woman tries that she'll regret it big time."

"Sorry to hear you had it so rough," Maya sympathized. "I've had my troubles too. I'm just getting over Chad's death. My boyfriend, Chad, died last year in an accident. He swerved to avoid a deer. It will take me a while to move on."

"What you need is a good man to set you straight and he's sitting right here," Connor said reaching over to put his arm around her.

Maya pulled away. "I'm not ready for anyone yet," she stammered. "Let's go get another of Herb's coffees."

Reluctantly, Connor dropped his arm and they made their way back down to the galley.

"I was wondering where you two were. I just made another pot of coffee. Are you game for another special?" Herb offered. Annoyed at being rebuffed, Connor shifted his attention to Herb.

"Did you monitor the whereabouts of the Coast Guard today?" he asked.

"Sure did," replied Herb. "Our fearless water boys are doing their usual patrol and are almost at Sara Bay. They should be up here within the next four days. I relayed the info to Mr. R on the 'sat' just before you guys got back from the Narrows."

Maya glanced inquisitively at Connor. "Why are you so concerned about the whereabouts of the Coast Guard?"

Herb shot Connor an anxious look.

"It's okay, Herb. I think it's time to let Maya in on our other job. What's the harm? We could always do with another pair of eyes on the Coast Guard. Besides, people can disappear without a trace in these parts." He laughed, inwardly thinking that if he showed he trusted Maya, he might be able to build more of a relationship with her— one with rewards.

Herb shot Connor another warning look. "I don't know, man. I'm not easy with this. We only just met this girl."

"The hell with it Herb. Cat's out of the bag now. Maya will keep her mouth shut. She knows what side her bread is buttered."

"I've made this deal with a former client who came on tour last year. The guy pointed out that since the *Ainslie* was well known around the area as a tour boat; it was the perfect cover for keeping tabs on the Coast Guard."

He grabbed a cookie and offered the canister to Maya. "My company was struggling to keep going in the economic downturn and here was an easy way to make ends meet. All I had to do was relay information, on the whereabouts of the Coast Guard, every few days to this guy's contact number in Mexico. By using a satellite phone for the transmission, the call is almost untraceable. I don't ask any questions why they want the info but I could make an educated guess … maybe drugs or smuggling. I don't really care. The money's real good."

Maya did her best to hide her shock and discomfort upon hearing what Connor was up to. It didn't help that the heavy meal and too much booze were catching up with her.

"Way too much information for me. I've gotta go to bed," she muttered. Although the boat was anchored in a sheltered cove, the floor seemed to be rising up to meet her feet. *Darn*, she thought. She had had way too much to drink. Trying not to stumble, she wove her way out of the galley.

"Night," called Connor. *Christ, I may have misjudged her after all.* He thought to himself.

"Night, guys. See you in the morning."

As she stripped off her clothes and crawled into bed, Maya felt uneasy. Although she admired Connor as a leader, she was less than enamoured by his come-ons.

Couldn't the man take a hint? She had told him about Chad. Exhausted and a little drunk, she closed her eyes and welcomed sleep.

The wind increased and the anchor began dragging on the sea bottom. During the night, the scraping sound kept Rachel and Don from sleeping well. Connor also lay awake, tossing in his bunk. Maybe he shouldn't have let on about the deal, he realized, but it was too late now. The fewer people that knew about his business the less chance there was for a slip-up. The girl was an enigma. He didn't even know her last name. Eventually, he succeeded in convincing himself that Maya probably had some secrets of her own. She'd keep her mouth shut—she'd better.

Chapter Eight

No one was in a particularly good mood the next morning. Some of the passengers were slightly hung over, and most had endured a fitful night punctuated by the harsh grating noise of the anchor as it snagged on the ocean floor. Maya sat sucking down black coffee hoping to revive her spirits. Today had been promising with the possibility of visiting the sea lion colony, but the weather sure wasn't cooperating. The wind had increased, and swells were rising. She could see white caps on the waves as she gazed out the porthole.

Herb provided a simple breakfast of fruit salad, yogurt, and cinnamon rolls fresh from the oven. Gradually, the mood lightened.

"Are we still going to the sea lion colony?" asked Sue.

Connor looked doubtful and said, "It looks pretty rough out there."

"It looks *really* rough if you ask me," exclaimed Rachel as she caught sight of the swells through the galley's porthole.

"We could make the run up there in the *Ainslie*," suggested Herb. "We can manoeuvre pretty close to the herd without spooking them too much."

"Yes, no point in taking unnecessary chances. We'll take the big boat," Connor agreed. Sue and Jake voiced their disappointment as they wanted to test their skills, but the rest outnumbered them.

Maya was happy that the excursion would be made in the larger vessel. She was uneasy about the clients' skill level for such swells. It would probably be beyond Rachel's endurance, and Sue and Jake tended to take chances. Around the shoreline, it was okay to be a bit less cautious, but out on the ocean swells safety was a different matter. Getting to an overturned kayak in such conditions would prove to be very difficult.

It took a couple of hours to motor up to the tip of the headland where the sea lion colony faced the open water. Once there, they were greeted by a fantastic display of sight, sound, and smell. The adult sea lions lounged on the rocks, seemingly oblivious to the intrusion. Adoring females surrounded huge bulls.

"The darker ones are the pups," Connor said.

The stench of raw fish guts drifted over to the *Ainslie* making the two couples and Maya almost gag. A deafening clamour erupted when the vessel got even closer. The males roared their defiance, and as most of the sea lions coursed into the ocean, the boat backed off. Maya was glad that Herb was observing proper viewing distance. The delighted guests clicked and whirred their various pieces of camera equipment. Finally, the *Ainslie* turned back down the coastline leaving the agitated mammals in peace.

As the *Ainslie* motored southward, towards Pantal Island, her passengers were treated to a rare sight, puffins floating in the rough sea. Rachel found it difficult to see the small birds at first, but once she started to look for their distinctive orange and yellow beaks, they seemed to be everywhere. Jake managed to get quite a few really good shots of the amusing birds that seemed to be top heavy with their thick beaks and stumpy bodies.

After lunch, Connor discussed the afternoon plans with Maya. "Would you be comfortable if we anchored out in this bay and kayaked over to that cove? Do you think our charges are up to it?"

Maya looked doubtfully at the rising swells, but she could tell everyone was anxious to explore more of the rainforest before their tour was over.

"If we go soon, before it gets any rougher, we should be fine," she offered.

Soon the kayaks were loaded and on the water. Paddling was a lot harder today. Thankfully, the couples had learned their lessons well and everyone rounded the rocky entrance and landed safely on the small sandy outcropping that posed as a beach. Dragging their kayaks up past the tide line, they secured them to heavy driftwood logs close to the sedge grass.

This island was crescent shaped with another beach just over a small rise. The group ditched their lifejackets and started through the sharp grasses to the beach on the other side. They were surprised to discover how different the scenery was on this side. The rocky beach consisted mainly of interconnected tide pools. Small crabs, sculpins, and minnows darted among the sea lettuce and sea anemones, and driftwood and shell fragments nestled in beside the pools. Delighted chatter floated in the salty air as the group poked and explored the tide pools.

Sue looked up and caught a slight movement from the grassy area. Three deer were staring down at these foreign creatures on their beach. She held her breath as they wandered close to her—so close she could smell the dampness from their hides. Their curious eyes gazed at her, and then they were off.

"Did you see that? They were so close," she exclaimed.

Jake smiled at her. It was a highlight of their trip for sure. His camera click was the sound that disturbed them.

"Hey, guys," said Connor, "remember the view from the cliff I told you about? Let's climb up and get a look."

With that, they all trailed back over to the cove, then shouldered their daypacks and started up through the dense rainforest. Squelching through mud and clambering over the huge nursery logs soon had everyone breathing hard. The steep deer trail wound its way up gradually and it seemed as though they were going at a snail's pace.

Eventually, they came to a small clearing that overlooked the cove. From there you could see the entire cove with its windswept islands and rocky shoreline. Waves surged and crashed against the rocks. Seabirds whirled and rose on the thermals as they hunted for food. The tip of the *Ainslie's* mast, rising and falling in the open surf, could be seen peeking over the outermost island.

"Let's stop here," suggested Sue. Her feet were soaking wet, and a blister was forming on her ankle just below the seam in her boot.

Everyone sank thankfully down onto whatever looked dry enough. Snacks and coffee were passed around.

"Wow, what a view," Jake exclaimed.

"You should see it from up there on the cliff face," Connor laughed. "It's enough to take your breath away."

"Not for me," said Sue. "My darn ankle has a blister. I'm hurting."

"This is good enough for me too," said Rachel.

"I'll stay with the girls," Jake said.

"Me too," answered Don. "This is plenty good enough for me. Thanks anyway."

Chapter Nine

After a fitful night leaning against the wheelhouse in the cold and wind, Connor got up stiffly and went down to the galley to rouse Herb. Hearing them talking, the guests quickly threw on some clothes and ventured out of their cabins to see what was happening.

"Herb and I are going to search the cove again. Conditions are reasonable and the light is getting better. I want all of you to stay put for now. I'll let you know if you can do anything to help."

Herb and Connor set out searching the waters in and around the cove. The wind had died down considerably but the sea was still turbulent swirling around the rocky shore. As they scanned the cove, the first thing they noticed was that the kayak was no longer beside the logs.

"Must have drifted out with the high tide and all this wave action," Herb observed. "Guess we should have collected it last night." He shook his head. "There goes three grand."

Connor suggested that they check the shore of the island to see if there was any sign of Maya there. As they searched, the only evidence of human presence they found were the footprints the group had left the previous day. The deer were back; feeding on the kelp that had washed up on the rocky beach across from the sandy landing. Gulls soared overhead and bees swirled in the sedge grasses. It was as if no tragedy had taken place, as if no life had been snuffed out.

Abandoning their efforts, the men reluctantly returned to the *Ainslie*. After boarding, Herb and Connor silently made their way to the wheelhouse. The couples, who had gathered on the deck, noticed the two men's sombre mood and asked no questions.

"*Ainslie* calling Coast Guard. *Ainslie* calling Coast Guard. Have an emergency situation. Need assistance."

"Coast Guard vessel *Keeley* responding. State the nature of your emergency."

With that call, the official rescue operation was set in motion. Connor was told that a helicopter would be dispatched from Port Franklin to help in the rescue effort. He was instructed to widen his search pattern and to remain on scene. The *Keeley* indicated it would change its course and rendezvous with them just after sundown.

Rachel sobbed quietly as they were told to look for a body now. There was little hope that Maya had survived. A disheartened group gathered on deck scanning the water while they waited for the officials to arrive.

The *whomp, whomp, whomp* of the rotors could be heard long before Connor spotted the rescue chopper. As the helicopter located the *Ainslie,* the pilot radioed to confirm the vessel's identity.

"Rescue Chopper 941 to skipper of the *Ainslie*. Do you see the chopper?"

"Roger, I have a visual."

"What's the status of your search? Have you located the victim?"

"Negative."

"Copy, will start our grid pattern. Maintain your current search pattern, and radio if you see anything significant."

"Roger."

After searching for over two hours, the chopper needed more fuel. The pilot contacted Connor. "Running low on fuel. Have to return to Port Franklin. The Coast Guard vessel *Keeley* is within half an hour of your location. Remain in search pattern until she contacts you."

"Roger. Thanks, you guys."

Shortly after six, the *Keeley* drew up beside the *Ainslie*, and two officers came onboard. After the formal introductions, everyone sat down in the main seating area around the large table.

"I know this is hard on you folks, but the sooner we get our questions answered the better. Memories are fresh now. Doubt can easily creep in later. Connor, I'll direct most questions to you, but the rest of you folks can jump in any time you feel you have something relevant to say."

With that said, Captain Dumont of the *Keeley* conducted a two-hour investigation. Connor stuck to his story that Maya had slipped after getting too close to the edge of the cliff. He had been unable to grab her in time before she tumbled over. The futile searches both last night and all of today were described in detail. Connor told them that he knew little about Maya, as they had only just met two days before she joined his touring company as a guide. He had not checked any references, and she had not spoken about any family. Since she had asked only for room and board in exchange for the experience of guiding on the West Coast, he had not filled out any employment papers. He knew only that she had worked as a guide for a kayaking company in the Gulf Islands and as a barmaid at the Sea Dog Pub in Port Franklin.

"Well, I'll leave you now," the captain said after his final questions were answered. "You can continue on your tour. You responsibility in the search is officially over. We will take it from here. I have all your contact information and will get in touch with you later."

As she watched the *Keeley* pull away, Rachel spoke up. "I think I can speak for all of us. Let's just go home." The couples nodded their heads in agreement.

"Yeah, let's go home," Sue said.

Connor climbed the stairs to the deck and entered the wheelhouse. Soon the *Ainslie* was making its way down the coast, a journey that would take two very long days.

****

The RCMP met the *Ainslie* as it tied up to the commercial float in Port Franklin.

"Oh, no, not more questions." Sue was impatient to get to the travel agency to rebook their return flight. She wanted out of this depressing situation.

"Sorry, madam. It won't take long. Captain Dumont gave us most of the info. We just have to clarify a few of the details."

The young constable went through the report as quickly as he could. Nothing could have been quick enough. It had been a very long and trying journey since they had left Pantal Island. By the time he was finished questioning them, Sue was close to tears and Rachel had a pounding headache.

The women ran up the street to the travel agency, getting there just before closing. Once the owners of the agency heard what the circumstances were, they stayed open long enough to book the couples' flights out the next afternoon.

At dinner that night at a local restaurant, Don brought up the fact that no one except the officials knew that Maya was missing and presumed dead. "What about her parents? Can you imagine if she were one of our daughters?"

"I *can*," Rachel said. "We need to do something. Let's get some posters made asking for information on Maya."

"I have some pictures of her I took by those waterfalls," Jake added. "We could use those and I'll put up a reward for anything that might lead to her identity."

The others readily agreed. Their flight wasn't until two o'clock the next day. There was time enough to put the plan into action—first the printers, then the police station to leave the posters and the reward money. At last, the two couples felt as though they were doing something proactive. But nothing would bring Maya back.

****

As Don and Rachel boarded the plane to Vancouver the next day, Rachel wished Jake and Sue well.

"This has been a vacation of a lifetime," she said. "Hopefully in time we'll be able to remember the adventures we had kayaking and the laughter and friendship that Maya gave so freely."

****

Connor reluctantly put in a call in to his best client, Mr. R., letting him know he would no longer be available for surveillance work. After the adverse publicity that Maya's death would surely draw, his business on the West Coast would probably fold. His tentative plan was to move the *Ainslie* down to the Baja and start a new company offering tours there. He would change the name of the boat and of the company. Besides, Mexico was hot. He was getting sick and tired of the weather up here.

Mr. R.'s cold, calculating tone implied retribution as he suggested that Connor's careless actions had compromised his operations. Connor knew if he wanted to stay alive, he would have to vanish.

Chapter Ten

As the cordless drill slowly ground to a halt, Mr. Rodrico quickly switched the battery pack. That was much better. They were running late. The transfer was scheduled for 2:00 a.m.

This was the first drop on the way up the coast. The freighter had made good time from off the Pacific side of Mexico to the coast of British Columbia. Juneau, Alaska was its main destination, but the Canadian connections needed their share. His organization supplied this northern half of Canada with a lot of cocaine.

Each man steadily worked at his section of the cabin. It was stifling in the enclosed space, and the sharp odour of sweat combined with the stale smell of cigarette smoke permeated the cabin. As the panelling came off, the off-white bricks of cocaine fell in a heap on the floor.

Grabbing the bricks, Mr. Rodrico repacked them in the sandy-coloured duffels. Ten bricks went into the false bottom of each duffel bag. He wedged a divider into place and then stacked cheap, offshore T-shirts and ball caps on top successfully hiding the contraband. Each kilo package of coke bore the logo of the Mangas, the Mexican cartel. There was a lot of money tied up in this cargo.

Rodrico wanted everything to go as planned this time, with no screw-ups. Last time, the Coast Guard had nearly discovered his shipment when they had inspected the vessel for evidence of illegal waste dumping. Just by chance, the Coast Guard had been in a hurry and had neglected to completely search the crew's quarters. Those false walls were pretty good though. Most of the crew were not even aware of the expensive insulation they slept beside.

Right now, this cabin's personnel were enjoying their evening meal. They wouldn't be back down until the last beer was consumed. Rodrico certainly kept his crew happy with good food and lots of booze.

The two workers, Jesus and Heratio, could speak very little English. He could depend on them to keep their traps shut in exchange for the huge bonuses he had promised them. However, they'd have to wait until after Juneau when all the goods had been handed off.

Finally, all the duffels were packed. The men hauled them topside. They piled them in a heap near the stern of the freighter; drawing a large grey tarp over the stash.

Anchoring the freighter just outside the entrance to Koony passage, Rodrico assigned Jesus and Heratio the watch. He bid the rest of the crew goodnight. One by one, the crew turned in for the night.

Several hours later, the soft beeping of his watch alerted Rodrico to the rendezvous time. The weather was cooperating and the seas were calm.

As his ship rode softly in the ocean, Rodrico scanned the night for signs of the fishing boat. A flickering portside light gave evidence to the boat's whereabouts. A brief signal passed between the wheelhouses of both vessels. The *Black Dawn* slowed its progress and waited off the stern. Soon the soft chug of a skiff's outboard drifted over the quiet seas. Diesel fumes mixed with the salty air.

"Identify yourselves," called Mr. Rodrico as the skiff approached.

"Rick and Mike Clifton from the *Black Dawn*. Vince sent us to retrieve some cargo. Do you have the stuff ready?"

"That's affirmative. Come along side," replied Rodrico.

The brothers, Rick and Mike, edged the skiff over to the freighter. Tying up to the ladder, they positioned themselves to receive the duffels. Jesus and Heratio lowered the heavy bags by a rope and pulley system to the waiting men. The strong and hardworking men laboured at a feverish pitch in the approaching dawn. After three trips back and forth to the fish boat, the transfer was complete.

The cargo was loaded onto the aft deck of the fish boat. Vince and his son, Jeff raised the trap door and jumped into the hold. Although twenty-one-year-old Jeff was capable and obeyed his father without question, Vince, a hands-on skipper, needed to make sure this particular cargo was safely secured in the hold.

The small catch of fish had already been scooped to one side. Rick and Mike threw the bags into the hold. It was nasty, smelly work in the enclosed space. The catch was over three days old and, despite ice and the cooler weather, rot had begun to set in. "Christ, this sucks," complained Jeff.

His father nodded. The men were more than grateful for the oilskins and rubber boots, and the kerchiefs over their mouths kept out most of the stench. They quickly covered the bags with a dark green plastic. Steel shovels scraped the sides of the metal hold as Vince and Jeff shovelled the now rotting fish over the heap of bags.

"All done, Dad," croaked Jeff wearily.

Vince and Jeff climbed out of the cavity and took turns rinsing each other off with water out of a hose on deck. Mind-numbing fatigue was written all over the men's faces. Fishing sure as hell didn't pay much anymore. Their latest catch was worth next to nothing, but these drugs would bring millions to the Mangas. Jeff and his dad expected to be paid handsomely for these few hours of hard graft.

****

After a several hours of smooth motoring, Vince saw the entrance to Bottle Neck Cove. He needed secrecy. It was too risky to enter the cove during the daylight hours. To pass the time, he set his lines and began trawling. The rest of the afternoon passed peacefully and the second hold was loaded with a small catch of pinks. He and his crew of three fished and chatted over the radio to the crews of neighbouring fish boats in the area.

"Seen any 'sporties' around?" asked one skipper, referring to the small boats based out of nearby fishing lodges.

Those tiny boats, usually holding only a guide and a couple of well-heeled clients, fished from dawn until dusk. Comfort was minimal, but most companies guaranteed a successful day. The guides were fiercely competitive; often giving the rival companies false information and speaking in coded messages to their mates. Another rivalry was also rampant. There was often friction between the commercial and the sports fishing boats. Each blamed the other for dwindling stocks.

However, today the commercial fishermen were having moderate success. Most were heading into the harbour after this day's fishing. Vince told the other fish boat captains, he needed to stay out longer to make up for the catch that had begun to go on him. As for the sporties, he didn't mind them at all. They were an inherent part of his operation. The small manoeuvrable boats were the next step in this transfer business.

The other fish boats started into port, leaving the *Black Dawn* alone on the chuck. Although Vince could see no sporties around, he decided to wait another hour just in case. Dusk drew in. After grabbing a quick supper of mac and cheese, Vince's crew brought in the lines.

"Okay, all eyes sharp!" he called. "This is one of the tightest passages I ever have to navigate. Mike and Rick stay on each side of the bow with those flashlights and call out the distance from any outcropping rocks. Jeff, I need you to watch the radar with me."

With those directions, Vince turned off all the *Black Dawn's* lights except for the running lights.

Going as slow as the engine would allow, he gradually steered into the bottle neck entrance. The wheelhouse glowed eerily from the green radar screen. Now and then, Mike or Rick called out the distance from the rocks. Slowly but surely, they conquered the narrow, rock-enclosed passage. As they rounded the last of the obstacles, they were shocked to find the *Cormorant*, a small government boat already at anchor.

"Damn, we have company! Those fish counters are at it again," Vince said angrily.

They had seen this boat before. The *Cormorant* provided transportation and accommodation to people who were employed to count fish in the various streams along the coastline. The counters would go ashore using a small dinghy, walk the stream, and count fish swimming upstream. Each stream was the spawning destination for its own returning salmon. Data collected by the fish counters was an important part of the fisheries' salmon run projections.

"Hello," hailed the *Cormorant*'s captain. "How in blazes did you manage to get in here? No one attempts it in your size of boat. I didn't even see your lights."

Thinking fast, Vince countered with bravado. "No problem for me and it's a nice sheltered cove. I come here all the time. Not much fun riding out there in the open when you can duck in here. Say, come on over for a drink later."

The government agent smiled and regretfully replied, "Thanks, but no. We're heading out at first light. Have to do the next section. It's going to take us at least two days before we can head up the strait. I'm used to seeing sporties in here, but not your kind. Anyway, good night."

After waving good-bye, Vince turned to Jeff.

"Bloody hell—we can't transfer tonight. We'll have to call Joe at River Bend and delay the pick up by at least four days," he said shaking his head.

Jeff nodded and rested his hand on the wheel as he scanned the cove for a good spot to drop anchor.

"Let me motor a bit out of the way and we'll drop anchor, well away from our friendly neighbours."

****

The captain of the *Cormorant* went below deck. After switching on the laptop, he searched for the *Black Dawn*'s records. Nearly thirty years in the business had taught him to trust his instincts. Those instincts were telling him something was amiss.

****

As the crew napped and spent the afternoon relaxing, Vince was making plans. They would have to wait until at least tomorrow evening to start unloading the bags. The *Cormorant* was leaving at first light, but there was always the possibility of the sporties popping in for lunch or a pee break. *Can't use the radio to contact Joe, but the 'sat' should be okay,* he thought. While he watched from the wheelhouse, the fish counters returned to the *Cormorant* in their Zodiac. He smiled and waved. Figuring they would all soon be tucked into their evening meal, Vince reached for the satellite phone.

"Hey, Joe, V here. Got in okay but have unexpected company. *Cormorant* is in with fish counters. Leaving at first light, but sporties are out this way too. Have to wait until tomorrow evening to ditch the cargo. Heard that the CG is out at Sara Bay as well. Perhaps pick-up should be delayed for a few days."

With the call completed, Vince set about making a quick fish stew from one of the morning's pinks. Fresh vegetables were low, but there were lots of potatoes and onions. His secret ingredient was a healthy dose of Szechwan sauce. His crew tucked eagerly into the stew and sopped up every last drop with bannock. After supper, beer and poker were the orders of the night.

The following morning shouted orders; the starting of the engine and rattling of the *Cormorant's* anchor chain signalled the government boat's departure. Once again, the crew of the *Black Dawn* could relax their guard.

Vince outlined the next part of the transfer to Jeff, Mike and Rick.

"Just before dusk, we'll get this stuff to the beach. Then you hide the duffels somewhere between fifty and seventy feet above the high tide line. Make sure you mark the location of each bag on the map. We don't need any screw-ups. Each bag has a number, and if they don't recover all the bags, they'll think we kept some. Mangas kill for much less than that."

The duffels would not be visible from the water. Their sandy colouring would blend in with the driftwood logs and forest litter. Every detail of the operation had been carefully planned. Vince was not going to deviate from his orders. The pick-up crews would leave his share of the money in a designated location in the undergrowth for later retrieval. Most of the revenue from this deal would be sent back to Mexico through the mainland channels, but the Mangas always paid him well. They were careful to keep each link in the transfer chain happy.

Throughout the day, the men tramped through the undergrowth looking for potential hiding spots. Twice sporties came in to the cove for necessities. Once the crew was on board, but the other time they were caught on the beach. A bit of chatting up of the guide and clients and an invite for beer soon deflected any curiosity that might have been aroused.

As the sun dipped lower in the sky, Vince decided it was time to start the transfer. He handed some of the bags down to Mike, Rick, and Jeff in the skiff.

"For God's sake, remember to mark the locations," he warned.

Several trips and three hours later, all the bags had been transported, hidden, and recorded.

"Let's get out of here," Vince said. "Same as before, so watch for those damn rocks." With that, Vince slowly navigated his boat once more through the difficult pass and out to the open sea.

Chapter Eleven

"*Cormorant* calling any Coast Guard vessels in the area. Non-emergency call. Switch to private channel 34."

"Go ahead, *Cormorant*, secure channel. Coast Guard vessel *Keeley* responding."

"Sam Williams here. We're supporting those fish counters in sector two. I want to report some suspicious activity in Bottle Neck Cove. While we were anchored there last night, the fish boat *Black Dawn* came in through that narrow opening. He was running with no visible lights except for his running lights and two deckhands with flashlights. They seemed pretty surprised to see us anchored in the cove. Said he goes there all the time, but that's a pretty big boat to go through that passage. The boat is registered to a Vince McLeod out of Port Franklin. He's been fishing these parts for the last ten years or so. No rap sheets or troubles that I know of. Something's not quite right, though. Can't put my finger on it, but you guys may want to check it out. We're continuing up the coast to Barkley Bay. Let us know if we can be of assistance."

"Roger that, *Cormorant*. Will pop in there on our way past. Thanks for the heads up."

****

"*Ainslie* calling Coast Guard. *Ainslie* calling Coast Guard. Have emergency situation. Need assistance."

"Coast Guard vessel *Keeley* responding. State the nature of your emergency."

"Yesterday we had an accident while on Pantal Island. Member of our crew fell off a twenty-foot cliff into the water. We were unable to locate her. Searched the immediate area until nightfall and again this morning. No sign of her. Winds in this area were bad last night. Her beached kayak is also missing. We presume it's been washed out to sea."

"Copy that, *Ainslie*. Describe the victim."

"Female in her twenties, dark hair, slight build, very physically fit. Name is Maya. No known last name. First trip guiding for us. She was travelling alone. I have no other personal information."

"Roger. Given the wind and surf conditions in your area, widen your search pattern and wait for our arrival. No matter how fit she was, be aware you're probably looking for a body. Survival is unlikely now. Do not leave the scene. Will radio for a helicopter out of Port Franklin. It should arrive on scene at approximately 14:00. The *Keeley* will be there as quick as we can but not before nightfall. Do you copy?"

"Roger, *Keeley*. Will widen search pattern and wait for the chopper."

Both messages came within minutes of each other. The sailors sprang into action. Headquarters dispatched a rescue chopper, and the *Keeley* changed course to head for Pantal Island. As the Coast Guard passed the entrance to Bottle Neck Cove, they saw the dark shape of a vessel coming out. There was no chance to intercept the *Black Dawn*. The emergency call took precedence. The *Black*

Dawn would have to wait. Whatever it was up to wasn't going away. The likelihood of finding a survivor in the ocean after that length of time was slim to none; the water around those parts didn't warm up much. Still, they had to try. The grim reality of the search began.

Chapter Twelve

Sounds of waves lapping at the shore, birds chittering in the cedars and bees humming in the salal gently nudged Maya awake. Stiff and sore from sleeping on the ground, she pushed the paddling jacket off her head and stood up. It took a few moments for her to orient herself to where she had lain hidden in the forest. She never wore a watch when she was on the water, preferring to eat and sleep by the natural rhythms of nature and her body, so judging by the sun peeking over the cedar trees; it was nearly nine o'clock.

The weather seemed to have calmed. Dragging out the navigation chart, she tried to find her position but realized it was futile without any lines of sight.

Gathering up her belongings, she made her way to the beach. She was immensely relieved to locate her kayak where she had left it in the darkness. She took stock of her supplies. Six granola bars, a jar of protein mix, and tea would not go far. Her water supply was very low. As she repacked the dry bag, she wondered how long she would have to depend on these supplies.

The harsh reality of her situation was becoming increasingly clear. Rescue wasn't likely. She couldn't risk using the radio this soon, as Connor could easily be monitoring it. No one even knew she had been travelling on the *Ainslie,* let alone where she was in this maze of islands.

She was so thirsty. Water was an immediate concern. She checked her leg but decided she'd better not remove the butterfly bandages yet, as she only had two more replacements. The skin around the wound didn't seem hot. Her leg didn't hurt as much as she thought it would.

Sitting down in the warming sun, she plotted her next move. Get water first, and then find a way out of this patchwork of rocky excuses for islands. Eager as she was to get on the ocean, she knew she wouldn't get far in the kayak without water, so she studied the shoreline carefully. Although she couldn't hear any rushing water, there seemed to be a gap in the trees towards the left.

Maya emptied out the first aid kit and put the contents in the mesh bag behind the kayak seat. Then she shook the protein powder into the first aid kit box. The jar that had held the protein mix would give her an additional container for water.

Grabbing the jar and her water bottle, she pushed to her feet and made her way over the shale and along what appeared to be an animal trail. She followed the path upward to the crest of a small hill.

This vantage point gave her a good view over the immediate seascape. Swearing softly, she chastised herself for not bringing the chart with her. Making mental notes, she plotted a conceivable course through the shallows. Then she moved on once again and crested another hill.

She could see evidence of a slight valley and hear the faint trickle of a stream as it wound through the cedars. Moving as swiftly as she could, she reached the tiny stream. Murky and rusty brown in colour, it looked horrible and smelled strongly of the cedar roots it flowed over. As she walked further upstream, she thought the water appeared clearer. Scooping some in her hand, she tasted the water. It had a slightly bitter taste but felt velvety smooth. She filled her water bottle and drank deeply. After refilling it and the jar, she paused to wash in the stream. The silky, cool water felt wonderful after the night she had endured.

Back on the beach, Maya ate another of her granola bars and sipped her water. It was time to start on her journey.

Loading her kayak with all her belongings, she donned her life jacket and pushed the kayak into knee-deep water. Straddling her boat, she carefully sat on the deck, inched back over the cockpit, lowered her bottom onto the seat and swung her legs forward into the cockpit. She fastened her spray skirt securely around the coaming.

A few minutes of strong paddling brought her to the entrance of the bay. Grabbing the chart from under her front deck cord, she studied her surroundings. Nothing looked as it had appeared from on top of the hill; nothing looked the same. Anxiously scanning the area, she set out in what she hoped was the right direction. Her deck compass indicated south, but she knew she could easily be heading into a blind passage and might have to retrace her route.

****

Maya was beginning to curse the one very big disadvantage of kayaks—since she was sitting so low in the water, she couldn't see around the next corner until she actually paddled her craft around it. Once again, her paddle struck a submerged rock. Once again, Maya found herself trapped in too shallow water with no option but to go back the way she had already travelled. It was bad enough during high tide, but at low tide most of these passages were impossible to navigate. Frustrated and exhausted by wasted effort and stress, she made for a small shell-strewn beach. She wearily dragged the kayak up into a tangle of roots and debris.

After drinking a limited amount of water, she set off to explore the secluded isle. A faint trail wound its way through the low-lying shrubs. She followed it upward until she came to a bluff overlooking the maze of tiny islands. Surprised by her lack of energy, she rested and took in the view.

Suddenly she heard a faint thumping sound in the distance. As the *whomp, whomp, whomp* sound became louder, she realized it was the noise made by helicopter rotors. Although she stared hard in the direction of the sound, the sun's glare prevented her from seeing which way the helicopter was flying. Was it Coast Guard Search and Rescue or simply a private craft ferrying fishermen to a lodge? Maya knew no one would spot her up here camouflaged by the sparse trees. She turned and fled swiftly down the trail towards the beach. Dashing desperately through the forest, she tripped over a large spruce root and hit the ground like a felled log, knocking the breath out of her as she crashed down hard. Fine dust from the dry forest litter rose in the air making it even more difficult to breathe. Scrambling to her feet as quickly as she could, she stumbled out onto the beach, gasping in pain. Tears welled in her eyes as she watched the helicopter disappear over the treetops. Maya sank to her knees in despair.

Although she knew that there was little likelihood of the chopper returning, she grabbed her paddle from the kayak and stood motionless on the beach anxiously listening for the return of the helicopter. She would wave the white-bladed paddle to attract attention. An eternity passed. No sound, no flash of light, nothing appeared out of the ordinary. The helicopter did not return.

Once again Maya trudged up the path to the bluff. As the salty breeze ruffled her unkempt hair, she gazed out over the kaleidoscope of islands plotting a path to more open water. The islands stretched for miles. Some were big enough to have vegetation, but most were mere wave-swept rocks lurking in the shallows ready to rip the bottom of the kayak. Towards the right, there seemed to be larger islands with less wave action. If she headed in the direction of the more open passes, there was a good chance the water might get deeper. The tide had turned. If she waited a couple of hours, most of the hidden hazards would be covered. It would take a while, but she was sure she could manage to get out of this maze by nightfall.

Returning to the beach, she sprawled in the shade of some bushes waiting for a higher tide. She ate one of her few remaining granola bars and contemplated her dire situation. Sucking back her panic, she forced herself to think positively. Her guiding skills kicked in as she took stock of her situation. She had survival tools, a little food, some water, a chart, and a compass. Her kayak was sound, and she knew how to paddle in most conditions. The cut on her leg didn't seem infected. She was alone, lost, and scared—but she was all right.

An eagle soared above her, working the thermal over the bluff. Seeing the magnificent bird rising and falling in the wind somehow gave her courage. Chad's mother had been a member of the Haida Nation. His sign had been the eagle, the symbol for strength. Maya would have to use her own resources and the eagle's strength to overcome whatever stood in her way on her journey to safety.

Packing away her gear, she launched her kayak into the soft swells of the incoming tide. She determinedly paddled the course she'd set in her mind while she had surveyed the seascape from the bluff. The water level was a lot better now with many of the rocks and ledges covered and passable.

After several hours and a few wrong turns, she found herself in a more open area. A harbour seal followed the kayak for a while, poking its head up every few meters. Its limpid eyes inquisitively following her progress.

The afternoon passed quickly, and the sun began to slide behind the islands in back of her. As dusk fell, she pointed her kayak towards one of the outer islands facing the strait. This would be home for the night. Paddling after dark was simply not feasible. Last night's adventures had proven that.

****

Seeing a small sandy beach surrounded by a thick growth of stunted cedars, she thought it would be a great landing spot. This side of the large island was a good place to camp, Maya decided, as it was sheltered from the offshore winds and had a good view of the strait.

Hauling the kayak out of the chuck, she secured the sleek craft to branches of a cedar tree. Unfastening the hatches, she removed her gear and made her way over the sand to the high tide line. Behind a pile of driftwood, she found a fairly level sandy area that might do for the night. By wedging the space blanket between a couple of logs, she managed to rig a shelter tall enough to lie down under. Searching the bordering forest, she gathered a few cedar boughs and handfuls of dry moss to complete her bed. These might serve to make her a little more comfortable and keep her off the now cooling sand.

She had to find food. The granola bars were running low and had only provided her with minimal paddling energy. Unfortunately, it was getting really dark and it was impossible to see beyond the faint beam of the emergency flashlight.

She knew she had to conserve the batteries, so she quickly collected small pieces of driftwood and pulled fibrous old man's beard from the trees. Scrabbling in the dry bag, she came up with the tin of matches. Then, after setting the old man's beard inside a pyramid of driftwood, she struck a match and lit her meagre fire. She didn't worry about anyone seeing the flames. Since the helicopter had not flown over again, she knew there was little hope of rescue. She would have to get out on her own.

By using the light given off by the fire, she managed to gather bigger pieces of driftwood and more dry cedar branches. Adding these carefully, she nurtured her fragile fire.

The fire soon provided welcome warmth, but Maya knew she still needed food. With no container to cook anything in, she was restricted to whatever could be consumed raw. Hunger pains gnawed at her stomach, and her head was beginning to ache. Visions of potatoes, coffee, and homemade bread danced at the edge of her mind. She would have to reserve her remaining granola bars for emergency situations.

Since darkness had closed in, she was reluctant to wander far from the fire, so digging for clams and gathering berries or seaweed would have to wait until daylight. She pulled out the first aid kit and scooped a good portion of the dried protein mix into the water jar. Sipping slowly, she pretended it was a milkshake.

As her hunger pains lessened, the events of the day caught up to her. She was bone weary. The warmth of the fire made her sleepy. Maya picked up the emergency flashlight and made her way down to the water's edge. After taking care of her toilet necessities, she returned to the safety of the fire. Shucking out of her paddling shorts and T-shirt, she pulled the grey sweat suit on and jammed her hat on her head. Maya knew she would lose a lot of body heat if she left her head uncovered. Throwing more driftwood on the fire, she gathered up her life jacket for a pillow, her paddling jacket for cover, and her paddle for protection, and then slid under the space blanket. After a lot of shuffling, wiggling, and moving around, she finally got comfortable. She drifted off to sleep lulled by the sounds of ocean waves breaking on the beach and the comforting crackling of the driftwood fire.

Chapter Thirteen

A heavy slithering sound woke Maya at first light. Startled out of a deep sleep, it took her a few moments to figure out that she was lying curled up in her makeshift shelter. Again the heavy slithering sound reverberated in the silent dawn. *What on earth could that be?* As far as she knew, there were no snakes on these islands. *Snakes can't swim this far, can they?* She thought. Peering out from under the low-slung space blanket, she came face-to-face with a huge river otter.

With its fur sleek and shining from seawater, the large animal had obviously just come from catching breakfast in the bay. Slimy mucus flew from its snout as it whipped its head around to fully take in his surprise visitor. The otter dropped its fishy breakfast and with a throaty hiss, fled into the nearby bushes.

Maya laughed in relief. Company and now here was breakfast! Rescuing the fish from the sand, she put it on top of a low-lying bush. She was not about to lose that fish.

The weather looked promising. A slight breeze blew over the little beach, and the sea looked quite calm. However, glancing around, she saw clouds building on the horizon. She had no idea what the forecast was. The radio in the emergency pack was only a short-range one for guides paddling with their clients to contact the mother ship. It was virtually useless to her. The *Ainslie* and Pantal Island were too far away now. Besides, Connor was at the other end of the radio's range.

Stripping off her clothes, she waded out into the gentle surf. Lying down, she let the cold water lap over her body. She grabbed a handful of seaweed and smoothed it over her skin, then raked her fingers through her wet hair letting the sea rinse away the grime of the past two days. Chilled, she rose out of the water and shucked as much of the salt water as she could from her body and wrung out her tangled tresses. After using the top of the sweat suit to dry herself as best she could, she dressed quickly in her paddling clothes and spread the grey top over a nearby log to dry in the sun.

Now she had to cook that fish. Maya rebuilt her fire with more driftwood and old man's beard. The fire caught quickly as the coals still had some heat from last night's fire. Thankful that she had a knife in her kit, Maya set about gutting the river otter's gift. When she was little, her dad had frequently taken her fishing. His philosophy had been "you catch it, you clean it and you eat it." Her dad had taught her well, and in no time she had the gutted fish skewered on a fresh cedar stick. Maya added more wood to the fire and then let it burn down a bit. Squatting on her hunches, she slowly roasted the seven-inch fish over the coals. The delicious aroma of the semi-cooked fish made Maya almost sick from hunger. Unable to wait any longer, she stripped away the flesh from the stick and shoved it in her mouth.

Once again, the clouds gathering on the horizon gave her concern. The wind seemed to be picking up a little bit as well. If the weather turned, she might have trouble paddling in open water, especially since she was exhausted and hadn't eaten much the last couple of days. Maya decided to stay put on the island for the time being.

With her decision made, she tidied up her campsite and pulled out her chart. Judging from the lay of the land, this island was one of the last ones before the open waters of the strait that separated the outer islands and the mainland.

It would take several hours in good weather to cross the strait in a kayak. In bad weather, she risked capsizing in the swells. Performing self-rescue in ocean swells was dangerous. It would be foolhardy to attempt to cross such a big channel in anything but good conditions.

Other problems arose on long crossings too. Her legs might cramp from sitting so long. The very real need to go to the bathroom would also be a trial. In a pinch, she could stretch her legs in the cockpit. She knew it was possible but not fun for women to pee in a kayak, but only if the ocean swells were small enough not to risk tipping over.

Water was also a concern. She would not have enough water using only her water bottle and the protein mix jar. She had to increase her water storage capabilities. She would have to find more containers and a good source of fresh water. With this in mind, Maya set off to explore her temporary kingdom.

****

Making her way along the shoreline, she left the small sandy alcove and clambered over the slippery, seaweed-covered rocks and past the next point. Since she had excellent balance, she was pretty surefooted when jumping from boulder to boulder and traversing the many driftwood logs that seemed to litter the island.

The very next beach was chock full of logs and debris carried in on the currents that swirled around this part of the island. It was a treasure trove of junk and garbage. She found several plastic water bottles with Asian lettering on them. Piling them neatly on a flat rock, she explored further. Near the edge of the bushes she saw a piece of blue material. Curious, Maya scrambled over to it.

Memories of Connor and Herb's stories of lost and found adventurers came flooding back as she gazed at what appeared to be the leftovers of a campsite. An old blue tarpaulin was stretched between two stunted cedars and a large driftwood log. The thin rope that had held the tarp in place had come unfastened on the fourth side, leaving the material to flap in the breeze. Crude benches constructed from driftwood surrounded a charred, stone fire pit. Just as in Herb's story, there was evidence of a party. Beer bottles and a half-empty bottle of Yukon Jack lay abandoned in the sand. A large white Styrofoam cooler was wedged on its side against a chunk of rock. In the middle of the fire pit was a blackened pot with some unidentifiable substance crusted on the bottom.

Shading her eyes from the sun's glare, she scanned the beach for signs of the campers. There was no boat that she could see. No clothes or sleeping bags were left under the tarp. Dragging the cooler from its position against the rock, she opened it. The stench of rotten meat immediately overwhelmed her, making her retch. In the bottom of the cooler was what looked like a slimy package of congealed hotdogs. Obviously no one had been there for several days. She quickly replaced the lid, shutting in the nauseating odour.

Maya marvelled at her luck. She could make good use out of a lot of this stuff. Trying to untie the knots in the ropes proved to be impossible, as the salt air and winds had done a good job of tightening the fibres. So instead, she sawed and hacked at the ropes with her knife, preserving as much of the rope as possible, until the tarp was free. After folding the tarp to a manageable size, she laid it on the ground and then placed the crusted cooking pot, plastic water bottles, and the bottle of Yukon in the middle. Carefully gathering the edges together, she made herself a clumsy package.

Her journey back to her beach was much slower this time, but she had treasures. Treasures that would might make a huge difference to her chances for survival.

Back at camp, she once again took stock of her situation. The weather appeared to be closing in for a few days. Rain seemed very likely. The increasing wind had brought a chill to the air.

Rigging the tarpaulin in the trees, she constructed a barrier against the rain and wind that would come from the open ocean. She made a fire pit on the opposite side, so that the tarp would deflect the elements away from the fire and she would still be able to retain some warmth without getting smoked out. Dragging the cedar boughs and moss out from beneath her space blanket, she reconstructed her bed. This time she could use the blanket as cover.

Remembering her sweat suit top spread on the log, she dashed down the beach to get it. She hauled all her gear into the lean-to and retied her kayak further inland away from the high tide line. Next she gathered as many small pieces of driftwood and as much old man's beard as she could manage, piling it under the shelter within easy reach. Maya was quite satisfied with her cosy, little camp.

With the skies beginning to darken with the incoming storm, food and water were her next priorities. Using coarse sand and the salt water, she scrubbed the dirty cooking pot until there was no evidence of the unknown leftover food. Loading the clean pot with her water bottle, the protein jar, and the plastic bottles she had found on the rocky beach, she set off in the opposite direction from this morning's adventure. There had been no evidence of any streams on that beach. She would have to go further and probably higher to get to a source of fresh water.

Just as she was beginning to worry that there was no fresh water on the island, she heard the welcome sound of water tumbling down towards the sea. Climbing higher into the forest, she discovered a beautiful waterfall. Water cascaded over a mossy ledge and splashed into a rocky pool that was surrounded by ferns and mosses growing in abundance. A variety of birds flew in and out of the bushes and spindly trees.

Since there were few cedar trees in the vicinity, the water didn't have that pungent, earthy smell. Scooping the sparkling liquid in her hand, Maya tasted the cool water. It was refreshing and sweet. She filled every container she had brought with her. Most of the plastic bottles didn't have tops, so she had to wedge them upright in the cooking pot, packing them in with handfuls of moss. Slowly and carefully, she retraced her steps down the hillside and back to her campsite.

Once she was back at camp, she quickly set about collecting food. Down by the tide line, she used a flat rock to scoop away the sand, revealing a few clams and oysters. She gathered sea lettuce and another kind of seaweed that looked promising. Clinging to the seaweed was a small crab, so he was added to her assortment of edibles.

Using her knife, she managed to pry open the shellfish and scrape the slippery creatures into the pot. Squeamish about cooking the crab alive, she stabbed it and then threw it and the seaweed into the shellfish mixture. She covered the collection with some of the fresh water.

As the chowder cooked over the open fire, Maya thought of Herb's wonderful fish dishes. She had liked him and had enjoyed his company. He probably thought she had drowned. Instead, here she was creating her own chowder; she could hardly wait to taste her concoction.

Chapter Fourteen

Once again, Maya was awakened in the early morning to sounds that were hard to identify. Although she was a good distance from the water's edge, she heard what seemed like stones being turned as waves lapped at the shore. Half expecting to find her campsite almost under water, she peered out from her shelter. No, the ocean was still a respectable distance from the camp, and she could see her kayak still firmly tied to the driftwood.

Again the noise came. Quietly, holding her breath, she crept out of her blue tinged world and into the morning light. There, not fifty feet away was the river otter; flipping the discarded clam and oyster shells that she had thrown out last night. *For heaven sakes! I should be more careful,* she thought. If this had been the mainland, her visitor could easily have been a black bear. Lesson learned. She would have to be much more cautious and remember to cache her food when she arrived on the other side of the strait.

It drizzled with rain all day, forcing her to spend the dismal day sheltered under her makeshift roof, feeding the fire and occasionally foraging for dry wood and foodstuffs.

Alone with her thoughts, she grew tearful. So much had happened to her this last year, none of it good. After Chad was killed in the truck accident, her life seemed to implode. She had trouble getting out of bed, could no longer focus on her studies at the university. She withdrew from her friends. At the urging of her mother, she tried seeing the university counsellor, but it was of little use.

Needing a change of scenery, she packed up her belongings and left school. With her kayak strapped to the top of her reliable Toyota, she had travelled north looking for work. Most people had been kind to her, but work was hard to find.

Eventually she found a job working in the Sea Dog Pub in Port Franklin. The small, dark pub catered to locals and tourists alike. Occasionally there was live music on the weekends to help attract customers. She was friendly and chatted easily with everyone. Although the job wasn't hard, the hours were long. When the opportunity to work on the *Ainslie* came up, she didn't hesitate. She had lots of experience, as she and Chad had spent every summer since they met guiding for various kayaking companies. She loved kayaking, and with her excellent people skills she usually gave the clients a positive and memorable experience. Remembering those carefree summers with Chad brought tears and sobs. Giving in to her emotions, she sat in the shelter and wept.

As the day wore on, she became more and more despondent. Knowing that she could not take the chance of spiralling into a depression that would sap her energy and motivation; she decided to visit the waterfalls once again. *Keep busy and suck it up,* she told herself.

The skies had cleared a bit and the sun's warmth felt good on her shoulders as she made her way up the steep hillside. Maya heard the birds chittering in the salal and the bees buzzing in and out the Saskatoon bushes. There were berries ripening everywhere. Red Huckleberries seemed to be ready to eat and the Saskatoon's were starting to darken.

Reaching the waterfall, she stripped out of her dirty clothes and waded carefully into the rock pool. Feeling the bottom cautiously with her feet, she crossed the pool and sat on the mossy ledge just under the water spray. It was like sitting in the mist. Rainbows appeared through the spray and danced in the sunlight. The cool water cleansed her body and her spirit.

Reluctantly, Maya got out of the pool and dried herself off with her shirt. Since she was alone on the island, there was no need for modesty. Grabbing her grubby clothes, she gave them a good rinse in the water. After wringing them out, she gathered the clothes into a bundle and started back down the hillside.

The air cooled her skin. She felt a bit ridiculous tramping through the woods buck naked except for the Tevas on her feet. She could imagine Chad getting a charge out of such an absurd sight. Halfway down the path, she stopped to pick as many berries as her hat would hold. Eating handfuls of delicious fruit, she continued to her campsite, where she laid out her clothes to dry.

With her mood much improved, Maya set about digging for clams and oysters for supper. This time she would let them soak in a pot of salt water for a while to rid of the shellfish of the sand they ingested. Last night's supper had been more than a bit crunchy. She sat on a rock jutting out into the ocean and fished for a while using the emergency fishing gear and clam meat for bait. After successfully catching two small rock cod, she gutted and filleted them as best she could.

When the oysters and clams had soaked for a good while, she shucked them and combined all the ingredients, including some seaweed for a bit of bulk, with fresh water in the old cooking pot. Setting the mixture carefully over the coals in the fire pit, she waited for the slow simmering fish stew to be done.

To make the time pass while she waited hungrily, Maya tried fishing again. Watching the eagles soaring over the rocky point and occasionally diving into the water gave her an idea. The eagles knew where the fish were, so she would follow their lead. Maya relocated to the rocky point, cast out her line, and almost immediately caught a fair-sized salmon.

It was difficult to bring in the heavy, fighting fish on a hand-held line. She waited for it to take a rest and then jerked it out of the water. It landed with a flop on the rocks behind her. Immediately, screaming gulls surrounded her. Waving her arms frantically, she drove off the scavengers from her catch. Quickly, she gutted the salmon, throwing the entrails into the ocean. Once again, the air was filled with gulls screeching as they fought over the scraps.

Maya cut the salmon into long strips and skewered the pieces on cedar branches. After supper, she would roast these kabobs over the flames. She was planning to save the fish for the trip to the mainland. Even so, tomorrow she would need to gather even more food and get ready for the arduous journey across the open water.

Dressed in her dry clothes, she enjoyed her supper and washed it down with some tea from her emergency supplies. She then set about cooking the salmon pieces over the coals. There was some protein powder left, so she decided to mix up a thick soup-like mixture and poured it into a couple of the Asian water bottles. Since the containers had no tops, Maya used compressed moss to stopper the plastic bottles. The emergency kit, now empty, became a perfect canister for the roasted salmon pieces.

Remembering the otter's visit this morning, Maya opened the front hatch of her kayak and stored the bottles and the container of fish. She resealed the hatch with its neoprene cover and then secured the fibreglass hatch down with the cinch straps, making it safe from any midnight visitors. After cleaning the campsite, she washed the cooking pot in the ocean.

Darkness was closing in rapidly. Scrambling into the grey sweat suit, she got ready to turn in for the night. It had been days since she had brushed her teeth, so she improvised with a soft, frayed cedar twig. The pungent earthy smell tickled her nose as she scrubbed gently at her teeth and gums. Making sure she had the flashlight handy and her paddle beside her, she settled into her nest of cedar and moss.

Since she had not had much exercise that day, sleep proved to be elusive. She tossed and turned trying to get comfortable. She lay listening to the night noises coming from the surrounding forest. After what seemed like forever, Maya rummaged around and found the half-empty bottle of Yukon Jack. Taking tiny sips of the strong liquor, she drifted off into pleasant memories and eventually into a dreamless sleep.

Chapter Fifteen

She woke later than usual the next morning, with a slight headache and desperately thirsty. The nearly empty liquor bottle prompted her recall of the night before. Chastising herself for being so stupid as to drink when she was all alone on some godforsaken island in the middle of nowhere, she drank most of her remaining water.

Everything, however, looked so much better in the daylight and the sun was starting to show through the clouds. Today, she needed to get her act together and ready herself and the kayak for the crossing. The weather was improving, and with any luck she would be able to launch tomorrow.

Forming a mental checklist, Maya began addressing her tasks. She checked to see that the salmon stored in the hatch was still okay. She counted her water containers and realized that since she had used some for storing the protein mixture, she would have to collect a few more. Berries and granola bars would be easy to snack on as she paddled. With only two bars left, she would need to gather more berries. Aside from collecting food and water, she needed to check that the kayak was in good repair. It might be a good idea to try to make some kind of a sail that she could attach to her kayak. It would certainly help if she could take advantage of the wind on such a long paddle.

After finishing up one of the bottles of protein mixture, she set off to the rocky beach that was full of ocean garbage. This time she was lucky enough to find three two-litre bottles that were in pretty good shape. She also discovered some thin twine and two fairly-straight pieces of worn timber from a wooden packing case.

Returning to the campsite, she tried fashioning her sail. Reluctant to destroy her tarpaulin, she attempted to use the space blanket. The slippery material proved very difficult to work with, so she was forced to cut a piece from the blue tarp. Choosing a corner portion, roughly three feet by five feet, she used her knife to stab two rows of holes parallel to two of the edges.

Maya sewed the fabric with twine around the pieces of timber, wrapping the edges over the ends of the wood. She then bound the wood together at the bottom with the rope, forming a triangle of sail. Since she couldn't figure out a way to attach the sail to the kayak, she knew she would have to hold the sail upright with the bound end down in the cockpit in front of her. She was quite optimistic that it just might work.

She took time out from her preparations to fish for a while, successfully catching three small rock cod for supper. After gutting and cleaning them, she hid them in the kayak's front hatch. She had to make another trip to the waterfall to replenish her water supply and to gather berries. Maya didn't want the gulls or the otter stealing her prizes.

Gathering up her water containers, she set off once again to the oasis in the bush. The vision of the water cascading over the mossy rocks was a welcome sight, as the day was growing increasingly warm. She enjoyed the coolness of the water as she waded over to the deeper part and immersed herself in the refreshing pool.

Under the right circumstances, this would be close to paradise. Listening to the surrounding forest, it was not hard to imagine a long-ago culture living here on this island. The natives would have subsisted on food foraged in the forest, fishing, and gathering whatever shellfish were in season; their shelters would have been constructed mainly from cedar wood; there was an adequate supply of fresh water, and the small bay afforded shelter from the storms. Yes, this might have been a perfect place for a camp, especially a fishing camp, Maya decided.

She could have easily spent most of the afternoon lost in thought, but time was moving on. Dressing quickly in her discarded clothes, she filled most of her bottles and jars. On the way down to the beach, she filled the remaining bottles with berries. It was a slow trip back since she had so much to carry. The moss stoppers in the bottles worked because she was carrying the bottles upright, but she wondered how she would manage them in the kayak.

After ensuring the rudder was working properly, she emptied the kayak's front and rear hatches. She retrieved the first aid items from the mesh bag behind the kayak seat. While tossing the first aid materials into the front hatch, she realised she could use adhesive tape to seal some of the bottle tops. If she wedged the bigger bottles behind her seat, they would stay upright and be handy for her to reach. She sealed the smaller water bottles and put them into the front hatch along with the cooked salmon and most of the protein mixture. These supplies were for later, as she might be landing after dark and be too exhausted to look for food and water.

She gathered some small, dry pieces of driftwood and some old man's beard as fire starter and put them into the back hatch. Her tarp, clothing, and the rest of her equipment would go in the back hatch in the morning.

She sat on the beach, sipping her tea from a chipped cup she had found that morning, watching a most beautiful sunset. The small islands in front of her were silhouetted against the deepening orange hue. "Red sky at night, sailor's delight," Maya said to herself. Tomorrow was promising to be a good day, at least weather wise. Just as she silently hoped the crossing would go smoothly, an eagle took off from its perch in the stunted hemlock.

****

After a restless night of shifting and turning to get comfortable and dreaming of alternately pleasant and horrific scenarios of tomorrow's crossing, Maya was awake and eager to go.

She examined the wound on her leg. It was healing nicely and seemed to need no further treatment. She started to dress in her kayaking clothes. Since her legs would be tucked into the cockpit and shielded by the spray skirt, she put on her quick-dry shorts. She then layered her other clothing: sports bra, cotton T-shirt, and a quick-dry long-sleeved shirt. She would also wear her paddling jacket that she planned to store in the kayak's cockpit if the weather warmed up enough. Right now there was a cloudy, overcast sky and a chilly wind from the north.

While hastily eating some cold leftovers from last night's supper, she consulted the chart. She would reach a few scattered islands before she had to venture onto the open ocean. By leapfrogging from island to island, she could make quite a bit of progress before tackling the long slog to the mainland.

She set about packing the remainder of her gear into the back hatch. After stretching the neoprene cover over the opening, she fastened the solid hatch cover using the cinch straps. Then she secured the rescue float, pump, and spare paddle over the back hatch and wedged the homemade sail under the back deck chords just behind her seat. She stowed her remaining granola bars in her paddling jacket pocket and put the bottles with berries inside the cockpit beside the seat. Most importantly, the large bottles of extra water were squished in behind her seat back. Her stainless steel water bottle was located in its usual place within easy reach, under the front deck chord.

Reaching inside the kayak for her sunscreen that she always kept in the cockpit, she applied a liberal amount to her face, particularly to her nose and ears, and slipped on a generous amount of lip balm. Checking that her knife was in the pocket of her shorts, she put her tube of sunscreen and the lip balm away in her paddling jacket pocket. Then, after taking care of her toileting necessities, she was ready to go.

Maya folded and tucked the chart under her front deck chords. Then untying the kayak, she tugged it down to the water's edge. Like a ballerina donning a tutu, she wiggled into the spray skirt and grabbed her paddle. Wading out to knee-deep water, she straddled her boat and sat down on the seat with her feet remaining up. She removed her Tevas. She usually paddled bare footed, wedging her sandals between her legs and the side of the cockpit. With a quick flip, her legs were inside the kayak and she was paddling out to deeper water. Bobbing in the slight surf, she fastened her spray skirt around the coaming.

Everything was ready, so she set her sights on an island about half an hour's paddling time away, dug her paddle into the water, and began to put distance between her and the small island that had become home for the last three days.

A short time later, she approached her target island. A bevy of seals sunning on the rocky ledges looked up and dove into the sea as she got closer. Since she didn't feel like she needed to stop and rest, she kept on going past the island, fixing her sights on the next shallow outcropping of rocks. This time she was greeted by the clamouring of gulls as they whirled and screamed at her to get away from their nests. Their nesting grounds were quite flat and provided a good place to haul out for a pit stop. Taking care not to step on any shallow nests, Maya held on to her kayak's painter while she made sure her bladder was empty. Then after drinking from one of the bottles from behind her seat, she once again scrambled into the kayak, fastened the spray skirt, and left the safety of land. Now there was nothing but open water between her and the mainland. The seas were relatively calm with a slight swell. She felt nervous but excited to be finally on her way.

****

Two hours later, it was a different story. The winds had picked up, and the water was getting increasingly choppy. Waves splashed over the kayak's bow. Drawing on her inner resources, Maya steadily paddled on and on. She needed to keep paddling into the waves with steady timing or the kayak's momentum would be lost. She could not rest, as she would risk being blown off course and perhaps being hit broadside by the oncoming waves.

Muscles fatiguing, she began counting her strokes and resting two strokes out of every twenty paddling strokes. Eventually, numbing herself to the pain in her shoulder, she entered the zone. Time passed seamlessly as she paddled automatically, matching her strength to the ocean's heartbeat.

Rain drizzled down on her in typical West Coast fashion. Maya remained quite dry thanks to her paddling jacket's hood and the tight spray skirt. Her hands, however, chaffed with the cold and wet, slipped on the paddle shaft. Thankfully the wave action had lessened and a slight mist seemed to be forming around her. As the water calmed, she was able to stop paddling and drift for a few moments, easing the pain in her shoulder.

Running low on energy, she fished in her pocket and brought out a snack bar. Wolfing it down, she contemplated her next move. She hadn't been able to use her sail as conditions had either been too windy or dead calm, like it was now. She would have to paddle the rest of the way without assistance. For that she would need more energy. She felt around for a bottle of berries. She enjoyed the tart huckleberries while she bobbed gently in the kayak.

The mist thickened into fog, and she began to worry about losing her way. She might have to rely on her deck compass. Quickly, she took her bearings and noted which way her kayak was pointing. The chart indicated the mainland was to the northeast. With a final drink of water, she began to paddle again. This time she kept a close eye on the compass as the fog enveloped the kayak.

An eerie silence encompassed her as she journeyed on, straining to see where she was going. She felt as though she was drifting through an opaque world, alone with only the soft splash of her paddle for company. Floating through this silent world, she calmed herself with the knowledge that she had the skills to navigate her path even if she had to depend on the compass for guidance.

Suddenly a large shape loomed out of the fog. Just as suddenly, it disappeared again. Straining to identify what it was, Maya held her breath. Again the shape rose before her. A large eye peered at her and disappeared as the humpback whale slowly sank into the depths. Frozen with fear, Maya could only wait until it had gone. Silence once again descended upon the misty world. Long moments passed. She was alone again.

With renewed effort, she began paddling. God knows what else was lurking in the depths. Another hour passed with the fog beginning to dissipate. Small rocky islands appeared to her left. She altered her course and made for the nearest one. Finally, with a last few pulls on her paddle, she made landfall. With shaky legs, she managed to get out of her kayak and flop thankfully down on a tiny rocky beach. Hanging on to the painter, she lay back on the rocks and breathed a sigh of relief. She knew she must be close to the mainland. It was just a matter of resting, and with a couple more hours of effort, she would be there.

It was late afternoon and in the unsettled weather, the sky was already darkening. Downing the last of her berries, she glanced anxiously around, noting that the sea was still relatively calm but the wind seemed to be picking back up. Maya relaunched her kayak and set off with renewed drive towards the shoreline now etched on the horizon. Reaching the headland two weary hours later, she started down the coastline looking for a good campsite.

Eventually she spotted a small creek trickling into the ocean. Having had more than enough paddling for one day, she decided that this cove would have to do for the night. It was going to be extremely difficult to beach here, as the shoreline was mainly barnacled rocks and slime covered driftwood. However, there appeared to be a small meadow up on the hillside, and she could fetch fresh water from the creek.

Hauling up her rudder, she paddled into the cove until she felt the kayak graze the rocks under the water. Wedging the boat's nose between two submerged rocks, she placed her paddle behind her and on another rock. With a supreme effort, she levered herself out of the kayak and onto the sharp rocks.

Reaching for her Tevas, she jammed them on her feet. She jumped into the water and began wading knee-deep towards the shore, towing her kayak behind her. Shaking with cold and fatigue, she struggled over the submerged granite and eventually lifted the nose of the kayak onto the unforgiving beach. Then grabbing the back toggle, she used the next wave to lift and float the body of the kayak further onto the rocks. She repeated this sequence until the boat was no longer in immediate danger of floating away.

With the kayak gripped by the rocks, she quickly unloaded her belongings, carrying them far up the beach. Finally, the boat was light enough for her to haul it up on her shoulder and stagger with it to refuge. Tying the kayak to an overhanging spruce bough, Maya sank gratefully down beside it in the driftwood. She was proud of herself. She had managed to survive crossing a strait that most people would never dream of attempting without a power-assisted vessel.

Chapter Sixteen

Joe sat in his well-worn camp chair, in the early evening, surveying his camp. This was no ordinary fish camp. Located in one of the best fishing areas on the coast, it had easy access to both fresh and salt-water fishing. Clients either flew by floatplane, landing on the Skitstul River, or drove the rough thirteen-kilometre dirt road in a four-by-four to get to this little piece of heaven.

They paid big bucks too. The average stay was four days at $795 a day. Of course, that included some air and/or ground transportation, all meals including alcohol, accommodation in luxurious double-walled safari tents, top of the line fishing gear, expert fishing guides, and use of Mustang marine suits and rubber boots. The processing of the guaranteed catch (filleting, vacuum packing, flash freezing, then boxing and shipping the fish to the client's home town) was also provided.

River Bend Fishing Camp had an excellent reputation. Joe was known for the quality of his service and the cleanliness of his facilities. His superb fishing guides also helped to set his camp apart from the other outfits in the area. Bob and Tim were his lead guides and had been with him for several years.

From where he sat on the hillside, outside his secluded high-walled tent, Joe could see the whole setup. A lodge and kitchen were located in an old, remodelled log house.

This was where the clients ate and relaxed after fishing all day. Clients could lounge in the comfortable, overstuffed leather furniture that surrounded a rustic stone fireplace. A large plank table, set up close to the kitchen, provided enough space for customers and guides to share home-cooked meals. Pictures featuring previous customers with their record catches, stuffed trophy fish, and some olden-days' fishing gear decorated the log walls.

The sleeping quarters were huge off-white safari tents, equipped with bunks, tables, and chairs. Usually two to four men occupied each tent. Crisp linens and heavy duvets covered the bunks. There was always a good supply of thick towels available.

A short distance from the tents was the washhouse complete with solar composting toilets. Thanks to the gravity-fed pipe system from the nearby creek, water was available for a quick wash. If they wanted to, the fishermen could use the outside showers supplied with hot water heated by electricity-producing solar panels. Most of the electricity for the kitchen and laundry facilities came from the diesel generator. Joe was careful to run the generator only during the day and watched the consumption like a hawk. One thing Joe hated was waste.

He fed his customers well. The kitchen freezers were packed with high-quality meats, and the fridges held plenty of fresh fruits and vegetables. Of course, there was always fresh fish available from the day's excursions. These good-quality homemade meals were based, for the most part, on recipes left by his one-time partner.

Occasionally, he missed having Sue around, but he was the first to admit that his gambling had ruined their relationship. Right now, Charlie was his cook but there were problems. He was unreliable and surly with the guides.

Then there was the booze. Fishing camps run on liquor, and at this one there were no limits. After an exhausting day, the men appreciated their beer with many of them enjoying hard liquor as well.

Yes, it was a good deal for sure. He didn't stint on the value he gave his customers. They returned year after year and often referred the camp to friends and business acquaintances.

Joe, a balding, beer-bellied man in his late forties, reflected on his little operation. Yes, he provided the best of the best. The fishing guides were young, capable men, who had for the most part grown up in this section of the country. They knew these waters well and knew where the fish hung out at certain times of the season. Joe could easily guarantee each fisherman at least one day of successful fishing. He could also guarantee big money for some of his guides, as fish weren't the only catch around there.

Two years ago, Mr. Rodrico had approached Joe with a deal he couldn't refuse. He offered to pay handsomely for Joe to be part of a drug ring importing drugs from Mexico. Joe was needed to transfer drugs that had been hidden in remote bays to various large centres such as Sumac and Franklin, and up into Alaska.

A fishing camp was the perfect cover for such an operation. The small sports fishing boats could, without attracting attention, easily nip into the drop-off beaches and pick up the stashes. Frequent comings and goings of vehicles with clients and supplies provided a way to smuggle the drugs—stuffed in false compartments, empty containers, or the recycling—out of camp.

The plan had seemed to be well thought out, and Joe needed the money. He didn't give a shit about drugs. If people were stupid enough to get hooked on coke, that was their problem. Drugs were not his vice; gambling was. He owed thousands to the casinos in both Franklin and Sumac. The lucrative deal let him pay off his debts and provided the means to carry on rolling the dice.

Joe belched and took another swig of the gut rot the cook passed off as coffee. Yup, you put in a long day here, sometimes working till past 2:00 AM. While the fishermen had their evening meal and toasted the day's exploits, the guides filleted and packed the day's catch, cleaned and restocked the sports boats. The clients enjoyed sitting around in the rustic lodge near the stoked stove. Jokes, tall tales, and laughter topped off a great day spent riding the waves trying to catch the "big one."

Usually the beer, good food, and tomorrow's early start prompted the men to weave their way to the sleeping tents before midnight. After the last guest had turned in, some of the fishing guides began their second shift. Not all of the guides were in on the deal, but most were. Like Joe, they needed the quick money. The rest simply looked the other way and minded their own business, as jobs were scarce in these parts.

Joe was a good employer who paid a decent wage and looked after his men. Besides, no one messed with Joe. He had a reputation of being ruthless. If you got on his wrong side, you suffered the consequences. It was not uncommon for Joe to talk with his fists and every now and then, rumours surfaced about someone who may have gone missing from River Bend.

As Joe sat in the gathering dusk his thoughts turned to his ex-wife, Sue. He still could remember their last time together.

Sue had been tidying up their sleeping tent and had come across his bankroll stashed in the cushioned back of his old recliner. He had plans to use the cash on the weekend when he went into Franklin. She was sitting in the dilapidated chair waiting for him.

"What in hell is this for?" she yelled as he pushed open the tent flap.

Leaping to her feet she brandished the rolled up wad of cash. "You son of a bitch. You swore you weren't playing anymore. The bank called on Monday about the overdrafts."

He could not deny the evidence she waved in front of his nose.

"It's only till I get us out of the hole," he shouted. "There's a big game this weekend. High rollers."

Sue sank to her knees in despair. "You really don't give a shit about me do you? You swore you'd quit."

"Sue, Sue stop it. Get up for God's sake," he begged, trying to pull her to her feet.

She did get up but turned away from him, disgust written all over her face. Grabbing a large packsack she began stuffing some clothing, her jewellery and the money into it. She went over to his jacket and wrenched the truck keys from the pocket.

"Have a nice life," she muttered and left.

"For Christ sake, Sue. Get back here," Joe yelled chasing after her.

As he reached for her arm, she swung her fist catching him on the side of his head. Pain shot through him as his ear took the brunt of the blow.

"Leave me the hell alone," she gasped as tears rolled down her cheeks. "Leave me alone."

Pain clouded his judgement and he raised his arm hitting her across the face for the first and last time in their marriage.

She stumbled, regained her footing and took off down the path towards camp. As he stood in shock, having struck the only woman he had ever really cared for; he heard the truck start and Sue drive out of his life.

He didn't blame her for leaving him. He knew she was right. Over the years, sadness and loneliness had replaced the hot anger. He had sunk more and more into debt. Those cards never seemed to be in his favour these days.

Although it had been over three years since he and Sue had split the sheets, he could still see her face. Now it was too late. Too much had happened since and he had no idea where she had gone. He missed her horribly but never had been able to give up his true mistress—lady luck.

Chapter Seventeen

Bob, Joe's lead guide, shrugged out of his sleeping bag and made his way to the biffy. Pausing afterwards to rinse his teeth and splash water over his weathered face and neck, he grinned appreciatively at his reflection in the small shaving mirror. Women seemed to like his rugged looks and his well-honed muscles. It was time for some well-earned R and R. He would take a run into Sumac after this next job—score a little BC bud and find some willing chick to spend money on.

He shook his tousled blond hair and started off to the kitchen. First coffee, then chase Charlie up for the packed lunches that they took in the fish boats. Man that guy was lazy. The son of a bitch never had the clients' lunches ready until the last minute, and often they simply weren't up to River Bend's standards. Just yesterday, he had spoken to Joe about it. Joe had assured him that things would change or the cook was gone.

Miracle of miracles, Charlie was up and the lunches were lined up on the table. Noting Charlie's sour disposition this morning, Bob grunted his thanks, packed the lunches and a good supply of Coors into the waiting cooler, and headed out to the boat. After checking the fishing gear and gas, he headed back to the cookhouse for a breakfast of eggs, bacon, and Texas toast. He ate hungrily, washing the greasy food down with strong camp coffee. Wiping his mouth with the back of his hand, he got up and strode out to the sleeping tents.

"Hey, you landlubbers. Get your sorry asses out of bed. Boats leave in half an hour. With or without you." A chorus of mild curses and the sounds of men stumbling out of their bunks assured him that everyone was eager to get going.

"Morning," he greeted Phil and Harry as they jumped aboard his Boston Whaler. They looked ready and anxious for the day's adventures. Phil had brought along his own fishing gear, but Harry was content to use the camp's equipment.

"Using this baby today," Phil bragged, as he handed Bob his gear. "Picked it up in Blaine, just after we booked River Bend. Prefer my own equipment. Top notch. Should be, it cost a friggin fortune."

Phil's tackle was top of the line and brand-new. Last night, he had been boasting about his fishing experiences, but Bob had yet to see any evidence of his phenomenal talent. In fact, during the last two days, it had been Harry who had reeled in the best fish. One of Harry's salmon, a Chinook, had weighed in at forty-seven pounds. Phil was getting a little choked, so best he get something decent today.

He would take them out to Finger Point. They needed to head in that direction anyway. Bottle Neck Cove was over that way, and today was pick-up day. Joe had relayed him the message that had come in on Monday. A drop had been made, but the government boat, the *Cormorant*, was in the area. It was advised that they should delay collecting the goods by a couple of days. Today was Friday, so the coast should be clear.

Bob insisted the men put on wet gear and life jackets, and then he cast off. Soon the whaler was heading out into the morning light and into the rolling pitch of the seas. It was rough going until two miles south of Finger Point when the seas calmed to steady swells and the wind lessened to a slight breeze. They trolled for a while with no luck.

Impatient for success, Phil began to question Bob's ability to find fish. "Maybe we should be closer to that shoal," he whined. "The last guide I had positioned the boat right over a ledge, and that's where I got the fifty-pounder."

"For God's sake, leave the man alone," Harry insisted. "He found us lots of fish yesterday. Give him a chance. We just got out here."

Bob gunned the engine and brought the boat closer to the outcropping of rocks. Chances were good for rock cod, and if they were lucky, a salmon might be skulking around the perimeter of the ledge. Lucky they were. Almost simultaneously, both men got a bite. The next few minutes were spent in high excitement as one fish after another was reeled into the boat. Phil's salmon gave him a good run and tipped the scales at forty-nine pounds. Harry managed three smaller fish—two rock cod and a salmon that was just under fifteen pounds.

"Time for a beer!" yelled Bob.

They passed the morning fishing off of Finger Point and then moved on nearer to the entrance of Bottle Neck. By casual radio chatter between the River Bend fishing boats, the guides set up their plan.

"I'm having trouble with this damn motor again, Bob. Can you drop your clients off with Bill and come in to Bottle Neck and see if you can help me fix this thing once and for all? I'll off load Doug and Marie to Jordie's boat. No point in spoiling their day. Lots of room on Jordie's."

"Sure thing, Tim. You got tools?"

With that, the plan was set. The guides got rid of their clients and were free to head into Bottle Neck for the pickup. With just two boats, they would have to work hard and move quickly, but they had done this before. Everything usually went off without a hitch.

They scooted around the rocks that guarded the entrance and motored into the bay. Checking that they were alone, they anchored in the shallows, and then both men jumped overboard and waded to shore. After finding the map with the bag numbers and locations, Bob and Tim started dragging the duffels filled with cocaine out of the forest and down to the beach. Hoisting two bags onto their shoulders, they began ferrying the drugs to the sports boats and heaving them on deck. Halfway through their chore, everything went to hell.

Chapter Eighteen

Wednesday nights seldom surprised Hunter. Here in the RCMP squad room, it was the same old scenario with Captain Smythe droning on and on about the cutbacks and how everyone had to do more than their share. Government funding was always limited when it came to law enforcement. There was never enough money to hire the needed personnel. What more could they bloody well ask of him?

Hunter was already on the drug beat for the northern territory, plus his mandate included investigating the cases of girls that had gone missing along the highway to Port Franklin. That investigation had been going on for six years. Girls had stopped disappearing in the last two years, but the file had never been closed. Perhaps the killer had moved on; perhaps the killer was deceased; perhaps he or she was just getting better at selecting victims with no family ties.

Most of the females had been of Aboriginal descent and were last seen hitching a ride along the side of the road. One had been a male who wore his dark hair long and had probably looked like a girl at first glance.

Only three of the girls' remains had ever been found. Forensics had failed to turn up any traces of DNA, fingerprints, or useable biologicals. All had been strangled; their bodies wrapped in plastic drop cloths and dumped in out-of-the-way locations. The perpetrator had been very careful, always using the same method and always erasing any evidence.

Moose and deer hunters had found all of the recovered victims. The killer was obviously knowledgeable of the maze of back roads and secluded areas that surrounded highway 43. By the time the girls had been discovered animals and time had done their job. Identification had been made through dental records and in one case a distinctive jacket left on one of the skeletal remains.

Hunter felt sorry for the families of these victims, but he felt even more compassion for the relatives and friends of those they had never found. It must be an impossible burden to bear, not knowing what has happened to a loved one. Those missing girls were constantly on his mind as he travelled the corridor between Fort Sumac and Port Franklin.

His prime responsibility was investigating drug trafficking. Since the opening of the deep-water port in Port Franklin, there had been a dramatic increase in the flow of heroin and cocaine to the north. Checks and raids on freighters, fishing vessels and container ships had yielded minimal results. Given the limited manpower available, it was impossible to examine more than a small percentage of the cargo entering the busy terminal. Besides, Hunter felt the port was too obvious. His instincts told him to look for another way that the drugs might be smuggled in.

One of his sources in the drug world had heard a rumour that a shipment of Mexican drugs was due at any time. A spike in violent incidents and shakedowns indicated the streets were starving for drugs. The gangs were getting antsy. Something was coming down, but the hows, whats, and wheres had yet to be determined.

According to the Coast Guard logs, just three weeks ago, the captain of a government vessel, the *Cormorant,* had reported suspicious activity in the vicinity of Bottle Neck Cove. Apparently, a fishing boat—the *Black Dawn*—had been spotted in the narrow-necked cove. Boats of that size seldom anchored in such places, given the number of larger and safer harbours available around there. The skipper of the *Black Dawn* had checked out okay, but the captain of the *Cormorant* still had his doubts. Perhaps this next trip to the coast would bring him closer to some answers.

He would be posing as an American tourist interested in a high-end fishing experience. This undercover assignment would give him a pleasant change from his usual highway patrolling. As he travelled, he would be able to strike up conversations with the locals about fish camps in the area. Conversations often led to gossip and innuendo, especially after he had bought a couple of rounds in the bar.

Competition was fierce among the various lodges and fish camps. They each had a fair idea of how profitable their rival's operation was. If anything generated suspicion, it was an outfit doing a little too well for its capacity. It would be a good place to start his investigations. Hunter's expense account was limited, but he could persuade Captain Smythe to loosen the purse strings to spring for a few days of fishing.

The only item of interest on tonight's agenda was the loss of a kayak guide from the *Ainslie,* a sixty-eight-foot vessel, serving as mother ship support for a group of kayakers off the outer islands. Evidently, the female guide had fallen from a cliff while hiking, and in all likelihood had been swept out to sea.

A search had been launched involving the Coast Guard, the *Ainslie,* and two Search and Rescue helicopters, but no trace of the woman had been found. Since the Coast Guard vessel, the *Keeley,* had been the primary vessel for the search, it had to abandon following up on the dubious activity that had been reported in the Bottle Neck sector.

The guide was described as a pretty girl in her mid-twenties with dark hair, 5' 3" in height, and with a slight build. According to the employer's limited information, the girl's name was Maya, but little else was known about her.

Everyone onboard the *Ainslie* had spoken highly of Maya. In fact, the clients had printed posters and provided a substantial reward seeking any information about the popular guide. These posters, distributed to the officers, were illustrated with pictures of the young girl. The photos had been taken by a guest on the kayaking tour. Although the search had been dropped, it was hoped that they could find someone that might recognize her, so the next of kin could be notified.

Hunter sighed as the captain wound down his briefing and his fellow officers collected their gear. He was tired and needed some shut-eye. He would be working alone this time and had to pick up his truck and camper and fishing tackle before heading out in the morning. It was getting late and he still had groceries and gas to get.

Luckily his camper was outfitted for the season, since he had already been out camping and canoeing with his nephew earlier this summer. One of these days, he might have a family of his own. Until then, his nephew Kyle fit the bill nicely. His sister, being a single parent, certainly appreciated having a break now and then. Ten-year-old boys could be quite a handful. Kyle, with energy to burn and a healthy curiosity, was no exception.

****

Just six kilometres out of Bainsbridge, near the junction of the Skitstul River and the estuary leading to the sea, Hunter spotted a diner. Its lights cast a welcoming glow over the parking lot. In the growing dusk, he noticed two transport trucks parked roadside with their engines idling. A couple of small cars and a van occupied parking spaces in front of the diner.

Pulling in beside a rusty Chevy, he switched off his engine and climbed wearily out of the cab. Stretching his back, he strode casually towards the swinging screen door. Odours of deep-fried food and fresh coffee met him as he swung open the door. It had been a long day, and he was eager for some decent coffee and a burger.

"Evening, sir. Sit anywheres you want. I'll be right with you." The young girl flashed him a warm smile, as she cleared off a large table.

"No rush. Whenever you have a moment." Hunter took a booth near the window.

He glanced around at the diner's other occupants. The road-weary truckers looked at him and then resumed their conversation. A young family seemed to be just about finished with their meal. Picking up the tab, the guy went to pay while his wife led the toddler to the washroom. An older gentleman and two teenagers sat at the remaining tables. These were locals, and they were in no hurry to leave. Hunter made eye contact with the older man giving him a brief nod.

"Coffee?" The young waitress had come over with a menu in her hand. She was dressed in tight jeans and a neat white T-shirt. With her long blonde hair and casual makeup, she looked to be in her early twenties.

"We're out of the special, but the hot beef sandwich is good or the salmon burger."

Hunter held out his cup for her to fill.

"Salmon burger, with lots of fries and salad if you have some." He scanned her name tag. "Sally, come chat when you got a minute. I need to find a good fish camp around these parts."

She bustled off to place his order and came back with the cutlery rolled in a serviette.

"You want mayo or tartar sauce on that burger?"

"I'll take the tartar sauce, thanks."

Several minutes later, as Hunter enjoyed the surprisingly tasty burger and munched on fries, the truckers paid up and left. The teens ordered more cokes and resumed their sporadic conversation punctuated with giggles. The girls glanced his way and giggled some more. Most women, including these young girls, found him attractive even when he was out of uniform. His dark eyes and hair gave him a ruggedly-handsome appearance. Over one eye, a pale scar curved upwards, hinting at an action-filled life. So far though, no one had interested him enough to commit to a long-term relationship. No matter, he had lots of time. He was only thirty-six.

Sally plonked herself down on the bench seat opposite him, interrupting his thoughts. She had brought the coffee carafe and an extra cup for herself. After filling their cups with hot coffee, she looked at him and said, "You were askin' after fish camps? I might know of a good one up the road a ways."

"Yup, I'd like to fish for a while since I'm up this way. Just drove up through the province from Washington State. I'm on my way to Alaska. Looking for a real top-notch outfit. I got money."

"Well, I've been going out with this guy Bob the last while. Drop-dead gorgeous and loaded. Anyways, he works at this camp called River Bend. From what I hear, it's pretty good. They guarantee you catch fish, feed you good, and there's all the booze you want."

Sally turned to the older gentleman sitting alone. "Hey, Mike, what do you know about River Bend? You know, Joe's place on the river?"

The older gentleman looked up from his paper.

"It's pretty expensive, but they say Joe gives you your money's worth. Guides are hardworking and they get results. My boy, Rick works there. He makes a whack of cash. Joe sure pays his men well."

"Yeah, Bob always has a ton of money to blow. Not that I mind, I like being spoiled." Sally grinned and got up to clear off the empty tables, pausing to refill both men's cups.

"Come set a while. I'd like to hear about the fishing in these parts," Hunter invited.

Mike joined Hunter at his table and the two of them talked fishing for a while. Mike had lived in the area a long time and knew it well. He favoured fly-fishing on the river but enjoyed salt-water action as well.

"Do you think they'd have any vacancies at River Bend?" asked Hunter. "Sounds like a decent place, but I only have a few days before I have to be in Juneau. Can you give me a number to call?"

"No, sorry I can't," replied Mike. "Hey, Sally, this joint got Internet? They probably got a Web site."

"Can't let anyone use the computer. I can give you Bob's cell, and he could ask if there's a space for you."

Sally gave Hunter Bob's cell phone number, and Hunter took his leave.

"Night, Sally. See you, Mike, and thanks for the info."

It was getting late and he still had to find a spot to pull over for the night.

In the parking lot, Hunter put in a call to Bob.

"Hi, Bob got your number from Sally at the diner. Hey listen. I'm looking for a fishing trip, say three or four days. Mostly interested in salt water. Wanna get one of those Chinooks. Sally said there might be space at River Bend. Thing is, I'm just passing through and it needs to be now. I can pay cash."

Bob seemed a little irritated that Sally had given out his cell number but relaxed as he listened to what Hunter had to say.

"Okay, man. What's your name and number so I can get back to you? We had a cancellation for Friday, but I don't know if Joe's filled it or not. Would Friday be good for you?"

"Sure, that's only the day after tomorrow. Find out and let me know ASAP." Hunter gave Bob his name and number and then hung up his cell.

After travelling down the highway for a few kilometres, he saw a rough dirt road leading to to a small lay-by that looked like a reasonable site to overnight. Since the truck was parked on a slant, he jockeyed it around making his camper as level as possible. As far as Hunter was concerned, there was nothing worse than sleeping with your head downhill. He had to run the front tires up on the chunks of two-by-sixes he always carried in the truck. By the time he had finished monkeying around, Bob had called him back.

"All set for Friday. It'll cost you $3,000 for four full days of fishing, all inclusive. You up for that?"

"Sure am," Hunter replied.

"Okay, then. Meet the van at the 7–11 in Bainsbridge at 6:30 PM on Thursday night. Do you need tackle? We can supply fishing licences at the camp." A few more details and everything was setup for the fishing trip.

It was too late to start a campfire. Hunter locked the camper door, put his firearm beside the bunk, and turned in for the night. He had all the next day to nose around and gather more information about the area.

Chapter Nineteen

Barbara was slumped at the receptionist desk, massaging her temples. Pain radiated from her jaw line to her cheekbones. A steady misery gripped her head like a vice. Three extra strength Tylenols and four cups of coffee were not helping at all. *Damn, she'd have to take one of her last Percocets.*

The vet, Dr. Stilman, had just left for lunch and would not be back for at least an hour. Time enough for her to scavenge the remainders of the Ketamine, the anesthetic, he'd used this morning; choke down her tuna sandwich and swallow her little helper.

Last night had been really rough. John had been in a panic. His latest plaything had died. This one had lasted quite a while, though. It had been well over six months since she had picked her up just outside of Talmont. Now everything would start all over again.

In her mind, she relived the scene that greeted her when she arrived home last night.

"You're late again. I've been waiting for hours. Where have you been?" screamed John. He swung his huge body down the steps and over to her as she got out of the dark blue Honda. Sweat poured down his livid face.

"Nowhere, just to the grocery store. It's Tuesday, I always go to the store on Tuesdays," Barbara said, hastily reassuring her agitated husband. "What's got you all upset now?"

"The mouse died. Guess the cat played a bit too rough. There's blood and guts everywhere."

"Not again, John. Not again!" Barbara stared at John.

"Where am I going to put this one? We've just about run out of places to hide the bodies. That old mine shaft collapsed and we can't risk dumping them in the bush anymore since they found that one beside number 31 road."

"Beats the hell outta me." He turned and went into the ramshackle farmhouse.

She unloaded the car and joined him in the kitchen. John sat nursing his third scotch. Sarah was in her usual place on the sofa watching a *Mash* rerun. The mentally challenged girl enjoyed the theme music and hospital scenes in this old series.

"Hi, Mommy," she called as Barbara began to put away the foodstuff. "Did you have to fix any puppies today? Any of them die?"

"Hey Sarah. How was your day? No, none of the puppies died today. Dr. Stilman did a good job."

"Good job for him. I like puppies. I don't like it when they die," Sarah stated flatly.

Barbara glanced over at John. He was well into his drink but thank God he usually remained reasonably sober until later in the evening. She depended on him to look after Sarah while she worked at Stilman's. If she hurried home after work, she knew her daughter was safe. Sarah kept to herself for the most part playing with the kittens or watching endless episodes of *Friends* and of course her favourite, *Mash*.

Thankfully, John paid scant attention to Sarah. Barbara made sure Sarah ate her porridge in the morning, and then it was his job to feed her the lunch that she left for the two of them in the fridge. Her daughter was capable of getting her own drinks and snacks so long as the food didn't need heating up. They couldn't trust her to use the stove. Often in the afternoon John would lock the farmhouse door and disappeared into his shop that was adjacent to the garage.

It was far from an ideal situation but in this remote location she had no other option. Few people outside of her family knew about Sarah. She had been born when they lived in the Territories. When they moved here, she had home schooled her daughter fearing she would be teased and bullied in a regular school. When Sarah had reached whatever limited potential she had, the teaching had stopped. She seemed happy enough.

John had never forgiven Barbara for having a handicapped child. He blamed her side of the family for diluting the gene pool. He even accused her of having had an affair that resulted in this slow child.

One saving grace was that John was not attracted to either his blonde-haired daughter or for that matter to Barbara anymore. He saved his energies for his little playthings insisting that his wife bring him only slim girls with long dark tresses. Young Aboriginal girls seemed to please him the most. Still, Barbara lived in constant fear that he might turn to their daughter one of these days. Although Sarah had the mind of a five-year-old, her body was that of an attractive young woman. Barbara kept supplying him with these unfortunate girls, hoping she might be able to keep her daughter safe. Better some no name runaway, than Sarah.

After Sarah had gone to sleep for the night, she and John locked the farmhouse door; crossed the yard and entered the shop. Switching on the fierce overhead lights, Barbara steeled herself for what she might see. True to his word, there were guts and blood everywhere. It was a testament to his depravity. The poor girl lay face down on the cold concrete floor. Her arms were bound behind her and a crude gag was held in place by electrical tape. John had taken his hunting knife and had carved his victim. Sticky rust-coloured blood pooled everywhere.

"Christ John, what did you do?"

"She said no once too often," he stammered. "I didn't mean for it to get so out of hand. Barb you gotta help me get rid of her, please." He collapsed in a heap with shaking shoulders, harsh sobs escaping from his open mouth.

"It's too much. I can't take it anymore. This has got to stop. Get up for heaven's sake. Crying sure isn't going to help now," she shouted in frustration. "Shut up."

John's head shot up at the sound of his wife yelling at him. She had no right to speak to him that way. He'd show her who was boss. He leapt to his feet and crossed the floor. Grabbing her by her arm, he shoved her roughly against the wall. The back of Barbara's head hit the wall and she slumped to the cold concrete. Red waves of pain spilled over into her eyes as she squinted at him in the harsh glare of the fluorescent lights. She had gone too far.

"John, John. I'm sorry. I'm just so damn tired. Of course I'll get rid of her. Just like I always do. Please don't hit me, please."

He backed slowly away from her and rubbed his hands over his face.

"Okay bitch. Shut your mouth and I'll let it go for now. What are we going to do with her tonight? It's too late to dump her. Too hard to drive those roads in the dark."

"I still have to find a place to put her. I told you the mineshaft collapsed after the spring melt. There might be another shaft nearby or some kind of animal den. Won't be able to tell until light," Barbara told her belligerent husband.

"Well, I can't have her stinking up my shop. Let's drag her into the root cellar, until you find a place."

They half-dragged and half-carried the body over to the root cellar near the barn and shoved it out of sight behind the potato barrels. The cool temperature in the root cellar would keep the body from decomposing too rapidly. Tomorrow she had to wash it with disinfectant and rub it with lye.

Barbara spent the better part of the night scrubbing the shop's main floor, the small toilet, the sink and of course the narrow cot where most of the cutting had been done. The stench of the coagulating blood gagged her as she worked at the stains with an old scrub brush. Wearily she dumped the last bucket of bloody water into the lagoon and put away her tools.

She didn't allow herself to think until she was standing in the shower with hot water cascading over her exhausted body. The enormity of her horrific life overwhelmed her. She wept. There was nothing she could do. She had to protect Sarah. She was as guilty as John was. She picked up the women; she dumped their bodies; she was guilty.

Pulling herself out of her reverie, Barbara got up and swiftly locked the door to the clinic. She turned the closed sign in the window towards the parking lot. Sometimes clients dropped by at lunchtime to pick up medications or to book appointments. She did not want to be disturbed.

Digging in the waste bucket beside the operating table, she located two syringes of the anaesthetic. A small quantity remained in each of the tubes. Quickly removing the plunger from one of the syringes, she emptied the clear liquid from one syringe into the other and capped the needle with a small rubber tip. She slipped the drug into her purse. There would be enough to immobilize her next victim but definitely not enough to kill. Dr. Stilman liked using Ketamine so there was a good chance there would be more leftovers soon.

After emptying the waste containers and washing down the operating room, she reopened the clinic. Harold, the old guy from down in the village, was waiting impatiently.

"How come you were shut? Been waiting for a good ten minutes," he complained.

"Sorry, sorry. What can I do for you?" Barbara asked, ignoring his question. "Need an appointment or meds?"

"Just some Stilbestrol, Molly's piddling again."

Barb checked the file and saw that Molly's check-up was due. "Best I book you in for Molly's check-up as well. She was due over three months ago. We've been having some cases of distemper over in Port Franklin. Just a matter of time before it shows up here."

"Sure book it. Molly's my baby girl. Don't want anything to happen to her," agreed Harold. He looked towards his vehicle where Molly waited anxiously in the driver's seat with her feet on the steering wheel. "Yes, she's great company that one."

As Harold left the clinic, she glanced at the clock. It had just turned one. Today was going to be a very long day. Her second shift would start as soon as she got home.

****

Driving along the back roads towards home, Barbara came to the entrance to the old mine site. She parked well off the road and swiftly ran along the dirt path that led to the well-camouflaged shaft. Hidden in the scrub, the shaft's greying timbers blended with the birch and poplar trees. Tugging and lifting the boards that shielded the opening; she peered into the hole. Most of the tunnel had collapsed in on itself leaving just a meter or so of space. There was not enough room to wedge a body and to cover it as well.

As she trekked further into the woods, Barbara kept her eyes open for more upright timbers. Over to her left, she found another abandoned shaft. This one was much more promising. The boards that covered the opening were rotting and easy to remove. Dust and mouldy spores flew from the wood as she pried it away. Cold, damp, earthy smells rose to meet her as she bent down and peered into the cavity. The dim shaft seemed empty. Just to be sure she dropped a stone into the hole and listened. There came a reassuring sound of it hitting water several feet below. Looking around she fixed the shaft's location in her mind and retraced her steps back to her car.

It was dark by the time she reached the farmhouse. All the outside lights were off except the one over the porch. John sat waiting on the steps.

"Any luck?" he asked as she climbed the stairs and sat down beside him.

"Yeah, found another shaft. You and Sarah get some supper?"

"We heated up some of the leftover stew from the other night. None left for you though," John answered and went inside.

She heard him pull the tab on another beer.

****

A week later they wrapped the now putrefying body in the drop cloth and attached meat hooks and ropes through the plastic. Dragging the dead weight, they managed to haul the carcass over to the Honda and heaved it into the trunk.

Barb then checked on Sarah, who was sleeping soundly in her princess bed, and went out the front door, locking it behind her. John was coming with her. It was far too difficult to carry or drag the body through the uneven bush at night by herself. They had to get this done.

John made his way slowly, swearing as he once again tripped over a hidden root. Built like a line backer and out of shape, he found the trail very hard going. Gasping for air, he sat down to rest at the opening to the shaft.

"Give me a minute."

Barbara waited swatting mosquitoes away from her damp forehead. She lifted the hair from the back of her neck and was immediately rewarded by several of the biters taking chunks out of her exposed skin.

"Hurry up and get your breath. They are eating me alive," she exclaimed.

Undoing the hooks and ropes, they positioned the plastic wrapped bundle over the hole. They heaved it into the shaft; hearing a solid thunk as the body hit the wall and then a splash as it hit the water at the bottom.

Chapter Twenty

Exhausted by the long crossing and the tension-filled day, Maya knew that she had little energy to spare. The sun was already starting to disappear behind the islands that shielded the entrance to this rocky beach. The clouds had begun to gather, bringing with them the possibility of rain. She had to pull herself together and get settled for the night.

Opening the container of fish, she ate slowly, checking for bones. She washed the dry roasted salmon down with a bottle of water. Dessert was more berries, huckleberries that she picked from the shrubs near the beach. Making sure there were no scraps left to attract wildlife, she rinsed out the containers and stored them and the rest of her food in the front hatch of the kayak. Since there was no point to making a fire at this late hour, she started to think about her shelter.

The log she sat beside was well above the high tide mark. Since she had used most of the rope on the sail, only short pieces of rope remained attached to three corners of the tarp. There was not enough rope to fasten the tarp to the bushes or driftwood. Too tired to think of a solution, she put on the dirty sweat suit and pulled socks over her feet. To protect her legs and scalp from biting insects, she tucked the grey pants into her socks and jammed on her toque. There had been no bugs in her other campsites, but here there were lots of mosquitoes. The boggy ground beside the creek was a prime breeding ground for the aggravating insects.

After hollowing out a shallow indentation in the sand, she put her life jacket down as a pillow. She laid her flashlight and paddle within easy reach of her temporary shelter. Sitting in the middle of the blue tarp, she wrapped the material around her like a cocoon, making sure she could draw part of the covering over her face. She lay down, curled up on her side, and fell fast asleep.

Nasty, stabbing pains seared through her midsection, causing her to draw her legs up tight against her belly. She tossed and turned on the sand, only to be driven out of her shelter and down to the water's edge. Crouching in the shallows, she relieved herself. Stumbling back up the beach, she lay down again only to be urged back to the water again and again. Finally, the pains eased. She slept.

****

The sun's rays beating down on the tarp made Maya extremely uncomfortable in her blue cocoon. Shaking off her wrappings, she rose to meet another day. She stripped off the sweat suit and immediately appreciating the cool breeze on her legs.

Her stomach felt bruised. Nevertheless, she drank the last of the protein mixture, hoping that it would not upset her tummy further. As she munched on one of the three remaining granola bars, she surveyed her surroundings.

There wasn't much to the rocky beach. The creek had slowed to a trickle that she could hardly hear as it traced its way to the sea. There was no place to dig for clams, and the shore was too rugged to support any quantity of berries. Fishing was a possibility, but she could fish elsewhere. Faced with limited sources of food and water, she decided to continue on her journey down the coast. She would have to rest later.

****

Getting her kayak out to sea proved to be as challenging as her efforts to beach last night. Trying to float the loaded kayak back out over the sharp submerged rocks took a lot of dexterity. Maya judged each wave as it came into the cove. She held her boat taut as a wave crested, then pushed the kayak up and forward as the surf receded. Several minutes later, the kayak was bobbing in waist-deep water.

Using the paddle float, she managed to swing her leg over the back deck of the kayak, inch closer to the cockpit opening, slide belly-down into the cockpit, and then rotate her torso until she was facing up. She was now sitting with her legs in the boat, ready to paddle. Fortunately, she had been trained in several methods of self-rescue; her guiding skills were certainly coming in handy for situations like this.

Consulting her chart, she saw that the nearest settlement was days away. The coastline was rugged and dangerous. Hidden shoals and ledges lurked beneath the waves. She hugged the shoreline for the most part, avoiding swirling water that threatened to draw her kayak into the larger rocks. Paddling was hard, and she tired quickly. Forcing herself to keep on, she slowly continued southward towards safety.

By mid-afternoon, Maya was in distress. Her arms ached and her shoulder had started to spasm. She had pushed herself to the limit. Her body was telling her that continuing on much farther was simply out of the question. Checking the chart, she found a sandy beach about an hour's paddling distance away. She gathered up her remaining strength and carried on towards the beach. Finally, a narrow strip of beige sand appeared to her left. Crying from relief and fatigue, she landed on the fine sand.

An eagle lifted off from a branch high in one of the spruce trees bordering the shore. It circled curiously over its visitor, and then returned to its perch. Another eagle approached, flew over the beach, and landed farther up in the trees.

Maya spied what appeared to be a nest in the fork of a tree. She sat watching the birds for a while, discovering more and more "golf balls" in the branches. The white-headed birds of prey seemed to be everywhere. From where she sat, she could count at least nine, possibly ten.

Remembering the uncomfortable night she had spent on the rocky beach, she set about making camp. She dismantled the sail, salvaging the rope. She then tied that rope to the ends of the ropes on the tarp. Stretching the blue material over driftwood logs and up into a small hemlock, she fashioned a lean-to. Once more, she hauled her things out of the hatches and stashed everything under the tarp.

Searching through the undergrowth, she managed to find some dry moss and soft cedar boughs for her bed. She should be warm and dry tonight. The weather had really improved, so there was little chance of rain. The lean-to should keep out any wind if the weather turned blustery.

Next, she turned her attention to building a fire pit and gathering dry wood and kindling materials. Sitting around a fire helped pass the time and somehow made her feel less lonely. She was really beginning to yearn for the sound of human voices. She missed having someone to share thoughts and ideas with. Longing to feel someone's arms around her, she wanted Chad desperately.

Snatching up the emergency fishing tackle, she headed over to the water's edge. There she found a strong piece of driftwood and used it to dig up some razor clams. Some were for dinner and the rest for bait.

Thinking back to her first gritty clam meal, she left most of the clams to soak in the cooking pot filled with seawater. Hopefully, the clams would spit out all the sand before it was time to boil them up. She climbed up to an overhanging ledge and began skewering the clam meat with the hook. Then with a wish and a prayer, she threw the line into the sea below.

The line barely reached the water, let alone had enough leeway to sink deep enough to attract fish. She moved down off the ledge and waded out to a half-submerged piece of granite. Sitting with her butt in the water and her legs splayed, she once again dropped the line into the ocean. Jigging the line up and down in slow motion, she waited patiently for a bite. Her hook caught nothing but the bottom, ripping off the clam meat. After re-baiting her hook, she tried again.

Just as Maya was about to give up, she noticed two eagles circling the end of the narrow beach where the shore once more turned to rock. As she watched, one of the eagles dove feet-first into the water and brought up a thrashing fish in its talons. Hurrying over to this end of the beach, Maya set up again. If the eagles were successful here, then perhaps she would be as well.

Thanks to Chad's totem, she caught enough for supper. Gutting and cleaning the fish at the edge of the beach, she then let the sea scatter the offal.

She was running low on fresh water, so she collected her empty plastic bottles and wandered up the beach into the surrounding rainforest. Having to climb up and over the fallen logs and through the sharp sword grass made the trek difficult. She could hear faint sounds of water flowing down a distant hillside.

Getting hotter and hotter as she wove her way through the quiet forest, she let her mind wander to the events of the past few days. Things had been very tough and she was still afraid that Connor might be trying to find her. Luckily, the cut on her leg had not become infected but she could not survive much longer on meagre rations of fish, berries, and clams. She needed to get to civilization as soon as possible.

There was always the chance she could be rescued, but that seemed more and more unlikely as the days passed. No one knew she was making her way down the coast. They were probably convinced she had been swept out to sea. Although they would have expected to find her beached kayak, the search party may have assumed that given the weather conditions at the time, it had drifted out to sea. No, rescue was highly unlikely. She would have to get herself out of this mess.

Lost in these thoughts, she walked straight into a cloud of black flies swirling up from the undergrowth. They were everywhere, in her mouth and up her nose. Coughing and spluttering, she waved her hands frantically around her head. In the chaos, she lost her footing and slid feet-first down an embankment to the creek bed.

Heavens! She should have been paying more attention to the terrain.

A sow black bear and her cub startled by the noise looked up, turned, and splashed upstream. Pausing some fifty yards away, they resumed turning river rocks over in search of food. Water glinted off their lush black fur. Rocks chinked and rattled as the bears' claws scrabbled at the creek bed. Maya could hear them snuffling and snorting as they rooted for food with their noses.

Their surprise visitor did not appear to be a threat. For all the bears knew, a log had tumbled down the bank. Luckily, the wind direction was downstream, so Maya's scent drifted away from the mother and cub. Ignoring the scrapes and scratches on her legs, she watched in fascination as the bears foraged. This was the closest she had ever been to a bear in the wild. The sow softly grunted at the cub. Tiring, the young one leaned against the sow, resting. A faint woof came from the sow and both bears vanished silently into the rainforest. Laughing softly, Maya realized she had been holding her breath.

After making sure the bears were well and truly gone, she retrieved the scattered plastic bottles. Filling them was an easy task as the creek ran fast over some decent sized stones. She dipped the bottles into the cool rippling water that pooled in the sunlight. She rinsed the blood off her legs and examined the scratches. Not bad, she had received worse scrapes falling off her bike when she was a kid. Feeling light-hearted after witnessing such a beautiful scene, she smiled as she made her way back through the forest to the narrow beach.

Supper that night was the fish she had caught off the ledge. The fish, clams, and seaweed made a filling and tasty stew. After eating as much as she could, she washed out the pot and boiled some of the creek water. Throwing two tea bags into the old container, she let them steep.

Before it got too dark, she arranged her sleeping area and put all leftover food and supplies back into the kayak's hatches. This was obviously bear country. She knew it would be wiser to cache her supplies in a tree, but all the nearby trees were too stunted. A bear could easily reach the food by standing on its hind legs. However, it would have difficulty tearing open the sealed kayak hatches. Besides, she didn't have much food left anyway.

After washing and toileting, she donned her usual night garments: sweat suit, socks, and toque. She built up the fire and sat sipping her tea in the fading light. As the stars came out, she crawled under the lean-to, covered her body with the space blanket, and fell asleep listening to the surf gently swish over the sand.

****

With the sun starting to peek over the tops of the dwarfed trees and filter into the lean-to, morning came early for Maya. Although she was anxious to get in her kayak and carry on with her journey, she had to take time to get food for the day. She wouldn't get far on her remaining snack bars. By dangling the hook and line near yesterday's successful hole, she managed to snag a couple of small rock cod. While these fish were simmering in the cook pot, she gathered a few Saskatoon's from nearby bushes. Although her body was probably in need of some sort of starch, she knew her knowledge of coastal plants was quite limited. She chose to just get the fish, some sea lettuce, and only a few berries rather than risk another upset stomach.

The sun was high in the sky by the time she climbed into her kayak. The horizon seemed unusually hazy, but she wanted to travel soon since the low tide was making the shoals more visible.

In the calm seas, paddling was effortless. She made good progress as the shoreline changed dramatically from jagged granite to soft sandstone. Wind and water had sculpted the beige cliffs into undulating mounds and caves. Erosion had carved away large portions of the shoreline, forming almost tunnel-like structures. Nesting birds darted in and out of homes burrowed in the cliff faces. Some of the caves appeared to go into the cliffs forever. Maya wondered if fishermen or perhaps this area's Aboriginal peoples had ever used any of the higher caves for shelter. As she paddled on, she scanned the sandstone for a glimpse of petroglyphs or perhaps some ancient rock paintings.

While she kayaked close to the shore during the low tide, she was treated to a fantastic display of tidal life. Purple, orange, and beige sea stars clung desperately to the rough sandstone, occasionally falling with a soft plunking sound as they dried out. Soft-sided sea anemones and spiky urchins were visible in their underwater world. As she passed through kelp beds, ghost crabs silently disappeared beneath the undulating fronds. Moon jellyfish joined the underwater parade, floating like transparent globes in the warm currents. Occasionally, she would notice a seal poke its nose above the surface, watching her progress with dark limpid eyes.

As she paddled slowly through this magnificent display, Maya began to feel the cool fingers of the incoming fog. Within minutes, the fog enveloped the kayak, sealing her off in a damp, alien world. She could scarcely read her chart. Holding it within inches of her face, she estimated her position. Bottle Neck Cove looked to be quite close.

Engine noises suddenly reached her ears. Surrounded by the thick fog, it was impossible for her to pinpoint the boat's distance or direction. It sounded like a small vessel, but she couldn't be sure. Stuffing the chart into the cockpit, she picked up her paddle tethered in front of her, readying herself for evasive action. Just as suddenly as the noise had come, it disappeared into the fog.

She shouted for help, but her voice was swallowed by the heavy greyness. No response came out of the eerie haze. Screaming louder, she called again and again. There were no answering shouts, no throbbing engine noises, nothing.

Unable to see where to go, she floated in the gentle surf. Gradually the fog lessened. She was able to make out the shoreline. Hugging the shore, she cautiously made her way towards Bottle Neck Cove, almost missing the narrow entrance. Guiding the nose of her kayak through the passage, she moved silently into the beautiful cove. Waterfalls seemed to be everywhere, tumbling in the now sunlit sky and rushing eagerly into the sea. A pristine beach spread out in front of her, promising safety.

She beached her boat beside a sizeable creek. Lining her kayak, she forged her way up the creek and into the tranquil forest. Part way up, she found a small sandbar. Wedging the kayak into the sand, Maya tied the painter to some branches. Flopping down on the grassy bank, she sat warming herself in the sun. All around her, the forest came alive with sounds of insects, birds, and the faint rustling of the wind in the trees. The air was perfumed with the scent of grasses, cedar, and berry blossoms. Maya relaxed dozing in the sun's rays.

Waking up a short while later and becoming aware of how hungry she was, she left the kayak where it was and crossed over the rocky point to a small beach. There, she searched for clams and oysters. She found several razor clams and a few butter clams.

On her way back to the creek, she found something else. A dirty beige duffel bag lay hidden in the undergrowth about thirty feet above the high tide mark. Curious, she crouched down, unzipped it, and examined the contents. It was filled with neon coloured T-shirts and matching ball caps. The bag seemed too heavy for just clothing, so she rooted underneath the shirts.

A stiff divider lifted away from the bottom of the bag. Maya saw several packages wrapped in heavy plastic under this partition. There was a symbol resembling some kind of an insect perhaps that of a scorpion, emblazoned on each brick-sized package. She had seen this symbol before on the news. Horrified she realized these were drugs, probably heroin or cocaine. Looking around, she could now see other bags hidden here and there in the bushes and behind rotting trees.

She stood up and all hell broke loose.

She stared straight at a stunned face. Turning to flee, she ran stumbling through the bush towards her kayak. Heavy footsteps closed the gap. Rough arms grabbed her waist and hurled her to the ground. She was dragged kicking, screaming, and flailing towards another man waiting on the landing beach. Since her brawny captor outweighed her by far, there was no escape.

Chapter Twenty One

Bob stood shell-shocked for a moment. His brain whirled, sifting through the impossible scene in front of him. Where had she come from? Did she know what was going down? Who in the devil was she? One thing was for sure; he couldn't let her get away. She had obviously seen the drugs hidden in the duffel.

As she took off running up the trail, he knew he could easily catch her. For a big man, he could move quickly. He sped after her, grabbing her around the waist. Dragging her down, Bob pinned her arms to her sides.

"Keep still, bitch. And shut the fuck up!" The small, dark-haired girl was a fighter, kicking at his shins and screaming at the top of her lungs. He swung his fist, catching her on the side of her jaw.

"I said shut the fuck up!"

"What's going on?" Tim yelled, hearing the commotion in the bush. He dropped the bags that he had been transferring to his shoulder and began running towards the screaming. The sight of Bob yarding Maya along behind him, kicking and fighting all the way, greeted him.

"Who's that little witch? Where'd she come from?"

"Beats the hell outta me. More to the point, what are we going to do with her? She's seen the drugs, man. She was looking right in one of the bags! Joe's gonna love this!"

Bob threw Maya down hard on the sand. She scrabbled backwards to get away. Reaching out with his foot, he slammed it into her thigh. She stopped moving and stared fearfully up at the two men.

Keeping an eye on their captive, Tim and Bob discussed what to do. Neither man had the stomach to kill her, but they knew they couldn't let her go either. They couldn't take the chance that she might somehow manage to get to the authorities.

"How'd you get here?" Tim growled. "There ain't no boat on the beach."

"I'm just kayaking down the coast," stammered Maya in a voice so faint the men had to strain to hear her. "Just let me go," she sobbed. "I won't tell a soul what I've seen. Honest, I won't tell. Who would I tell anyways?" Tears streamed down her terrified face.

Bob fired questions at her. "Where's your damn kayak? Are you alone? No one would be stupid enough to travel these waters alone."

"Yeah, well I *am* travelling by myself. Look, just let me go and it'll be the last you'll ever see of me," she pleaded.

Bob glanced at Tim ruefully. "No can do. You know too much. The higher ups would have offed you already. Tim, raise Joe on the radio and see what he wants to do."

"Best not, Bob. Radio ain't secure. Can't risk the sporties coming in here and finding this cock-up. Let's just get her back to River Bend or get rid of her here and now."

"Can't kill her without Joe's say. Go get the duct tape from the boat, and I'll watch her."

Tim grabbed two more duffels and waded out to the boat. Snatching up the tape, he quickly made his way back and over to Bob. He handed him the tape and his fishing knife.

As the knife came towards her, unsure of Bob's intentions, Maya scrambled backwards. A few quick wraps of the sticky grey tape, and her wrists were bound tightly. The men then securely fastened her legs together at the ankles.

Leaving her lying on the sand, they completed collecting and loading the bags onto the small boat.

Tim waded up the creek and found Maya's kayak wedged in the sandbar. Dragging it downstream, he brought it over to the beach.

"We can't leave this here. Someone might be looking for this chick. What'll we do? Scuttle it out in deep water?"

"Yep, best we do that," agreed Bob. "If we open those hatches, we can get enough water in to sink her. Take the ballast out too. And bury her stuff."

Tim and Bob began dismantling the kayak. Maya watched, as her only means of escape was rendered useless.

"You gotta take a leak?" Tim asked the frightened girl. "It's a long way back to camp. We don't need you messing yourself."

Maya nodded frantically.

Dragging her into the undergrowth, he untied her ankles and pulled down her shorts. Giving her no privacy, he watched as she relieved herself. He yanked up her pants and ignoring her pleas for looser tape, tightly rewrapped her sore ankles.

Down beside the water line, he hauled her up and over his shoulder, then sloshed towards the boat. Onboard, Bob was waiting for them. He grabbed her under the armpits and heaved her onto the deck.

Most of the boat's deck was filled with fishing gear and of course the duffel bags. Bob pushed Maya down onto the steel decking amongst the bags, forcing her to lie on the cold surface. Before they covered the drug-filled bags and Maya with an old tarp that smelled strongly of used oil, the men checked the map and bag numbers one more time, to make sure they had not left any of the contraband. Each bag was worth a fortune and they did not want to be accused of stealing any. The gang was unforgiving. Retribution would be swift.

After lacing the kayak's tow rope through the deck line, Bob started the engine and steered the Boston Whaler through the narrow passage and out into the open ocean.

"This is good enough. Plenty deep," Tim said as they got out into deeper water.

Bob set the engine on idle. Working quickly the two men prepped the kayak by ripping off the hatch covers to expose the empty hatches. They used an oar to push the kayak under the surface, filling the front and back hatches as well as the cockpit with the salt water. They scuttled the kayak. Tim boarded his own craft and the men trawled as they slowly made their way towards the river estuary. Anyone watching would think they were simply fishing on their way into port.

The swells increased. Soon the two men had to reel in the gear and give up the pretence of fishing. With the boat bouncing headfirst into the waves, Maya was thrown around the deck, bruising herself badly on the legs of the seats. Eventually, she managed to wedge herself between the side of the boat and one seat.

It was almost evening when the boat reached the river mouth. They were in no hurry to get in before dark, as they couldn't unload the bags until the clients had turned in for the night.

Cooling ocean breezes chilled Maya who lay on the cold hard deck. She moaned as she shivered and tried to get warm.

"What's wrong with you, princess?" Bob looked at her from his position at the wheel. He could see her legs protruding from under the tarp. Part of him felt sorry for her obvious discomfort; grabbing a jacket from the deck storage compartment, he jammed it roughly around her body.

"Get used to it. Life sure ain't gonna be pretty for your sorry ass."

Since the camp was now only a couple of kilometres away, Tim grabbed the duct tape again and ripped off a piece. Hauling her head up by her hair, he plastered it over her mouth.

"Can't trust you not to scream your fool head off."

Maya gagged and fought to get her breath. Blood rushed to her head as she desperately tried to overcome the claustrophobic sensation. Steeling herself, she made herself slowly breathe through her nose, calm down, and stop fighting against the horrible tightness. Just a small portion of her nose was left uncovered. She had no idea how long she could remain in control and not panic. Survival instincts had kicked in. As hopeless as the situation appeared, she was determined these men would not win. She had to stay alive. It was just a matter of time before they made a mistake and she would escape.

****

Dusk was beginning to settle over the river as Bob and Tim slowly approached the camp. Laughter and loud, drunken voices drifted out to them on the cooling evening air. The other guides, Jordie and Bill, were doing their part of the plan; liquoring up the clients. Nothing could be unloaded until the last customer had gone to bed.

Just to be on the safe side, the guys moored the boat out of sight on the far side of the fuelling dock. Leaving Maya lying bound and gagged beside the bags, Bob and Tim made their way over to the lodge. Jordie came down the steps to meet them.

"Had to limp all the way home with that bloody engine conking out twice on the way back. It's gonna be a long night fixing the sucker. Gotta eat first. Where's the damn cook anyway?" demanded Bob.

Seeing the cook cleaning up the kitchen he asked, "Any leftovers? It was rib night wasn't it? You must have some leftovers or did these greedy guts chow down the lot?"

As Tim and Bob sat eating their late supper, they were treated to tall tales of how successful the fishing had been after they had offloaded their clients to the other boats. Everyone snickered at Phil's exaggeration of the huge fish he'd lost.

"Must have been at least fifty pounds, the way it pulled. Crappy line broke right at the last second."

The fishermen certainly had enjoyed a fine day out on the water. Most of them were staying another three days, so it wasn't long before they turned in for the night. They had learned that five o'clock comes awfully early. Plus, the fresh air, good food, and too much beer combined to make even the hardiest of them long for some sleep. Gradually, the lanterns in each of the sleeping tents were extinguished. The staff sat around killing time drinking coffee and beer in the kitchen.

"Evening, fellas."

Bob and Tim glanced up as Joe entered the kitchen. Even if he weren't their boss, Joe would have commanded their respect. He was an imposing figure of a man with a husky build, balding head, and bushy grey beard. He strode purposefully, not wasting any effort. Grabbing a beer from the cooler, he settled into a creaky old rocking chair.

"How'd it go out there?"

Tim shot an anxious look at Bob. "Not so good. Got the merchandise, but got something extra. You are not going to like this." He looked at Bob. "Bob, you better do the telling."

Bob cleared his throat and went on to tell Joe the details of the pickup in Bottle Neck Cove. When Bob had finished talking, Joe sat for a while thinking. None of his men dared say a word. This was a huge problem and one that would not go away easily.

"Best you all get busy unloading the bags. Bring the girl over to my tent. It's a fair distance from camp, but even so, keep the gag on. Don't want her disturbing our guests." With that, Joe stood up and walked out of the kitchen and up the well-worn trail to his private tent.

By the time Bob had carried Maya through the woods to Joe's tent, River Bend's boss had a plan. The girl was a liability, and the easiest thing to do would be to kill her and get rid of the body in the lagoon. Still, that was easier said than done. He had made several men who had double-crossed him disappear, but killing a woman didn't sit well with him. No, he'd make use of her.

His cook was on his last chance and he needed someone to help clean. Right now the guides took turns mucking out the washhouse and cleaning up the clients' quarters. They did it, but it was a lousy use of their time, especially on transfer nights. Those nights, he needed all of his men to unload the drugs and store them until they could be hidden for transport. Stashing the contraband into the containers, false-bottomed trunks, and other compartments took a lot of their time as well. Yeah, this little bit of extra cargo could be worth her weight in gold. First he had to control her, and then train her. Something told him the training might be the best part.

"Hey, Joe. You in there? I brought you a present."

With those words, Bob entered the high-walled tent and deposited Maya at Joe's feet. Joe took one look at Maya and laughed. This was going to be easier than he had thought. In front of him was a filthy wraith of a girl, barely 130 pounds, soaking wet. Her greasy brown hair partially hid a soft jaw line that was already beginning to swell from Bob's fist. Dark, terrified eyes stared at him, while smothered moans escaped from behind the slash of grey tape. He grabbed her face and stared directly into those panicked eyes.

"Listen very carefully. I don't repeat myself. Nod your head if you want to live."

Maya quickly nodded.

"Good. Now promise you will not yell or scream if I take the tape off."

Again, Maya nodded.

"Good, we have progress. I'll take off the tape and untie your hands and feet. Remember that *I will kill you* if I have to. Understand?"

Maya nodded a final time, and Joe motioned to Bob to remove her restraints.

Maya's legs gave out and she slumped to the floor. Hauling her up by her shoulders, Bob dragged her over to a chair and shoved her in it. The stench of diesel fuel, dirt, and human waste rose from her.

"Christ, you need cleaning up," Joe said. "Take her over to the washhouse and scrub her down."

Following Joe's orders, Bob half-dragged and half-carried Maya to the showers. Stripping her naked, he shoved her under the outdoor shower. Handing her a bar of soap, he told her to scrub. Maya wasn't quick enough for Bob's liking, so he grabbed her by the hair and proceeded to wash her like a rag doll.

As humiliating as it was to have someone scrubbing harshly and pawing at her, it also felt good. The warm water cascaded over her shoulders, easing the pain. It was wonderful to get rid of the stench and dirt of the last few horrible hours. He chucked her a towel that she thankfully used to dry herself and to shield her body from his prying eyes. After she pulled on a baggy old T-shirt that Tim had brought over from Joe's, she untangled her hair with someone's discarded comb. Bob glanced at Tim.

"Do you think that's good enough?"

"Sure thing. Hey, better than before," replied Tim as he took hold of her arm and began marching her back towards Joe's tent.

Maya struggled briefly but soon realised that it was useless trying to pull away.

Joe was waiting for them. He smiled at Maya as they entered the tent.

"You clean up pretty nice," he said. "Sit down and eat. You fellas go help stash the cargo."

Maya's eyes went to a small table holding a plate of food. There was a ham and cheese sandwich, a package of potato chips, and a can of cola.

"Sit down and eat, I said. You look like you haven't eaten in days."

Maya didn't need another invitation. She sat and devoured the sandwich in four unladylike bites. Savouring the potato chips one at a time, she watched Joe warily. The room was very hot and everything started to sway slightly. She drained the soda and reached out to put the can on the table. Realizing too late that she had been drugged; she looked up helplessly as she slumped slowly off her chair.

Joe carried her to a cot placed beside his bed. She was out for now. He yanked the T-shirt down over her legs and covered her up with a rough camp blanket. Then he fitted a large tie wrap snugly around her wrist. Threading another tie wrap through it, he attached that to a chain fastened to one of the cot's legs. If she woke up before morning, she wouldn't be able to run. The boats usually left around 5:30, so as long as the guests were out fishing, he didn't have to worry about her making noise. The education of this sweet, young thing would begin when the camp was empty.

****

Several times during the night, Maya roused from the drug-induced sleep, only to be drawn back in to the heavy blackness. Her mouth felt like dry cotton and her uncooperative limbs did not seem to belong to her. She was disorientated and incoherent.

As morning came, the drugs started wearing off. Gradually in the strengthening light, she could make out her surroundings. Lying as still as possible, she listened to the sounds of Joe snoring in his bunk. She jerked her arm upwards and found that she was chained to the cot.

Joe startled awake with the rattling of the chain against the metal frame.

"Well, we're back in the land of the living." He chortled. "You were gone quite a while. Those sleeping pills must be stronger than I thought. We're going to get acquainted now that the camp is deserted. I'll take you around and show you the layout. First, let's find you some clothes and then get some grub."

"Please, just let me go. I promise I won't say anything about the drugs. What you do is your business, not mine," Maya said trying to bargain with her captor.

"I was only kayaking down the coast. How was I supposed to know about your operation? No one would believe me anyhow."

"Maybe you can earn your freedom. But for now, if you do what I want, I'll let you live. If you don't cooperate, you won't live to see tomorrow's sun—that's for certain. There's no one around here for miles, so there's no point in taking off. Besides, Bob's a real good tracker. He can find anything in the bush."

Joe cut the tie wrap from around her wrist. He turned and rummaged in a box, coming up with a pair of knit shorts and a bright pink top that had been left behind by some fisherman's wife.

"Throw these on. Let's get going."

Joe confused Maya. One minute he was friendly, and the next he was ruthless. Maya silently nodded, turned her back, removed the T-shirt she had slept in, and put on the clothes. She smiled tentatively at him and was rewarded by a flickering smile in return. She wanted to appear willing in order to gain his trust.

Joe pushed her ahead of him up the trail to the washhouse. While she went into the outhouse, he waited for her just outside the door. Then, they went into camp and over to the lodge.

True to his word, the camp was deserted. Joe had fired the cook that morning and the guides were all out in the boats with the clients. No one was due back for hours. He knew who was catching fish and where the boats were because he was constantly in touch by radio. His men didn't make a move without his say.

He showed Maya around the kitchen and indicated where the supplies were kept.

"You have any skills in the kitchen? Can you handle this stove?" he asked as he fried up bacon and eggs for breakfast.

"I'm not bad at the basics," answered Maya. "And my grandma taught me how to make bread and pies."

He was also pleased to find out that she had cooked for a couple of kayak adventure companies and was used to feeding a crowd.

"Well you can always follow Sue's recipes. You can't screw up worse than my last cook. Lazy dickwad. Camps like mine run on three things: fish, booze and good grub…in that order. First two, I deal with and now the food is going to be up to you. It better be up to scratch if you know what's good for you. You can always become fish bait," he stated flatly.

Maya nodded and tucked into the fry up he shoved in front of her. Having had no fat in her diet for days, the eggs and bacon tasted wonderful.

Finally, she raised her head and smiled tentatively at Joe.

"You cook a fine breakfast. Thank you. All I've had for the last while has been gritty clams and boiled seaweed. This is delicious.

"How come you were out there by yourself?" questioned Joe.

Maya startled and understood she was on the point of giving away too much information. For all she knew Joe might know Connor. They both were involved in drugs.

"Ummm- I just decided to do the coast by myself. You know eco-warrior sort of thing. Wanted to prove a woman could do it, I guess. Would've made it except for Bottle Neck Cove."

"Shoulda had more sense girl. The West Coast is very unforgiving. Weren't your parents concerned... a boyfriend?"

Maya looked away and said nothing.

He knew she was being very careful not to reveal a lot of personal information. No point in questioning her further. She had shut down. *Fine,* he thought, *let the girl keep her secrets for now.*

"Okay, show me you want to live. Show me you can earn your keep. Here's Sue's card on venison stew. Get to work if you know what's good for you," he said as he shoved her in the direction of the pantry.

While he watched, Joe had Maya prepare tonight's meal, venison stew and sourdough biscuits. She then made several apple pies and a huge chocolate cake. There was no time to bake bread for tomorrow's lunches, so Joe defrosted some of the bakery bread from the freezer.

Just after one, he made grilled cheese sandwiches. Maya's contained a little extra—more sleeping pills, though not last night's extreme dosage. He took the sleepy girl back to his tent and laid her on her cot.

As she drifted off to sleep, she felt him chain her up again.

Joe left for town. There were things he had to get.

His first stop was the pet store where he bought a costly, electronic dog-restraint system. The expensive setup for dogs 100 to 150 pounds included a lightweight receiver collar with soft probes, a transmitter with adjustable levels of correction, an alarm that would activate if boundaries were challenged, boundary posts, and rechargeable batteries. Next he shopped at the local department store where he bought ladies underwear, a couple of pairs of knit pants, a pair of shorts, several cotton tops, and a heavy sweater. He also got a couple of large towels. At the drugstore, he got shampoo, soap, a toothbrush, and other necessities. While at the department store and the drugstore, he spun a tale of his sister's kid coming to visit and the airline losing her luggage.

Joe got back just in time to welcome the first of the returning boats. As usual, the clients were tired but happy. The fishermen enjoyed Maya's venison stew and biscuits. Several asked for seconds of the chocolate cake. After the guides had processed the day's catch, cleaned and restocked the boats, it was their turn to be equally impressed with the food. It seemed as though Joe had found himself a darn good cook this time.

While the clients enjoyed the free flowing beer and whiskey, Bob and Joe set up the boundaries for the dog-restraint system. The area covered took in Joe's tent, the washhouse, the outhouse, the docks, and the lodge. Joe altered the collar changing the buckle to a two-hole arrangement that would take a tie wrap.

"Thanks Bob. See you tomorrow." Joe turned and left with the collar and transmitter, striding up to his secluded tent.

The girl was lying chained to the cot waiting for him to return. He quickly closed the gap to the cot and sat down heavily on the narrow bed. Before she could move, he had the collar around her neck and had pulled the tie wrap tight. Without access to scissors or a sharp knife, there was no way of getting the tie loose. He would be watching her in the kitchen, so there was little chance of her freeing herself in there.

"Let me explain the deal here." In a monotone voice, Joe began to tell Maya how life at the camp was going to be. She would have to cook, clean, and do whatever he asked. She was in no way ever to talk to any of the clients and only to the guides if he gave her explicit permission. She would be allowed to have privacy in the washhouse and outhouse, but at all other times she would be watched or chained to the bed. He showed her the various components of the restraint system. Then he gave her a taste of the charge, full force, at maximum level of correction.

Maya's hair tingled and her lips went numb. A strange metallic taste poured into her mouth. The agony was unbelievable.

Chapter Twenty-Two

The lights were off in the farmhouse when she got home. Through the well-lit shop window Barbara could see John pacing back and forth swigging from an open bottle of scotch. It was only six o'clock. What was going on? With her heart in her mouth, she quickly ran up the steps and tried the door. It was locked. Fumbling in her purse, she found her key and unfastened the scruffy peeling door.

"Sarah, Sarah. Are you in bed already?" There was no answer. "Sarah," she called raising her voice in alarm. "Sarah. It's mommy. Are you sleeping?"

A small whimper came from inside the bathroom. "Mommy."

Barbara tried the door. It didn't open. Sarah must have locked it from the inside. "Sarah unlock the door. You know you're not supposed to lock the door. Open the door."

"I can't, I don't remember how," Sarah answered.

"Okay Sweetie. It's okay. Mommy will get the pointy stick and open it from this side. Just wait."

Sarah fell into her arms as she pushed the door wide. "Mommy I'm sorry. I was bad. I locked the door but I was so scared. Daddy scared me."

"Did you try to go in the shop?" asked Barb. "You know daddy doesn't let you in the shop."

"No, I was a good girl. Daddy scared me," said Sarah and erupting in tears.

Barbara gathered her weeping daughter into her arms and stroked her head. Slowly the girl settled down and gradually the story came out.

"Daddy started drinking his beers and forgot to give me my spaghetti lunch. I got the big chair and got the chips out of the snack cupboard. And I got a thing of chocolate milk out of the fridge. I'm a big girl I can feed myself but I really wanted spaghetti, you know.

I played with Smokey for a while on my bed but daddy came in without knocking. That's rude. He looked all funny and smelled like beer. Daddy said he wanted to play mommy and daddy. He told me to get my shoes on and to come over to the shop. He looked at me real funny. I know I'm not to go to the shop. Why did he want me to go to the shop, Mommy? I told him to go away. I told him I wanted to play with Smokey. He stared at me funny and said, 'dumb blonde.' What's a dumb blonde mommy? He went back out to the shop but I was scared. So I hid in the bathroom, but you can't hide if the door is open so I locked it. I'm sorry, Mommy. I was a bad girl. I locked the door."

As Barbara rocked her frightened girl in her arms, she felt cold fingers of dread close around her heart. The urges were getting to John. It had been too long since his last companion. She'd have to go trolling.

****

First she tried hooker alley. It never ceased to amaze her how this area of town was always so busy. There were plenty of women standing around in their high-heeled boots and short skirts but none fit the bill. Most were too old and those that were young enough had blonde hair or hair that had been streaked with bright pink or purple. She spotted an Aboriginal girl over by the thrift shop.

"Hi. You want some work tonight?" she asked her as she rolled down her window.

"Don't swing that way, lady. Besides, Lessies don't pay good enough. Gotta go." The girl jumped into the black Lincoln that had pulled up behind Barb's car.

After spending a good part of an hour scouring the area for other possible candidates, Barbara called it quits and moved off down the street. Perhaps she'd have better luck out at the junction.

The junction of highway and the river road was often a good place to pick up hitchhikers. Tonight, she saw that there was no one waiting for a ride. She carried on up the highway for several kilometres, still no luck. When she spotted a patrol car cruising down the other side of the road, she understood why no one was thumbing a ride. Picking up hitchhikers was illegal in this area. It would cost you dearly in fines. Giving up, she returned to the farm.

"No luck tonight," she said as she came into the kitchen. She was relieved to see Sarah in her usual place on the couch watching TV. "I'll cruise past the tree planters camp tomorrow after work."

"Best you do," grunted John. "Blondes are starting to look better and better."

"If you know what's good for you, you'll leave her alone. She's your daughter," she hissed.

"So you say. I'm not so sure," John sneered as he crashed his fist down on the table.

"Get some grub on the go. I'm starving." He got up, crossed over to the couch and deliberately sat close to Sarah.

****

There were three tree planter camps in the vicinity. Slowly Barb cruised by the one farthest from town. She saw two girls together hitching into town but neither looked right. Besides, she couldn't handle two. She only had one syringe in the glove compartment.

Out past the Bastin Lake camp, she saw one other person. Heading on up the road she found a turnaround, turned and cruised past again. It was a male.

It was getting late and she was growing concerned about Sarah's safety. She headed for home.

Bad news greeted her as she entered the dishevelled kitchen. Pots and dishes were still on the counter as she had left them this morning. John hadn't done a thing.

"Damn pipe to the lagoon is blocked," he said. "Have to get an industrial snake. Can't rent one until the weekend. No clean towels or underwear."

"Isn't that just great. I'll have to stay in town tomorrow after work and do the laundry at Soo Ling's. Can you see to supper for you and Sarah? Not sure when I'll be finished. Shouldn't be too late if I can get three machines," Barb said.

"We have any frozen pizza? That would be quick and easy," suggested John.

****

The next afternoon, Barb struggled into the Soo Ling Laundromat with three large cloth bags.

"Thanks," she said as a nice young man held the door for her.

Quickly, she grabbed the first three machines she saw empty. She had already sorted the clothes at home so it was just a matter of adding detergent and selecting the temperature and wash cycle. Adding coin after coin into the machines, she noted how much the cost had gone up since the last time she was here. Prices may have risen but the place was certainly no cleaner.

"Major bucks ain't it," observed a voice beside her.

She looked up and smiled at the dark-haired young woman feeding coins into the next washer.

"Yes, it's quite a lot. I haven't been here for a while."

As Barb sat flipping through a grungy magazine, she carefully scrutinized the girl. She was the right height but her dark hair was a bit too short. Still, she was a strong possibility. Her washers stopped and she transferred her clothes to the big gas-heated dryers. The girl stuffed her few items into the machine beside Barbara.

"This will take a while," noted Barbara. "Let's go grab a coffee across the road, my treat."

"That would be great. I haven't had anything all day. Just got in from the prairies. Left home with hardly any cash and had to come wash my clothes so I can go job hunting tomorrow."

Barb smiled. "In that case let me spring for a muffin as well. Welcome to Bainsbridge."

Limping slightly as they left the store, Barb suggested that they take her car.

"I know it's just across the street and down a little way but my foot is really bothering me."

"Okay," said the young woman and got into the Honda.

Just as she turned to speak to Barb, she felt the needle plunge into her arm. The effects of the drug were immediate. Spiralling down into a world of hazy darkness; she spun in and out of consciousness. Trying to speak was impossible. Trying to move became more and more difficult. Quickly, she became immobilized and sat slumped over in the front seat.

Barb started the car and eased out into the street. Driving cautiously with one eye on her victim and the other on the road, she made her way to the riverbank. She parked and shut off the lights. The girl was too heavy for her to move by herself so she slid the seat back as far as it would go. She pushed her down until the defenceless woman lay crumpled up on the floorboards. Running around to the trunk, she took out a tattered emergency blanket and draped it over the inert form. The woman's eyes stared at her as the blanket fell, mutely pleading for release.

Waiting half an hour, with the girl in the car under the blanket, was nerve racking. She hoped the dosage was sufficient to paralyze her until they reached the farmhouse. Barb restarted the car and drove to Soo Ling's, where she calmly collected her clothes out of the dryers.

"Thanks so much," she called to the bored young teen behind the counter.

She left and drove steadily out to the farm. Parking in front of the shop she went to get John.

John met her on the front steps. He had seen her park at the shop and knew what that meant.

"Sarah's watching *Mash*. I'll lock the door. What's this one like?" He was like a kid at Christmas.

They carried their prey into the shop and through to the small walled-off room. There they threw her onto the narrow cot. John was breathing heavily and not just from exertion.

"Rebecca will be fine. She'll do the trick," John said raggedly as he named his victim. "Rebecca. Yes, she'll do the trick."

With that, Barb turned on her heel and left the shop, shutting off the main lights as she went.

"I was scared again, Mommy. Daddy tried to touch me. He called me his fancy girl. What's a fancy girl, Mommy? What's a fancy girl?"

"Don't worry about things like that anymore. Daddy will leave us alone. I brought him a new toy. He will be playing with it in his shop. Remember; don't go in the shop. There are too many sharp tools. You could hurt yourself. You have to stay in the house and play with Smokey. Smokey needs a friend. Smokey needs you to love him. See here's Smokey now. Cuddle up and go night-nights. She smoothed her daughter's hair and tucked the blanket around her and Smokey, who had crawled under the covers. 'Shh, go night-nights."

****

As he methodically stripped off her dirty T-shirt and jeans, John checked over his new prize. She had that unwashed road weary smell he so enjoyed. The hair wasn't long like he liked but it would grow. The newness and stillness of the inert woman quickly inflamed his desire. He made quick use of his prey. Tomorrow she'd remember nothing. He'd have to teach her all over again. That was the fun part.

He gave her another little dose of Special K and went into the tiny bathroom to wash up. After he was done, he put the fluffy pink towel on the hook beside the chipped sink. May as well make her feel welcome; she'd be here for a while if she was any good.

Chapter Twenty-Three

Maya didn't think things could get much worse. From the moment she was captured on the beach to the horrible boat ride to the camp, she had been in pain. The right side of her face hurt like hell from where Bob had hit her. Her legs and body were bruised from hitting the metal legs of the boat's seats. The skin around her mouth and her lips was almost raw from the adhesive in the duct tape.

The pain delivered by the tightly fitting collar, however, was the worst she had ever felt in her life. As it subsided, she gave way to retching and shaking. She gazed mutely at Joe, knowing there was nothing she could do. She was totally at his mercy. She curled up in a ball, whimpering like an injured dog.

"I'll leave you awhile to think things over." Joe left as suddenly as he had come.

Gradually, she gained control of herself. She reached up to her neck with her free hand and felt the collar. The buckle had been removed and the collar was held together with a rigid plastic strap. Tugging at the tie with her fingers proved to be a futile effort. Nothing budged or loosened. She couldn't even get up as she was still chained to the cot. Frantic thoughts threatened to overwhelm her. Steeling herself to be calm, she lay there thinking.

She had to gain Joe and Bob's trust. Let them get complacent and drop their guard. She would have to do it slowly to be believable. She knew how to cook; she could clean. She prayed that was all they would want. Although the restraint system appeared to be foolproof, its energy source was batteries—and they wore down didn't they? Perhaps Joe would forget to recharge the batteries, or maybe the transmitter would fail. Possibilities flooded her brain.

Someone from the camp or maybe even one of the guides might help her. One of the fishermen might get suspicious and wonder what she was doing in the camp. They might think the odd collar was not just a fashion statement reserved for the young. Or maybe Joe could change his mind if she was really nice to him and let her go. She dug deep for any vestige of hope.

After what seemed like forever, she heard the sound of the entrance zipper being pulled down. Joe had returned. He unshackled her. Marching her outside, he showed her the boundaries and threatened to activate the shock system again.

She let tears well up into her eyes and looked at him beseechingly.

"Please no. It hurts so bad. Please—please don't. I promise I'll do as you say."

Joe grinned and activated the system.

Unable to control her reaction, Maya writhed on the ground. Unclenching her jaw, she gazed at him with wounded eyes. Saliva gushed from her mouth, pooling in the dust. She was rewarded with a flash of regret on Joe's face. As she whimpered and moaned, he hauled her to her feet and dragged her down the trail and into the main part of the camp.

Seeing her frantically look around for signs of other people, Joe laughed. He explained that the camp was usually deserted from 6:00 in the morning until about 7:30 at night when the boats returned for the day. From six in the morning until six in the evening, she would be expected to get everything done. After that, she would be confined to the tent. He couldn't take the chance of her running into one of the fishermen or a sympathetic guide.

She knew that he would be able to monitor her movements even if she were out of his sight; the alarm would vibrate on his wrist if she challenged the boundaries. Shrugging her shoulders helplessly, she asked Joe what she would be doing. She listened carefully as he told her about her new camp duties. Cooking seemed to be the most important. That she could do. The cleaning of the toilets, client tents, and washhouse wouldn't take much skill. It appeared that they shipped out most of the laundry, and the guides took care of the sports boats and processing the fish. Joe took care of the general handyman chores and the running of the camp.

****

True to his word, Joe woke her every morning at 5:45. This gave her time to visit his outhouse, dress, and then wait for him to escort her to the kitchen.

He came for her as soon as the last boat had left the dock. He had already cooked and fed the clients their breakfasts of eggs, bacon, and hash browns. Huge slabs of her home-made bread and large mugs of camp coffee completed their meal. The guides had collected her ready-to-go lunches that she had made the day before and put in the large cooler.

Since the camp menu rotated every week, Maya soon got into a routine. First, she made the bread dough, leaving it to rise while she prepped the vegetables and meat for the evening meal. Next, came whatever cookies, pies, and cakes were required for the next day's lunches and that evening's dessert. The ovens were a good size, so if she planned well, she could get everything cooked within her limited time frame.

By the time the sweets were cooked, she was able to start baking the many loaves of bread that had been left to rise in pans. Maya then concentrated on the evening courses and preparing sandwich fillings. Sue's recipes were easy to follow.

Gradually, she suggested other items that she knew how to cook well, including chowders, soups, and her special chocolate fudge cake. These dishes proved to be very popular with both the clients and the staff. Joe began to appreciate her efforts and skill.

Most of the cooking chores were completed by three, leaving the rest of the afternoon for cleaning the washing facilities and tents. The sheets were only changed if there were new clients. Dirty sheets were loaded into large cotton sacks belonging to a laundry in Dunsmere.

There was too much work for one person to get done, so Maya was grateful that Joe was not a lazy man. They usually worked side by side in the kitchen. He helped with the cleaning as well. Trying to seem friendly, she chatted while she worked with him. She told him stories of kayaking, university, and travels without giving out any important personal information.

Eventually, he started to reveal more and more about himself. She listened as he spoke of his troubled childhood back on the prairies. She saw that this self-made man was very proud of this fishing camp; it meant the world to him.

Underlying this confident air of his, she detected trouble. She wondered *why he needed the drug operation and the fishing camp. From what she could tell, he loved running the camp and took pride in giving his customers quality service. What was hanging over his head, making him deal in drugs?*

The last chore was making up the lunches for the guides to take in the boats on the next day's excursions. By the time the cleaning was completed, the loaves of bread were cooled enough to slice. As Joe fed the loaves into a slicing machine, Maya filled and double wrapped each sandwich. Adding cookies, fruit, and perhaps leftover salad, she then bagged and tagged each lunch with the guide's name.

Some clients had special dietary needs, so each guide was responsible for packing the correct lunch into softsided coolers for the day on the water. The previous cook had been able to prep the lunches first thing in the morning, but of course that was out of the question for Maya. In order for him to keep Maya out of sight, Joe now had to cook breakfasts and didn't have time to deal with lunches. Holding well-wrapped food overnight in the huge walk-in cooler did not seem to be a problem. Never one to do half a job, Maya tried her best to provide well-cooked food.

Joe was receiving lots of compliments about his food. Yes, the girl was working out fine.

Shortly before six, she knew Joe would escort her back to his secluded tent. Thankfully, he had stopped chaining her to the cot and she was able to move about the tent in relative freedom. Searching for any sign that someone could be missing her, she pored over every magazine and newspaper that came into the tent. Either no one was aware she was missing or Joe carefully screened each paper before he let her read it. Once when she was reading the port section of the Franklin paper, she scanned the Coast Guard report. Buried in the incident report were two brief lines about a kayaking guide missing and presumed drowned somewhere off Pantal, a small island on the west coast.

She shivered with the sudden awareness that no one would be looking for her now. Everyone thought she was dead. Her parents were used to her going off with Chad and being out of communication for months. Now that she was alone, they might become alarmed, but not for several weeks. Her sensible parents knew they had raised a strong, independent child capable of looking after herself. *If they only knew,* she thought. *If they only knew what a predicament she was in now.*

Evenings passed slowly. Left to her own devices, Maya took to snooping, trying to discover what made her captor tick. While she listened for the sounds of Joe's footsteps coming up the trail, Maya searched through the various boxes that littered Joe's tent. She was always careful to replace everything exactly the way she had found it. She came across several old photos of Joe and a large blonde woman. This must be the Sue he had talked about. In the photos the couple looked happy enough enjoying adventurous times in the bush. It was clear that they had been very much in tune with one another. Both seemed to love the outdoors and a simple way of life. Maya wondered what had happened. Did Sue leave or did she die tragically?

Unexpectedly, she stumbled upon the answer. A handful of poker chips and drink coasters from a casino in Fort Sumac revealed Joe's secret. Of course, he gambled. It all made sense to her now. Drugs and gambling often went hand in hand. You could make a lot of money transporting and selling drugs. What better way to pay off gambling debts? Joe would not want to risk losing his beloved fish camp to debtors. The out-of-the-way location, access to offshore boats, hidden coves and bays, young men eager to make big money—it all made his operation a perfect cover up for smuggling.

Maya still had many unanswered questions though. How did the drugs leave the camp? Were all the guides in on it, or just Bob and Tim? Did any of the clients know? One thing she knew for sure—they would never let her go alive.

****

Suddenly, the atmosphere around camp changed. The guides were preoccupied and Joe was tense. Thursday usually meant a big clean up as most guests arrived on Fridays. Also, on every second Thursday, the delivery truck arrived from Fort Sumac with supplies for the camp. The white four-wheel drive van bumped and jarred its way over the thirteen rough kilometres of dirt road carrying everything from frozen foodstuffs, basic groceries, fuel, and booze to clean laundry. It left again early Friday morning with empty barrels, containers, and dirty laundry. All the guides were at River Bend on Thursdays. No one had the day off as all hands were needed to unload, reload, and to look after any guests that had an extended stay.

This Thursday was no exception. Harry and Phil left by floatplane, but the four other guests from Alaska were staying on for another week. Tim was assigned to take them out to an exclusive fishing area. This prime area was a fair distance away and would require them to overnight on a nearby island. Camping gear, extra food, and of course lots of beer were loaded on to Tim's boat. Joe saw them off around six and went to get Maya.

"No guests for supper tonight, but we have to feed the guides and the driver," Joe smiled. "An easy day. We'll just have burgers, fries, and pie. You can manage that on your own. Best make up some extra bread though, for lunches and for later. It's gonna be a long night." He led her down to the kitchen and warned her not to talk to anyone.

Bob rushed into the kitchen and reported that the truck was on its way in. The driver had called from Dunsmere to make sure they didn't need anything extra. Maya tried to blend in to the background, pretending to be busy slapping around the bread dough. She caught a look pass between Joe and Bob. They both left to stand outside the kitchen door and carry on their conversation. Obviously something big was happening; something they didn't want her to know about. With her curiosity thoroughly aroused, she carried on with her chores, straining to hear what they were saying.

"Yup, the system works well. Those containers are great and thank God no one ever checks Roy's van with sniffer dogs," said Bob.

"Doubt if Mitzy would let another dog anywhere near Roy. Jealous little thing," laughed Joe. "Funny little mutt, keeps him company though."

"Roy does a real good job chatting up the highway guys. Think everyone knows his stories about his wife and those two teenage girls of his," added Bob. "Rodrico sure did well hiring him."

"He could hire the Pope for all I care, just so long as drugs get to the warehouse and money gets in my bank," Joe said as he glanced through the screen door checking to see what Maya was doing.

Raising his voice, Joe told her, "Best you hurry. The guys will be getting hungry soon." Maya looked up and nodded.

"Time to secure our girl?" asked Bob as Joe rejoined him on the steps.

"No, I don't need to chain her. It's such a pain in the ass. She never leaves the tent… too afraid of the collar! Besides, I'll keep an eye on her. You and the boys can manage to load by yourselves."

"Christ, Joe, it'll take all night if you don't supervise. Some of the guys are new at it. You have all the compartments mapped out in your head," argued Bob.

"Okay, fine. I'll slip her some of my sleeping pills and she'll be out."

Just as Maya was finishing up the blackberry pies, the rest of the crew came in for supper. Maya served up the burgers and fries, keeping her head down and not uttering a word. She could see Joe watching her carefully from the rocking chair, and she noticed Bob fiddling around in the kitchen over by the stove. *Okay*, she thought, *he's putting the pills in one of the burgers.* Joe must have told him to do it while she was busy feeding the crew.

Going back into the cooking area, Maya could see two burgers wrapped in tin foil and some fries wrapped separately.

"Need something?" She asked Bob quietly.

"No, just fixing a burger for myself. Yours is over there for later." With that, Bob turned and left the kitchen, strolling down the path towards the fuel dock.

Shortly before six, Joe took her back to the tent.

"Is it okay, Joe, if I sit outside for a while? There are no customers in camp."

"Sure, I guess it won't hurt. Eat your burger, and I'll be back in half an hour."

Maya dragged out a wooden chair from Joe's tent and moved it over into the sunshine. The cooling air was pleasant on her face and neck. The kitchen could get quite hot with the stove going in such warm weather. She raised her hair up off her neck and allowed the cool breezes to refresh her. Out of the corner of her eye, she saw Bob watching her every movement. She was not surprised. He waited until Joe was out of sight and then came up beside her. *What did he want?* She wondered.

"Evening," Bob said. "Brought you a little something to cheer you up."

He produced a small flask and offered it to her. Judging by his slightly slurred speech, she could tell he had already been enjoying himself. Best keep him friendly, she thought, remembering his fist on her jaw.

"Sure, haven't had a drink for ages." She seized the flask and took a long pull of the fiery liquid. Coughing a little, she swallowed and gave him back the flask with a smile. "Thanks."

They sat for a while appreciating the night air. Not much conversation passed between them as Bob was constantly on the alert for Joe's return. As they passed the bottle back and forth, Bob shifted his leg so it brushed up against Maya's. She stiffened and then made herself relax. She needed to gain his trust as well as Joe's. More chance for her to stay alive if both of them liked her. A little competition might come in handy.

Suddenly, she heard Joe's footfalls on the dusty path. Bob melted away into the bush and hurried back down to the camp.

"You haven't eaten your food yet? Best you do before it gets stone cold."

While Joe went into the tent, she slid the burger under her thigh and started to eat the fries. Listening to the rustle of clothing as Joe changed into warmer gear for the evening's work, Maya then shoved the burger into a crevice between two logs. She balled up the tin foil and put the crumpled paper beside the half-eaten fries.

"Get in here," demanded Joe. "Time you got inside. Remember, if you don't want a taste of the collar, you'll stay put."

Maya nodded meekly and yawned.

"I'm awfully sleepy for some reason. Guess I'm coming down with a cold or something. Gonna lie down for a while anyway," Maya muttered.

Crossing over to her cot, she lay down and pretended to drift off to sleep. Listening intently, she heard Joe come over and stand looking at her. Then she felt his hands on her. He rubbed them over her breasts and down over her stomach. *Oh, God, no,* she panicked. She rolled over slowly, feigning sleep. He continued exploring her body with slow wandering hands.

"Joe, you ready?" Bob had come looking for him.

Joe sighed and left the tent, closing the zippered entrance on his way out.

"She's out for the count. How many tabs did you put in the burger? She went down fast."

Maya let out a slow breath. That had been close, too close for comfort.

She sat up and listened for any trace of the men returning. She heard nothing but the usual night noises. Carefully, pulling on her sneakers, she crept out of the tent and into the surrounding bush. Staying within the restraint boundaries, she made her way silently towards the fuel dock. The van had been pulled up beside it, and the guides were busy hauling out sandy-coloured duffel bags from the fuel shed.

She recognised the bags, of course. They were identical to the ones Tim and Bob had loaded onto the boat in Bottle Neck Cove. Hiding behind some thick, stubby spruce trees, she crouched down to watch.

The guides unpacked each sack carefully, piling the brick-shaped packages on the ground. The van looked as though it was in a shop being repainted. Side panels had been removed. The trunk's lining lay discarded in the dirt. The wheel wells were exposed, and the roof lining was hanging down as well. As Maya watched, fascinated, each part of the van was stuffed with the off-white bricks.

Next, the guides started to dismantle several of the containers that had once held the camp supplies. About one third of the container was double walled. The bottom was also double. Cleverly, the drugs fit in between the two linings. Once sealed, no one would be able to see any difference between the containers that held drugs and those that did not.

While Maya stared from behind the spruce screen, she saw them empty and repack the laundry bags. The rest of the drugs where hidden amongst the dirty linens. No wonder Joe had wanted her out of the way of this business. Yes, she had to admire the careful planning that had gone into the whole operation.

Rough hands closed around her mouth, and she found herself being dragged out of the bushes.

"What do we have here, Joe? Look who's been spying."

Tim hauled her to her feet. There was no escape. Joe incapacitated her with one shock.

Helpless, she mutely begged with her eyes. One more shock and she lost consciousness.

****

Maya came to, shackled to the cot. Dried blood, from the damage her teeth had done to her lips, filled her mouth with a revolting metallic taste. She gagged and choked. She desperately wanted water.

Slowly, the memory of the previous night filtered into her foggy brain. She began to recall the scene in the woods, and she remembered the sinking sensation she had felt when those arms encircled her. Then she remembered the wracking pain, as she was shocked into submission. Joe had carried her limp body to his tent and had stripped her naked. Silent tears had coursed down her face as he raped her again and again. She sobbed as she recalled the callous, violent sex, so unlike the gentle lovemaking she and Chad had enjoyed. Her body cringed as visions of Joe plunging into her flooded her mind. Turning her head to the side, she vomited onto the floor.

She heard the tent zipper being yanked down. Moving as far away as possible on the narrow cot, she brought her knees up protectively. As Joe gazed down, she could tell he was ashamed at what he had done.

His tone, however, gave no hint of this.

"Need any more of last night's medicine? The boys would be more than willing. Best you listen, listen real good. Any more nonsense like the stunt you pulled last night and I'll take you out in the bush and shoot you. Understand? You know way too much, now."

Maya numbly nodded her head. She had lost this round. All the progress she had made in gaining Joe's trust had been erased; she was back to square one. She wondered how much worse things could get.

As Joe reached for her wrist, she shrank back trembling. He released the tie wrap and yanked her to her feet.

"Time to get on with the chores," he said as he pushed her towards the washhouse. "Go get cleaned up and be up at the kitchen in five. Don't make me come get you."

She stood for as long as she dared under the hot shower, trying to scrub away any traces of Joe. Tears mixed with the cascading water as she recognized things would never be the same. Hauling herself out of the comforting water, she dressed and hurried to the kitchen.

She moved through the following days as if she were in a fog. Any glimmer of hope had been eradicated. Although Joe didn't shackle her to the cot, the collar was still around her neck and he was now demanding oral sex. He seemed less worried about her running into the guides, but she was kept hidden whenever the guests were in camp. Once or twice she had seen guests when she had visited the outhouse, but always from a distance. She was never able to make contact.

She heaved a sigh of relief when she found she had to ask Joe to get her some sanitary supplies. At least, that dreadful night had not resulted in a pregnancy. Joe actually seemed to prefer oral sex, so if she continued to service him that way she should be all right.

As the days wore on, Joe appeared to relax. He became quite careless and used to her presence in the camp.

Occasionally she was able to walk along the riverbank and immerse herself in the shallow pool beside the sandbar. She welcomed the cool water after a long and tiring day in the kitchen.

She saw there was lots of evidence that the weather was starting to change. Chattering squirrels loudly challenged each other while they guarded their stashes of pinecones. Sometimes small advance flocks of Canada Geese dotted the skyline as their annual migration got underway. Bears were coming down in the cooling dusk to feed on the salmon that strayed too close to the riverbanks. Leaves took on the heavy dusty look that heralded their demise. Although the August days were hot and humid, she knew fall came quickly to these northern parts.

Maya worried that her days were also numbered. *What would happen to her once the camp closed for the season?* She very much doubted that she would be allowed her freedom. *How could she make herself indispensable after the clients had stopped coming?*

She had no ideas or solutions. She would have to escape before it was too late. For now she would concentrate on being friendly, on making herself useful and getting them to believe she'd given up on freedom.

Joe started to permit her to sit outside the tent during the evening hours. From her vantage point, she could watch a pair of nesting eagles as they tirelessly hunted for prey to feed their eaglets. At first, there had been two young birds in the nest, but eventually the stronger eaglet had pushed the other out of the nest. Even though she knew this is what usually happened in the eagle world, she couldn't help but grieve for the unfortunate, young nestling. The adults would constantly call to each other as they approached the nest. Watching the eagles gave her some peace. Eagles are a symbol of strength. Chad would have wanted her to be strong.

Chapter Twenty-Four

Hunter woke at the crack of dawn. He never slept much past sunrise, needing only a few hours shuteye each night. He had been like that since he was a kid. His had been a great childhood filled with many pleasant memories. Although his parents had been strict about morals and behaviour, they had been lenient with him when it came to allowing personal freedom. As a reliable man with a strong, independent character, Hunter had already been promoted to a senior position on the drug squad. His colleagues respected his leadership skills.

Hunter never reluctant to speak his mind, usually managed to temper his candour with friendly humour. He had a good group of friends, mainly on the force. Girlfriends came and went, never staying long enough to form a lasting relationship. He soon realized that most women were put off by his dedication to police work. His career was his priority and he had yet to meet someone who would take precedence. In addition, few women put up with the reality that his undercover work took him out of town and out of communication for weeks on end.

Now that both his parents had passed on, his sister, Susan, and her son, Kyle, were his only close family. Given that most of his assignments dealt with dangerous gangs trafficking in drugs, Susan was deliberately kept ignorant of the details of his police work.

Feeling too lazy to cook and more than a little hungry, he decided to return to the diner for breakfast. As he swung the door open, he found himself hoping that Sally was working this morning. No such luck; a large-bosomed woman wearing a uniform that was much too tight greeted him. Betty, in her late fifties, was friendly enough. Turned out she was a cousin to Mike and already knew all about his fishing inquiries.

"Did you get fixed up at River Bend? Mike said you were asking. It's a good fish camp. That Joe's a weird duck. Keeps to himself. Most of his guests are satisfied though, and lots of young guys from 'round here have worked for him one time or another."

Hunter smiled. She should be good for some gossip. Some of his best tips came from lonely waitresses who loved to pass the time of day.

"Yeah, called Sally's fella and he set me up for Friday. What do you know about him? Sally seems like such a nice young thing. It would be good to know she was with someone half-decent."

"Oh, Bob you mean? He's nice enough. Loves to flash the cash, but so do all those guides from River Bend. Rumours have it there's more going on there than just fishing. Too much money floating around, if you ask me. Then again, maybe Joe just pays well. You gotta pay well to keep the young guys on steady. A camp is only as good as the fish it gets, and they know where the fish is."

Hunter settled down to a huge breakfast of bacon, scrambled eggs, hash browns, and toast. He drank his vitamin C and charged his batteries with the diner's fresh-perked coffee. As usual, while he ate, he checked out the other customers. An old couple sat in the corner booth, myopically reading sections of the newspaper. The other tables were occupied with truckers fuelling their bellies for the long road trip to the Interior.

Hunter considered diner breakfasts were often the best value for your dollar. You usually got what you ordered and this meal was no exception. After polishing off the last of his eggs, he sat sipping his coffee.

"Hey, Betty," he called to the waitress. "Fill 'er up again, please. Come sit if you have time. Perhaps you can tell me how to pass the day around here. I have to meet up with the River Bend van just past six tonight."

"They ain't got no van. You must be going in on the delivery van that drops their stuff off the second and fourth Thursdays in the month. It leaves the 7-11 at 6:30, regular as clockwork. Some of the guides catch a ride in that way too."

Betty got back to answering his question. "Well, let's see. The fish hatchery in Bainsbridge is pretty interesting. There's the float in one of those old riverboats from the 1800s—takes about four hours though. You might not get back in time. Town isn't bad. Has two pubs and a mall. Earl runs the sporting goods store on the main street. He knows all there is to know about fishing in these parts. He could tell you how to catch that Chinook you're after."

After chatting a while with Betty, Hunter paid his tab and left a generous tip.

"See you later," he called as he strode out the door.

"Yeah, see ya. Good luck with that fishing."

He carried on into town. After making inquiries as to where he could leave the truck and camper for a few days, he went downtown to the sporting goods store. Introducing himself to Earl, as an acquaintance of Betty, he began making casual conversation.

He discovered there were three fishing camps in the immediate area, but Joe's had the best reputation and seemed to make the most money even in this harsh economic time. Earl told him that although they ran up a huge tab, they always came through with the money by the end of the season. He bitched about carrying the other camps on into the winter and then some.

When Earl's wife came in to relieve him for lunch, Hunter offhandedly invited Earl for a brew at the local pub. Never one to pass up free booze, Earl eagerly accepted. The two men crossed over the street to a rather dingy looking bar.

Several regulars looked up from their pints as Earl and Hunter entered the dimly lit bar. It took a bit for their eyes to become adjusted to the gloomy atmosphere after being outside in the brilliant sunshine. The air stank of stale cigarettes and beer. A couple of men recognized Earl and invited them to join their table.

"Missus let you out, did she? Who's your friend?"

Earl introduced Hunter as an American tourist, here to do some fishing.

"Told him one of the best camps is Joe's. Turns out he's booked there tonight. He wants to land a Chinook. Be lucky if he does. Run only just started up this way. Heard tell of some guy landing a fifty-two-pounder last Wednesday, a spring though."

"Where'd he go for that, Earl? Off Rainbow Reach or Bottle Neck?" asked the younger of the regulars.

"Bottle Neck. Most of the big ones hang out there."

The waitress came over and stood waiting for their order. In the bar's humidity, her limp blonde hair was hanging straight over her weary shoulders. Impatiently, she flicked at a fly crawling across the back of an empty chair.

"What'll you have, fellas? Ain't got all day while you try to impress studly here." She gave Hunter a wink. "They gas all day about everyone else's luck. Never seen them go out fishing themselves yet!"

"Couple of drafts, please. And whatever these two are having—my tab." Hunter returned the wink.

He sat nursing his draft, needing to keep a cool head while he was on the job. Earl and his friends had no such concerns and accepted Hunter's hospitality each time he offered. As the beer flowed, so did the innuendoes and speculations about Joe's extraordinary business success. For the most part, there were no concrete facts, just chatter tinged with envy.

Next the conversation centred on missing fishermen and boats. There had been a good number of wrecks along this part of the coast. Hunter paid close attention when they mentioned the missing sea kayaker. Must be the same one they were briefed on in the squad room. The story had grown bigger as most do over time. Apparently, the owner of the *Ainslie* had offered up a ten thousand dollar reward to anyone who found her dead or alive. There had been several sightings of the young female guide, including some fishing boat catching a glimpse of a kayaker in the fog a mile or so off the entrance to Bottle Neck Cove. Another sighting had the kayaker in Skagway, Alaska. Still another had her seen in a mall in Franklin. A ten-thousand-dollar reward often brought about a lot of sightings.

None of the tips usually panned out, just like those in the missing girls' investigation. Years had gone by, and many of the friends and family of those missing girls had mortgaged their homes and taken out loans in an effort to post rewards. All to no avail; the few leads that had sounded promising had failed to produce any results. The killer was just too careful. The countryside around there was just too isolated.

About three o'clock, Earl's wife, a tall redhead, came barrelling through the door.

"What in hell are you up to, you drunken sod? There's me stuck on my own, minding your damn store, while you're in here drinking your face off."

Earl just smiled and reached out his arm. Catching her butt in one of his big mitts, he gave her a squeeze.

"Hon, I'm just waiting on you. Thursday's a shit day at the store. You could've been over an hour ago. You knew where I was. Sit down. Hunter, my man, get my old lady a brew."

Around five, Hunter called the afternoon quits. He had a couple of things to do before he met up with the van. First, he put in a call to headquarters, letting them know he was going fishing for the next few days. He checked with them on a few facts about Bottle Neck Cove. That name had come up several times over the last two days. It was confirmed that it was the location of suspicious activity report received by the Coast Guard, some three weeks ago. Apparently, it was also reputed to be an excellent fishing area. Hopefully, the guides at River Bend would be willing to take him out there. He could be persuasive, especially if he greased a few palms. That's what expense accounts were for, weren't they? Hunter went by the ATM machine and withdrew several hundred dollars in fifties.

He pulled into the service station where he had arranged to leave his truck and camper. Grabbing his duffel with his clothes and what fishing gear he had, Hunter then unloaded his gun and packed it and the ammunition in the bottom of the bag, under the clothes. Slinging the bag over his shoulder, he locked the camper and truck up and wandered over the road to the 7–11.

"Evening. You guys know where I catch the van going to River Bend camp?"

"Yup, you're right in time. There it is pulling in now."

Hunter watched as a short, wiry man parked at the gas bar and got out of the cab. The driver waved at the service attendant, who switched on the gas pump. Several minutes later, the tank was full and he came in to pay.

"Hey Roy, got a passenger for you tonight. Says he needs a ride to River Bend. Must want to try his luck catching a one of those Chinooks," called the attendant to the van's driver.

Roy nodded to Hunter.

Hunter smiled offering out his hand.

"Hunter's the name. Good of you to take me. Heard the road is pretty rough and don't feel like beating up the truck and camper. Have to make it all the way to Alaska in it. No point in pushing my luck when you're going that way. Thanks." Hunter climbed in the passenger seat and chucked his bag over the seat.

The entire van was packed with all sorts of goods. There were several large Styrofoam coolers, boxes of fruits and vegetables, cases of canned goods, flats of beer, boxes of hard liquor, and sacks that probably contained linens and towels. Lined up along the back was a row of red Gerry cans filled with fuel.

Suddenly Hunter felt a wet nose nuzzle his ear. Mitzy, Roy's whirling dervish of a dog, had found a new friend.

"See you've met Mitzy," laughed Roy.

The lively little mutt leaped over the back of the seat and into her master's arms. Licking his nose and panting with excitement, the fluffy white dog greeted him like a long lost friend. There was obviously a tight bond between them, Hunter observed, probably born from many long hours on the road.

"Settle down, girl. Behave yourself."

Mitzy licked him once more and then returned to her bed in the back of the van. She circled her box twice, snuffled, and settled down for the journey. With the dog settled, Roy gunned the van into action and set off down the very long, thirteen kilometres of twisting ruts.

****

By the time the van had made its way over the rough road to camp, Hunter and Roy had become well acquainted. Roy loved having a captive audience and filled Hunter's head with all kinds of trivia from his life.

Hunter learned how Roy had met his wife while driving a taxi back when he was a teenager. Their match was destiny, and their two teenage daughters were payback. It seemed like they had no end of trouble from these girls. From what Hunter could understand, they were pretty normal girls getting up to what most young people did these days: partying, boys, tattoos, and hooking off school. To hear Roy tell it, they were off the rails and bound for trouble.

Hunter breathed a sigh of relief that he didn't have to worry about such things. His nephew was only ten and more interested in hunting and fishing than the opposite sex. Still, he knew the time would come when Uncle Hunter would pale by comparison to a night out with the guys.

As they skidded around blind corners and over washboard, he took the time to survey the surrounding countryside. There were several places you could hide a truck and camper. Closer to the actual camp was a small lake with a forestry campsite at one end.

"What's the name of this lake?" Hunter asked Roy as they drifted past.

"That one, I don't know. Not that familiar with the names of all the lakes around these parts. That lake is fed by some small creek that empties in from under the highway. Pretty little lake."

One last stretch of bone-rattling washboard and they pulled into the camp parking lot. It was just after eight. Joe and Bob came out to greet the latest guest.

"Joe Cunningham, this is my place. This here is Bob who you already spoke to on the cell."

Hunter shook the outstretched hand, noting the confident air of the beer-bellied man. He saw that Bob hung back a bit, obviously deferring to the older man.

"Hunter. Pleased to meet you. Heard a lot of good things about your operation out here. You ready to show this city boy how to catch a big one?"

"We'll try our best. Got you over in that tent. Bob will show you around, then you guys come up to the kitchen for a night cap." With that, Joe turned and went into the lodge.

Bob picked up Hunter's duffel and was surprised by its weight.

"What you got in there? Lead weights?"

"Not much, just a little fishing gear. But you did say most of the boats had lots of saltwater tackle, didn't you? I'm not familiar with ocean fishing. This will be my first time out on the sea. Hope to hell I'm not seasick!"

"No worries. After three hours, you get used to anything. We have Gravol and these bands that go on your wrists. They were developed for pilots flying bombing raids over Germany during one of the world wars. Can't remember which one. I prefer the bands; you don't get sleepy. The bands work like acupuncture. I know—New Age crap. Don't knock it though. They work hot damn. Here's your home for the next four days. You get first pick of the beds as your tent buddies don't arrive until late tomorrow morning." Bob ushered Hunter into the off-white, high-walled tent.

Hunter glanced around inside the tent. It was well equipped with four cots, a few chairs, a small card table, and a couple of benches set along the back wall. The cots were already made up with sheets and thick duvets. Bottled water was set on the table, and towels were piled on one of the benches. Pretty darn good for a fish camp.

He put his duffel under one of the cots and followed Bob out to check the rest of the campsite. A couple of solar composting toilets and a washhouse were set apart from the sleeping tents. Shower stalls were outside the washhouse but faced the woods, giving a little privacy. Three more high-walled tents were set apart a little way from the client accommodations. These, Bob explained, were for the fishing guides. Joe had his tent up the path a ways.

They meandered down to the dock. Seven Boston Whalers, Joe's choice of sport boats, were lined up like horses at the trough. Each boat had its name and the name of the camp painted on the side.

"Pretty good little boats. They're very stable in swells. Have a rep for being unsinkable. Nice back deck with lots of room for fishing action. This here one's mine." Bob pointed to a brand new, top-of-the line Dauntless 230.

"At twenty-three feet, it can hold up to nine people if need be," Bob boasted. "You'll be fishing with me tomorrow."

"How many of us will be going?" Hunter asked.

"We never take more than four clients in each boat. Don't need to be tripping over people. We're out there to land fish, not to dance."

They walked over to the fuelling dock where a strong smell of diesel hung in the air.

"Stinks, don't it? The fuel barge had a bit of a spill last time he delivered. Diesel comes in by boat, up the river at high tide. Cheaper shipping it that way than trucking it from Franklin and in over the dirt road."

Bob showed Hunter the fish-cleaning station next. One side was open to the dock. It was an elaborate setup with enough room for six guides to work side by side. A stainless steel counter stretched the length of the three-sided room. Every so often, there was a catch basin for the fish guts attached to the counter. Bob explained how these basins were then dumped into large, covered buckets, which were later emptied out at sea. Hoses with strong pressurized showerheads hung overhead, ready to rinse the steel surface clean after each fish was filleted. The fillets were then taken to another room to be vacuum-sealed in heavy freezer bags, quick frozen, and packed in the boxes for shipment to the client's home.

Bob explained how each guide was responsible for processing his own client's catch. Each client's catch was kept separate from everyone else's, ensuring the customer took home the fish that he had caught.

The clean processing plant impressed Hunter. He could not detect any strong fishy odour, just the sharp smell of steel and disinfectant. Joe ran a pretty tight operation, he noted. Perhaps his reputation for having an excellent fish camp was well deserved.

After touring the camp, the men joined Joe in the kitchen. Joe was lounging in his favourite chair beside a low burning fire in the hearth. He waved his arm in the direction of the liquor stacked on a shelf in the pantry.

"Help yourself, or get a beer out of the fridge if you want. What do you think of my place? Pretty sharp, eh?"

"Sure is," agreed Hunter. "I'm real impressed by the fish processing plant. You got room to hold any fish I catch until I get back from Alaska, or should I arrange for a buddy to take delivery?"

"We have lots of storage right now. It's getting close to the end of the tourist season. Most of the regular fall fishermen have their fish shipped out right away or take it with them."

As Hunter was enjoying sitting and chatting with the two men, Tim came in.

"Evening," he nodded to Hunter as he popped the top off his beer. "You Bob's latest? Got yourself one of the best guides in the camp. He sure gives me a run for my money!"

Turning to address Bob, he asked what time they were heading out in the morning.

"If you get an early start, you might be able to get out off the pinnacles. Jason said they lost a big Spring there yesterday. Maybe I'll go with you. The rest don't get in until late tomorrow. Guess their flight outta LA got screwed up."

"Be great. We haven't fished together all season. I aim to set out at six." Bob smiled. He enjoyed spending time with Tim. He was one of the few guides that he really trusted.

Hunter took that as his cue to head off to bed. "Best I turn in then. What time is breakfast?"

"Round five," answered Joe.

Hunter crossed the camp over to his tent, grabbed his toilet kit, and headed over to the washhouse. After quickly sloshing water over his face and hands and brushing his teeth, he entered the composting toilet. Unfamiliar with these kinds of outhouses, he carefully read the directions printed on the door. It seemed simple enough. Do your business and then throw a scoop full of cedar chips down the hole. The system must work, as the outhouse was almost odour free. It looked like they kept up the cleaning pretty well too. As he left the toilet, he caught a brief glimpse of movement up the trail. He assumed it was Joe heading up to his tent in the woods.

He reviewed the day's events. So far, the camp seemed to be on the up and up to Hunter, however, was fully aware that time might tell a different story. He was keen to go fishing in the morning. Since he had not had any chances to go ocean fishing before, this would be a great opportunity to learn. Yes, he would learn new skills and be working at the same time. It was a good deal all around.

Chapter Twenty-Five

Hunter awoke to the sound of feet shuffling in the dirt outside the tent. He quickly reached under the pillow for his piece, then realized where he was. Right, this was the fish camp, and that was probably Bob coming to give him a wake-up call. It took a couple of seconds for him to orient himself to his surroundings.

"Okay, I'm up," he called before Bob had a chance to come inside. After hastily pulling on several layers of clothes, Hunter washed up and headed over for breakfast.

Joe, busy in the kitchen, looked up as Hunter strode into the lodge. Bacon was already sizzling in the pan and the coffee smelt good and strong. Grabbing a mug, Hunter poured himself some of the brew and sat down at the table.

"Morning, Joe. What's the weather for today? Same as yesterday or are we getting that system from the south?"

Joe grinned. "I'd say it'll be good out on the water, but the radio says clouds are moving in around two. One egg or two?"

"Two, thanks."

Hunter ate with relish, thinking that they cooked really well here in the north of the province. He hadn't had a bad meal since he got there.

Tim came in through the side door.

"Hey, what size boots do you wear? Think you need a large for the marine suit?"

"I'm a ten and a half boot usually and the large will be fine," replied Hunter.

Tim nodded and then reminded Hunter to bring a hat and to be at the boat dock in twenty minutes. The *River Girl* was all set to go as soon as he was ready.

"Oh, don't forget to sign the waiver. I'll leave it on the table for you," he said as he turned to leave the lodge.

Less than twenty minutes later, Hunter climbed onto the Boston Whaler and settled himself in one of the seats facing the back of the small boat. Bob gave him one of the collar life vests that inflate if a tab is pulled. He explained to Hunter that most fishermen preferred using these as they weren't bulky and didn't interfere with playing the fish. Bob insisted every client in his boat wore safety equipment since the camp's insurance policy demanded strict adherence to the boating regulations.

Soon they were chugging towards the mouth of the river, past Tine Island and further out to sea. As they left the bay, the swells increased to a soft rolling pitch. Hunter started to feel queasy; the eggs and bacon weren't sitting too well. He stood up to get out of the exhaust smell drifting from the motor and leaned against the side of the boat. Suddenly, he lost his breakfast over the side and weakly sat down in the shelter of the boat's windscreen.

Bob reached over and handed him the sea bands.

"Try these. We should be out of these rollers soon. This here is called the rubber room. Offshore currents stir up the water. The water can get pretty rough in this section."

Hunter stretched the knit bands over his hands, placing the plastic button between the tendons on the underside of his wrists. *New Age shit*, he thought to himself. Not ten minutes later, he felt well enough to venture out on deck once more.

"Hey, those suckers work. Thanks. Feels like the swells are lessening too."

"Yep, just about out of them," Bob said. "Keep the bands on for a while, till you get used to the boat. We'll start trolling off the pinnacles soon. That'll take your mind off your gut."

Tim got the trolling lines set with flashers and strips of herring. As Bob slowed the boat and started in on the first pass, Tim showed Hunter how to release the lines, clip on the downriggers with the ten-pound cannonballs, and let out more line for a good depth.

With the lines all set for trolling, there was nothing to do but wait for the bells to jangle. Pass after pass was made. Tim adjusted the lines to a deeper depth, and they made two more passes. As Hunter watched the gulls swirl in the sky and stared at the boat's wake, he thought it was all quite boring. They had been out there at least two hours and no luck so far.

Just as they started the third pass at the new depth, both lines went. Tim jumped up, reached over grabbing the rod out of its holder, and started to reel in the left rod. Bob slowed the engine to a crawl and went to help out. Tim was landing his salmon, so Bob went to give Hunter a hand. He was just about to shout directions when he saw that everything was under control. *Man, he was a quick learner*, Bob thought. The guy already had rod in hand and was steadily working the line.

Hunter could see the fish rising and falling in the water trying to shake the hook. Letting out some of the line, he gave the fish its head. Moving around the rear deck, alternately reeling in and letting out the line, Hunter played the fish until it was exhausted enough for Tim to get the net under it.

Tim hauled the net up and onto the deck. Thrashing and flipping, the thirty-pound spring was a sight to be seen. This spring had put up one tough fight.

Hunter was grinning from ear to ear, flushed with excitement. So this is what deep-sea fishing was all about! Hunter could hardly wait to land the next one.

Tim dealt a quick bash to the fish's head and it was all over. He threw the salmon into the cooler and reset the lines.

Shortly before noon, Bob signalled for them to bring in the lines. They had only managed to land one more salmon, a pink. He gunned the motor and moved to a new fishing spot.

"This here is one of my favourites. Don't usually bring clients here. We guides like to keep some hot spots quiet. Not much good for salmon, but we'll jig for rock cod off this shelf. Tim, set up the jiggers, will you? We should stop here awhile and then have lunch, in a bit, on that sand beach this side of Tine."

The men passed the time jigging the cod lines up and down as the boat slowly drifted over the rocky ledge. Hunter soon learned the technique of letting the line drift down, and then a few strong jerks, then drift again. For Hunter, the thrill with this type of fishing was actually feeling the cod bite. His arm jerked from the initial strike, as the fish took the bait. Then the steady pull of the cod, trying to escape its doom, followed. A couple of the six cod they caught fought almost as hard as the spring.

"What's the limit on cod?" Hunter asked.

"No worries, we have three guys in the boat. If fisheries come by, we'll divide the catch. No way for them to tell who caught what. Fisheries are pretty easy to spot. Their boat's big and slow moving. Besides, Joe monitors their whereabouts and that of the Coast Guard vessels on the VHS. Right now, fisheries are up the coast playing mother ship to a group of scientists hired to count coons on the outer islands. He hasn't said where Coast Guard's hanging. Want to grab a beer. We'll head in to this beach off Tine for a lunch break."

Bob started up the engine again and motored slowly towards Tine Island.

Ten minutes later, he cut the engine and the boat bobbed towards shore. Tine was mainly a bunch of rocks jutting out into the ocean, but a pretty little beach lay to the east side of the island. Bob hauled the outboard up and let the boat drift up onto the sand. Jumping out into the ankle-deep water, the guys sloshed to shore in their boots.

Tim had brought along the cooler and set it over by some rocks at the edge of the sandy beach. "I don't know about you guys, but I'm hungry." Tim started pulling out cold salad, thick egg salad sandwiches, chocolate cake, and of course beer. The guys tucked in hungrily, pausing only to wash mouthfuls down with the cool beer.

"Damn good food. Joe make all this?" Hunter asked.

"Heck, no. We got this girl that cooks for us. Little slip of a thing, but she sure can turn out a meal. Way better than that other bastard we had a while ago. He drank more than he cooked."

"Didn't see her last night or this morning. Joe cooked breakfast," Hunter observed.

Tim paused and thought about what he should say.

"No, you won't see her. She works the day shift when we're out on the water. Then she spends the rest of her time up at Joe's. Doesn't mix at all. I don't much care, so long as she cooks like she does." Tim reached for another piece of cake.

"Hey, look, we got cookies as well. Maybe save them for later in the boat."

After lunch, the guys trolled some more just northwest of Tine. All in all, it was a successful day. In addition to the six cod, they now had seven fair-sized salmon. None of the salmon had fought as well as the first one Hunter caught. Still, he was tired and happy as they motored up river towards the fish camp.

"Can I help you clean some of the fish? I'd like to learn how to fillet properly. Usually do a crappy job of the trout I catch."

"Well, I guess so," Bob said. "We provide the processing as part of the cost, but Joe won't mind if you watch. Might let you do that thirty-pounder you got. Best we weigh it first on the scale so we know exactly how big it is." Bob grinned. He liked this Hunter guy. He wasn't afraid of hard work and was real quick picking up on things.

Joe met the boat as it chugged to the boat dock. He had shuffled the boats around so that there was space to pull in and unload.

"How'd it go? Pinnacles live up to Jason's bragging?"

Tim nodded to his boss. "Yep, did okay. Six cod, seven salmon. Hunter landed a real nice spring. Gave him a good run. Okay with you if he wants to try his hand at filleting?"

"Sure, no problem. The girl made venison stew and it is ready whenever you get done. The other clients' flight was so fucked up, they don't get here until after ten now.

Come on up when you're showered." Joe moved on up the trail to his tent.

Hunter and the guides spent the next hour and a half cleaning and filleting the fish. By the time it was all done and they had showered and changed into clean clothes, the sun was setting and the air had cooled down considerably.

They wandered over to the kitchen and found an enormous pot of stew simmering gently on the back of the stove. Fresh sourdough buns were wrapped in foil in the warming oven. The incredible odours fuelled their hunger. Grabbing huge bowls, they ladled the pungent mixture into them and dove in. Blowing on their spoons to cool the stew, the men ate in companionable silence.

"I had a great day out there. Thanks, you guys," Hunter said between mouthfuls.

Bob and Tim nodded in agreement.

****

While the guides cleaned up the *River Girl* and gassed her up for the next day, Hunter went exploring around the camp. He noticed slim, steel rods with discs on top of them set out in a long rectangle. Looked like some kind of fencing system without wire. He had seen something similar at his friend Ed's place. He used a wireless fence to keep that ditsy dog of his from going onto the road. This apparatus wasn't quite the same but very similar. Appeared new, too.

Hunter traipsed around for a bit and then sat in a wooden deckchair overlooking the slow moving river. In mid-summer, this river meandered along, but he imagined that in spring it must be a raging torrent with all the snowmelt that would come down out of the mountains.

Stillness settled over the camp, punctuated once in a while by a burst of laughter or a shout as Bob and Tim readied their boats.

The mosquitoes began to come out as soon as the wind started to die down. Hunter went over to his tent and got out his insect repellent. Giving himself a liberal spray, he returned to the deckchair overlooking the river. To his surprise, Joe had pulled up another chair beside his.

"Great night, isn't it?" Hunter said as he joined the camp owner.

Joe grunted appreciatively. "They're all great nights out here. No noise, no traffic, no hassles. I love it here. Gonna retire here when I make enough money. Mind you don't need much if you got no debts. Yes, sir. Gonna pay off what I owe and call it a day."

Hunter could tell Joe had been drinking a bit, so he decided to probe a little.

"With a successful operation like this, you couldn't have many debts. Folks say you do really well every season, even now with the economy in the toilet."

Joe laughed ruefully. "Camp does fine. I just can't leave the casinos alone. Worst things ever invented. Cost me my old lady and almost cost me the camp last year. Yeah, worst things ever to come along."

"I don't bother with them much," Hunter said with a sigh. "Seen too much grief caused by the slots. You play slots, or are you more a fan of black jack?"

"Black jack and poker. Some real good games go on in Franklin and Sumac." Then, as if he knew that he might be talking too much, Joe shut up. They sat watching the river until Bob and Tim came to join them.

"What time did you say the other clients were coming in, Joe? It's getting on ten-thirty. It'll be a rush to get going in the morning if we're to get in a whole day's worth fishing." Tim sounded worried. "Where do you think we should take them if time is tight?"

"It's pretty good where we were today," offered Hunter. "I wouldn't mind the same place twice."

"Yeah, let's do that," Bob suggested. "Then we can take a bigger run out to the reef off Bottle Neck the next day."

Around eleven, they heard the rented four-by-four come to a halt in the dusty parking lot.

"Must be them." Joe got up and went to greet his new arrivals.

"Hello! Welcome to River Bend. You must be tired after the run-around you've had today. Tim will show you your tent. Drop your stuff off, and then come up for a stiff one."

Hunter and Bob rose and wandered up to the lodge.

After dropping their bags off, the newcomers entered the lodge and gratefully accepted the proffered drinks. As they sat down at the table, Joe served up some of the venison stew and chunks of crusty bread. None of the sourdough buns were left, as the guides and Hunter had polished them off earlier. Hunter studied the men as they wolfed down the savoury stew. They all looked like seasoned fishermen. It seemed as though they came up this way fishing every year, but this was the first time they had been to Joe's.

Mack and Butch were brothers from Maine, both in the accounting business. Mack had thin greying hair and a small build. His brother couldn't have been more of a contrast if he tried. Built like a tank, Butch was a bear of a man. He was at least six eight and had a fiery red beard and thick mane of red hair. The other two guys were also from Maine; Hank was a carpenter by trade, and Francois, his partner, owned a successful restaurant.

"If we're to have any sort of a day tomorrow, best we all turn in," suggested Bob. "Let me show you the facilities and where to meet us in the morning. You four will be heading out on the *Tide* with Tim. Hunter and I will be along too, but in the *River Girl*. No fun with too many in a boat. You guys are here to fish, not take turns all day. Maybe one of you wants to split off and come with Hunter and me. That would be two and three clients to a boat. Think about it."

With plans made, everyone turned in for the night. Hunter discovered that he still had the tent to himself. The others had requested they bunk together. The four guys had met six years ago while on a fly-in fishing trip in northern Ontario, and had travelled together just about every year since, so Bob had given them the next tent. It had been a long day. Hunter found himself getting more and more tired as he mulled over the day. Checking to make sure his weapon was within easy reach; Hunter gave up fighting the drowsiness. So far things seemed above board at River Bend but Hunter never let his guard down.

Chapter Twenty-Six

Saturday dawned clear and bright, but there was a chill in the air. You could tell fall wasn't far away. Hunter yanked a knit sweater over his fishing clothes and put on wool fisherman's cap. It would be even cooler out on the water. The rest of the guys had already washed and gone down to breakfast. Keen to be on the water, they were nearly finished with their food by the time Hunter walked in.

"Morning all." Hunter sat down at the end of the table.

Joe looked up from frying eggs. "Same as yesterday?" he asked Hunter.

"Yeah, great. Can I have some of that crusty bread instead of toast?"

"Sure thing," replied Joe turning to the stove to tend to the eggs.

Bob and Tim came in bringing the clients' survival suits and some deck boots. While the customers were eating, they carefully went over rules and regulations and then had the new comers sign waivers. Butch had a few questions about the new limits on Coho. Last year they had been allowed to take two a day. This year the regulations called for only four Coho in five days of fishing.

"Yeah, Fisheries is saying the run is low again. Personally, I feel it's the trawlers taking more than their share," grumbled Bob. He was referring to the rivalry between sports and commercial fishermen that had been going on for years. Each blamed the other when limits were low. No question about it though, the runs for both Coho and Chinook were decreasing every year.

"Well, up and at 'em. Meet you fellas on the boat dock in fifteen," said Bob.

Butch had decided to join Hunter in Bob's boat, leaving his brother Mack, Hank, and Francois to go in Tim's. Mack seemed to be a regular stand up sort of fellow but Tim raised his eyebrows as Hank and Francois climbed carefully on board. They were dressed in matching outfits, right down to the jaunty white Tillies on their heads. Both were athletically built and had casual, unassuming attitudes. Francois and Hank seemed to share an affectionate companionship that comes from being long-time partners.

Tim had long ago decided that he didn't give a shit what gays got up to behind closed doors so long as he didn't have to see them swish all day. He also didn't like it when some of the older guys brought their trophy wives along. Nothing was more off putting than seeing these old buggers feeling up these young bimbos whenever they thought someone might be looking. As far as Tim was concerned, they were out there to fish—not to show off to all in sundry.

Francois and Hank were already examining the fishing gear and seemed ready for some action. He'd do his best to find them fish. Bob always had better luck though.

The *Tide* and the *River Girl* motored out of the river mouth towards Tine Island. Hunter reached for the sea bands as they approached the rubber room. The ocean swells didn't seem to be as big this time. They had started out a couple of hours later than yesterday, so perhaps the tide had some bearing on the currents.

By the time they had set the lines and started trawling, Butch was into his second beer. Hunter thought to himself that the guy must have the constitution of an ox. There was no way he could drink this early or in these water conditions. Bob gave Hunter a knowing look as Butch reached for the second beer. It would take two of them to handle this guy if he became a belligerent drunk.

After several passes and having caught three spring salmon and released a dogfish, they decided lunch was in order. Bob reached for the radio.

"*River Girl* calling *Tide*, *River Girl* calling *Tide*. Heading to the sandy beach on Tine. You coming?"

"Roger that. Bringing up the lines now. You get anything? We managed four salmon, and one's a Chinook. Mack got it. Round ten pounds."

"Good on you," replied Bob. "Got a few, but just springs. See you in fifteen."

Lunch consisted of coleslaw, potato salad, and cold beef sandwiches seasoned with horseradish. Some oranges and oatmeal cookies rounded out the meal.

"Great food," Mack declared. "Way better than our last trip with Seven Seas. You guys really know how to put on a spread."

Once again, Hunter found himself wondering about this mysterious cook that kept to herself.

The afternoon passed quickly. Both boats caught their limit for the day and headed back early. As Bob neared the entrance to the river, he reached for the radio to call Joe.

"*River Girl* to River Bend, *River Girl* to River Bend. Come in Joe."

Surprised when his several attempts to contact his boss failed, Bob checked his radio. A lead was hanging loosely needing a screw. Tim's boat was already heading into the channel. He turned to Hunter with a shrug.

"Can't raise Joe. He always likes to meet the boats but the radio is out of commission. I'll have to fix it tonight."

"I'll give you a hand if you want," Hunter offered.

"Nah, no need. It's just a loose connection."

It was just around five when they motored up to the dock. With the exception of Hunter, the clients headed to the showers and then to the kitchen for beers.

While Hunter was busy helping unload the fish, he caught a glimpse of the girl scampering up the trail. One look at her face was enough to tell him she was scared to death. Joe was hurrying after her. Hunter noticed for the first time a small black shape, the size of a drink tetra pack, attached to Joe's belt. He stared at the girl. She was slim, average height, and had her dark hair pulled back in a ponytail. Wearing black knit pants and a pink top that was much too big for her, she moved swiftly towards Joe's tent. Oddly, she had one of those grunge or hip-hop collars around her neck. The fashion statement looked out of place with the rest of her clothes.

"Get a move on. *Move!*" Joe ordered the girl along.

Hunter's training and instincts as an investigator kicked in as he mulled the scene over in his head. Something did not sit right.

Leaving the guides to process the fish and restock the boats, Hunter grabbed a shower. He wasn't interested in a beer, so he sat beside the river again, relaxing in the last remaining warmth of the day and watching the slow moving water.

Suddenly things started falling into place. The black object on Joe's belt was a transmitter, and the fashion statement on the girl was the receiver. The son of a bitch had a dog collar on her. She was Joe's prisoner. She didn't keep herself away from everyone, *he did*. Christ, what an efficient, but cruel system that was. Those training setups would deliver one enormous jolt if calibrated right. Hunter figured it might be almost as good as a Taser for incapacitating someone. He had experienced the Taser's force during basic training for the RCMP; it wasn't something that needed repeating. The question was why was she a captive? What reason would Joe have for holding her here against her will?

****

Tonight's meal was corn chowder followed by BBQ pork ribs, mashed potatoes, and green beans. Apple pie sat cooling on the counter for anyone who had any room left.

After supper, everyone lounged around the fireplace swapping life histories and tall tales of previous adventures. Hunter stuck close to his basic cover story of being an American tourist from Washington State on his way up to Alaska. It turned out that Mack and Butch had driven up the Alaska Highway last year in July.

"Lots of bugs," Butch said. "Man, those black flies are vicious. Even the animals can't stand them. Saw moose in the rivers up to their nostrils trying to get away from the buggers." Butch did his best impression of a large moose struggling to breathe in the water. "Now's not a bad time to go. The bugs should be dying down by now. Either that or take snorkelling gear with you!"

More entertaining stories flowed, fuelled by beer and then the whisky. Each guest good-naturedly trying to outdo one another with tales of fish caught and wildlife triumphed.

The brothers both worked for the same company that had been founded by their father. Accounting was the only life they knew. Every year they travelled extensively trying to beat the boredom of a nine-to-five job. Mack, surprisingly, was the younger brother. He had been seriously ill after a trip to the Brazilian rainforest. He had picked up some parasite, and it had taken months of diagnostic tests and gruelling treatment to get over it. Although he joked about the drugs turning his hair grey, you could tell the ordeal had taken its toll on him. Butch consumed lots of beer, but it had little effect on the big man. He was nursing a huge grudge against his ex. He claimed that she was trying to turn his kids away from him.

Hank and Francois quietly took it all in, eventually adding their story to the mix. They both lived and worked in the same town. Hank enjoyed working with his hands and by all accounts was a darn good carpenter. The partners had completely renovated their loft. Francois owned a restaurant in the heart of the entertainment district. It was this successful business that enabled them to have at least one good trip a year.

Gradually the conversation wound down, and one by one the clients retired for the night. Soon, just Hunter, Joe, and Tim were left finishing up their drinks. A soft beeping came from Joe's belt. He quickly got up and went outside. When he returned a few minutes later, Hunter asked what was up.

"No big deal," Joe said offhandedly. "Have a no-wire perimeter setup to trip if a critter runs through. We've had trouble lately with bears, and a cougar was sighted crossing the dirt road that comes into camp. Didn't see nothing, but I gotta keep all you girls safe," he joked.

Hunter headed to his tent and went to bed fully clothed. After about an hour, he poked his head outside and listened carefully. There were no sounds other than the usual night noises coming from the surrounding bush. There were no lights visible except for the one hung outside the composting toilets. Slowly and quietly, he made his way along the trail that led up to Joe's tent. Pausing ten or so feet away from the side of the tent, he listened intently. Soft whimpering originated from inside the tent.

"Oh, no! Please don't make me. Please …"

"I told you not to leave the tent," Joe growled. "Now you owe me. Want a taste of the collar instead?"

"Oh, God, no!" The whimpering came again.

"On your knees. You know what to do."

Hunter thought quickly. He had to help—but how? He shuffled his feet loudly in the dirt.

"Hey, Joe! You got a minute? Sorry to bother you, man, but I could have sworn I saw that cougar over by the boat dock. Must be after the fish guts."

Joe swore under his breath, zipped up his pants, and headed out the door.

****

Early the next morning, Jason, one of the guides, returned after his days off. One of the locals followed behind him in an old beat-up truck. Earl, the owner of the sporting goods store in town, wanted to fish for the day. Of course, Hunter recognized him and shook his hand warmly. Joe readily agreed to Earl going along in the boats, insisting he go for free. It was good advertisement for his camp.

Jason threw the mail and newspapers he had picked up in town on the table. He poured himself a coffee and quickly scanned the news of the day. Joe gathered up the mail and put it in a pile with this week's flyers and other items to read later.

On top was a poster, of the missing kayaker, that was being circulated by the RCMP. As he ate his breakfast and chatted with Butch, Hunter watched Joe. Casually, Joe took up the poster, walked over to the counter, and put it under a pile of old flyers. Hunter was puzzled. What did the poster have to do with anything around here? Clearly, Joe didn't want anyone seeing it.

It was decided that Jason would take the brothers in his boat, the *Kingfisher*. Hank and Francois would go with Tim, leaving Bob to guide for Hunter and Earl. The guides collected lunches from the cooler and went to finish loading the compact sports boats. Soon the group was heading out towards Bottle Neck Cove, a fishing hot spot. By the time they arrived off the entrance to Bottle Neck, several sporties were already there, trolling back and forth in a wide grid. Radio chatter from the guides indicated the bite had fallen off in the last forty minutes.

"Heading out to Main Banks, nothing happening here," complained a guide from one of the rival companies. Several other sporties followed suit, leaving River Bend's boats alone.

"Those guys have no patience," Bob said to Hunter and Earl. "Just wait a few minutes and things should turn around. Tide is ready to turn, and if we let out a few more meters of line, we should snag a few off the shelf." Bob set out his lines and began the long sweeping passes. Tim and Jason soon had their boats going in a similar pattern.

True to his word, the fishing changed. Earl reeled in the biggest fish of his life. The enormous Chinook would tip the scales at sixty plus pounds. It was no fighter, though.

Once it struck, it hung on the line like dead weight for most of the time it took Earl to land it. Still, he was not disappointed; he had something to brag about now.

Just after one, the guides headed in through the narrow rock entrance to Bottle Neck Cove. Sharp jagged rocks constricted the entrance. It was easy enough for the small Boston Whalers to gain access to the cove, but any larger boat would have difficulty unless the captain really knew what he was doing. Going in there at night or in the fog could be a deadly proposition.

Lifting the outboards up out of the chuck, the guides let their boats glide in as close as possible to the shore. After dropping the anchors, the men waded in and set up on the beach. With huge driftwood logs and clean sand, it was a popular place for lunch.

Many small boats if caught in one of the fast-moving West Coast storms, took advantage of the shelter cove until safer conditions returned.

In some places, the ever-increasing temperate rainforest grew right down to the water's edge. Some tiny, white sandy beaches lay scattered in between patches of rounded pebble rock. Everywhere was littered with driftwood. In the curve to the north, where the beach ended and the sharp shoreline began, there were all kinds of beach debris. Plastic water bottles, sneakers, rope, plastic milk crates, and fishing floats could be seen hung up in crevices and under logs. It was a beachcomber's paradise.

Jason and Tim arranged lunch on a huge driftwood plank. Today's meal was cold leftover ribs from the night before, pita bread with humus, sliced cheeses and cut-up vegetables, cinnamon buns and coffee. As usual, the guests were impressed with the top-notch food. Although Hunter tried for more details on this mysterious girl who made all this delicious food, the guides were less than forthcoming.

Bob changed the subject and began talking about Bottle Neck Cove. In the 1800s, this cove had been known as a prime location to hide booty pirated from ships heading towards the ports that supplied the gold fields. All kinds of goods were plundered and then later resold to the unsuspecting and desperate miners. It was rumoured that after the gold rush, human smuggling was routed through this area, as well.

Hunter could see the possibilities. He wondered if this might be a landing spot for drugs coming up from Mexico and the South American countries. It would take a lot of manpower and some clever organization. Still, given the right connections, it could be done. Drugs were entering the North, and they were getting in somehow.

With lunch over, the guides hastily repacked the cooler, and everyone waded back out to the boats and hauled himself aboard. This time the passage through the narrow entrance proved to be more difficult. The tide had turned and the wind had picked up considerably. Tim led the way going at a snail's pace until he was well out from the jagged rocks.

Bob radioed Joe back at camp. Joe cautioned that the weather station had called for increasing winds and had predicted a strong possibility of driving rain. Much to the disappointment of the customers, the guides decided to call it a day.

"Don't feel comfortable about this front coming in. The swells are already two meters, and they're saying they could reach six. Let's head in and fish the mouth of the river if the conditions hold," Jason suggested over the radio to Bob.

"Yup, best we do that. No telling how long it'll take us to get back anyway." Bob gave a wave to the other boats and steered the *River Girl* into the oncoming waves.

****

It was a rough ride back. Everyone was glad to see the entrance to the river. The passage from Bottle Neck to the river mouth had taken well over four hours. Tired and hungry, no one suggested any more fishing.

Hunter had been busy thinking about his next move. Back at camp, he put his plan into action. Halfway through filleting one of the salmon, he gasped and bent over. Straightening up again, he continued filleting only to double over again.

"Hey, man, what's wrong with you?" Tim asked. "You okay?"

"Will be," Hunter grunted. "Got to go to the can."

A bit later, he returned and said that he'd better lie down for a while. "I must have eaten something that didn't agree with me. You guys feeling okay?"

Tim nodded his head. "Sure am, no problems here. Go stretch out for a while. Supper isn't for an hour. If you don't show, we'll save you some." With that, Hunter made his way to his tent and lay on his cot. An hour and a half or so later, Joe entered Hunter's tent.

"You feeling any better?" Joe asked quietly. Hunter briefly opened his eyes and weakly looked at Joe.

"Don't worry about me. I'm okay, forgot I can't take too much fat. Docs say it might be gall bladder acting up. One lot of ribs is fine, but two was a bit too much. It'll pass. I'm going to call it a night. I want to fish in the morning, so don't forget to wake me."

He turned over and pretended to go back to sleep. He heard the tent zipper close as Joe left as quietly as he had arrived. After waiting for a few moments, Hunter got out of bed and put on his shoes. Grabbing his gun from its hiding place, he peered out of the tent. Joe was almost at the lodge. Hunter judged he had maybe twenty minutes tops to get to Joe's tent and return.

Running up the trail, he covered the ground quickly. He discovered Maya sitting outside Joe's tent on an old packing crate. Holding his finger to his lips, he motioned for her to stay quiet.

"Hey, trust me, I'm a friend—a cop." He showed her his badge that was clipped to his gun holster.

Relief flooded her face as Maya stood up. He caught her just before she tumbled to the ground.

"Hey, no time for that, missy. We have to talk and quickly. I reckon we have twenty minutes before Joe comes along."

He got as much detail as he could out of her. She confirmed much of what he already suspected. Yes, she was the missing kayak guide. She had managed to travel down the coast by herself. A man named Bob had caught her finding drugs in a duffel bag that had been hidden in the bushes in Bottle Neck Cove. They hadn't known what to do with her, so they had brought her back here to this camp and to Joe.

Joe was controlling her with this awful collar. If she went out of bounds or didn't do as he said, he shocked her. Joe made her cook, clean, and do other things. At this, she bowed her head and looked miserably towards the ground.

Maya then told him about the drug transfer. The other night she had seen them packing the drugs into compartments in a van, into empty containers, and even into the laundry bags. She had been discovered as she watched and Joe had delivered more shocks.

Time was passing quickly. Hunter held the frightened girl in his arms and promised her that he'd get her out of this mess.

"It won't be soon, but I *will* get you out. Trust me. But I can't do this on my own. I'll have to get back up. Hang in there. Pretend nothing's different. I'll be back for you. In two days, we'll talk again if I can make it past Joe. Hang in there, Maya."

With a last squeeze of her shoulders, Hunter let her go and faded into the woods. Joe's footsteps could be heard coming up the path.

Chapter Twenty-Seven

Bob shook Hunter awake the next morning around 5:30.

"You up for fishing today?"

Hunter sat up slowly and rubbed his hands over his rough three-day beard.

"Hell, yes. Not going to let a gut ache stop me. Besides, if I skip the bacon this morning, I should be fine. What time are we pulling out?"

"Not till eight. We're only going as far as Puffin Island today. Some rich couple is flying in by floatplane and will meet us there. Off to the side of Puffin is a decent area to land the plane. Jason will pick them up. Apparently this couple goes from one fishing lodge to another all summer long. Must be nice to have that much money! Even with Earl gone we'll take three boats. The new people have requested a boat to themselves."

"Fine with me. Maybe Butch will join us, but he'll have to share the beer." Hunter grinned. He enjoyed Bob's company, and Butch was a downright good guy.

As he washed up, Hunter caught himself wondering how far Bob was into all this drug business. Maya had said he had clipped her a good one on the jaw. Although Bob didn't seem like the type to hit a woman, you never knew what might trigger someone to violence.

The day was clear and bright again. They made good time and passed Bottle Neck just before ten. Jason headed on up as far as Puffin and jigged for cod while he waited for the floatplane. Soon, they heard the drone of a light plane and watched it touch down within meters of Jason's boat. It was clear this couple was used to this kind of life. Their gear was packed in custom cases, and the transfer to the *Tide* took no time at all. They waved their plane off, and Jason moved up channel to get into a trawling pattern.

"Hey, Bob. How far down are you guys? Still using the hoochies?" Jason called over the radio. He was double-checking with Bob in case the conditions had changed while he had been waiting for the plane.

"Go another fifty feet or so, Jason. Bait and hoochies should still be good." Bob reset his own lines, and everyone settled in to wait. After trawling for only three hours, the boats had already limited out on salmon. They chose to motor on to Bottle Neck Cove for lunch again. This time, instead of getting right back out on the water, the group decided to comb the beaches for a while.

While the clients were scouring the beach for treasures, Tim and Bob had checked out the surrounding bush in case a drop had already been made. There were no duffels hidden in the forest, so they encouraged the group to search along the high tide line as well. Lots of interesting items were found including an old medicine bottle, an old-fashion washboard, a chipped plate, and a child's plastic toy elephant.

Much to the new couple's disappointment, the beach yielded no Japanese floats. Since this beach was popular with the sports fishing crowd, any floats would have long since been discovered.

After a brief snack, the guides loaded the gear and everyone back in the boats and motored over to a prime jigging ground. Dogfish after dogfish took the bait.

"What's with these damn dogfish?" Mack asked Tim.

"Oh, they're nasty. Gotta handle them carefully. Their skin is so rough that Aboriginals used to use it to sand their cedar carvings." Giving up the area to the pesky dogs, the group decided to head in towards camp. On the way, they tried a couple more shoals and snagged a nice ling cod.

Shortly before dusk, the three boats entered the river mouth. As usual, Joe met them at the dock.

"You can all head up to the lodge as soon as you get squared away. Tonight's our world famous salmon BBQ."

He greeted the newcomers and told them their pilot had radioed that the pickup was the following morning, around ten.

"Tim will show you your sleeping tent, washrooms, and the cookhouse."

With his guests welcomed, Joe went up to check on Maya. She had just finished putting the salads in the coolers and was slicing the loaves of sourdough bread.

"Get a move on, guests will be up here soon. You best be on up to the tent now." His hand hovered menacingly over the transmitter. Maya dropped the knife and started towards the door. She slammed straight into Hunter who had followed Joe up to the kitchen.

"Oh, sorry," she gasped, brushing past him. Without so much as a backward glance, she hurried on across the campground.

"Not very friendly, is she?" Joe commented to Hunter as he entered the kitchen. "Still, she cooks like a pro, so who cares."

Hunter stared after the frightened girl feeling helpless to fix her situation. They had too much manpower in this camp. He had to get backup. Besides, he knew he was getting close to solving the smuggling operation. Months of undercover work would be ruined if he tipped his hand too soon. More pieces of the puzzle needed to be solved. He wondered when the next shipment of drugs was due. They had been told in their briefing that drugs were getting scarce on the streets. Chances were pretty darn good that a shipment was on the way.

The new couple came in. They were impressed with the camp and complimented Joe on his excellent setup.

"Great place you have here, Joe. I'm thinking of bringing some of my managers up here for the team building session in June. Sure like that composting toilet system you have. Wouldn't mind putting one in on our property in Oregon," said Ray as he helped himself to a beer.

Nancy opted for some white wine.

Nancy and Ray were from Seattle. He ran his folks' chain of successful shoe stores that stretched from Seattle into the Midwest. Nancy was a stay-at-home mom to their three kids, ranging in age from thirteen to twenty-six. Ray was loud and jovial in comparison to his quiet, laid-back spouse. Surprisingly, she was the avid fisher.

The rest of the clients came in and found seats at the table.

As everyone waited for the salmon sizzling on the barbecue, Ray entertained them with fish tales from various locations along the coast. Money was no object to these affluent people, but their charming manner put everyone at ease. Nancy simply couldn't sit still and asked Joe if she could help with the preparations.

"Sure thing," Joe said. He was never one to turn down a willing helper. Besides, Nancy reminded him a bit of Sue. Not in her looks of course but in her quiet, efficient manner.

Nancy made herself at home in the kitchen putting finishing touches on the meal and setting the food out on the huge table.

What a meal it was! Once again, Maya's cooking skills impressed. It was little wonder Joe kept her around. Hunter was convinced Joe wouldn't kill her until he had to. Maya more than paid her way. She was one of his biggest assets.

The BBQ lasted long into the night with most of the guides and their clients becoming more and more rowdy. Butch and Ray drunkenly did karaoke to the country channel on the radio. Somewhere around two in the morning, it was decided everyone needed a dip in the river. Bathing suits were optional by this time.

Hunter played along, seeming to get as drunk as the rest of them. Weaving his way back to his tent, he called goodnight and disappeared into its welcoming depths. Once again he was bunking alone. Nancy and Ray had their own tent. He had hoped to go up to Joe's tent and pay a visit to Maya, but he had noticed Joe had not been drinking very much. It was too risky. He couldn't afford to blow his cover now.

Tomorrow, he would to catch a ride into town with Tim. Tim was going in to pick up some boat parts. Hunter would then collect his vehicle and begin to set up the team. Unfortunately, the poor girl would have to wait a while longer.

****

Joe sauntered out of the kitchen as Hunter loaded his gear into the bed of Tim's pickup.

"Did ya have a good time? How'd the salt water fishing compare to lake?"

Hunter laughed. "Let's say it's more like comparing a war to a battle. Man what action. I'm hooked! Thanks again."

Hunter turned with a wave and climbed in the white extended cab. They pulled out onto the dirt track and began the slow drive over the washboard road.

Chapter Twenty-Eight

John underestimated Rebecca's will to live. Despite the frequent injections of Ketamine and the continuous rapes, she clung to life, never giving up hope, waiting for a chance to flee. Her body became weak from malnutrition and her system fried from the repeated doses of Special K.

Once in a while she caught a glimpse of a large, blonde-haired woman bending over the bed. She was pretty sure that she knew her from somewhere but the memories were disappearing more and more each day. John kept her isolated in the small bedroom but occasionally she could hear him talking to someone.

"For God sake feed the girl. Here I brought you some soup and a cold sandwich for her. You must feed her or she will die from all the dope you're giving her," Barbara begged. She did not want to go trolling again.

"She doesn't seem hungry. Doesn't say much anyway. Still breathing, still warm to the touch." He snickered as he said the words. "Plenty more where she came from. Still this one's pretty good. Nice piece of ass."

"Getting way too skinny I'd say," Barb stated in a matter of fact way. She was careful not to anger John these days. The last time they fought she had to take a week off work because of a black eye that no amount of make-up would cover. She couldn't risk anyone asking questions.

As fall approached, John began leaving Rebecca untied but he still shut her in the small room. Once, he forgot to fasten the latch on the enclosure and she was able to wander about his shop, examining his tools and looking out the window. He discovered his error when Sarah spoke up at suppertime.

"Mommy, there's someone in the shop. I saw her in the window when Dad was out feeding the cows. She had a grey-coloured face and long dark hair. Why is she in the shop? I'm not allowed in there. Why is she?"

"Don't be silly, Sarah. There's no one in the shop," said John. "You watch way too much TV. It must be hurting your eyes."

Sarah reached up and rubbed at her eyes. "No, my eyes are still there. They're good."

"Christ," swore her father. "Dumber than a post," he muttered under his breath.

Barbara glared at John. She hated it when he talked like that. Sarah was very sensitive and it was so easy to hurt her feelings.

"Daddy's only kidding you. The neighbour lady was over getting a wrench for her husband. They had to fix their car." She smiled and ruffled the girl's blond curls.

Sarah turned back to the television unaware of the look that passed between her parents. John rose quickly and went out to the shop. Barb noticed all the shop lights come on and then the shouting began. Deliberately blocking out the violent images that began flooding her mind; she reached over and increased the volume on the TV. She couldn't protect the girl. She had to stay in here and look after her Sarah.

****

After a while, John found it less and less stimulating playing with his inert victim. He needed more. He began weaning her off the drug and beating her into submission. Then as he approached his climax, he wrapped his meaty hands around her neck and squeezed, choking her into unconsciousness. This became his new obsession. The more Rebecca resisted the more he enjoyed himself.

A black diesel truck pulled into the yard. John could hear it idling as he finished with the girl. He quickly latched the door and left the shop.

"Hey there. What can I do for you?" he asked the driver getting out of the cab. "You need something?"

"You John? Kevin from the wreckers told me you might have an axle for my old Dodge. Hope you don't mind my dropping by. Couldn't call first. Got no cell phone."

John looked at him suspiciously. He rarely got visitors and didn't much welcome them, especially the unexpected kind. This one seemed legit enough. He desperately tried to remember the conditions in the shop. Yes, he had closed her door but had he locked it?

"Yeah, I got a couple of axles that might do. Give me a sec and I'll shut the dog in. Not too friendly that one." He re-entered the shop.

"Get in your kennel," he demanded. "Get in." Quickly crossing the shop floor he checked on the girl and saw that she was lying sprawled on the bed just as he had left her. Latching the door and turning up the radio, playing on the counter, to muffle any noises she might make; he retraced his steps.

"I'm Stan," the trucker said as he offered his hand. "Like I said, I'm sorry for coming without calling first."

"It's okay now. My bitch is in the kennel. You can come in." They spent the better part of an hour sorting through parts and talking about rebuilding old autos.

"You want a beer? Got some cold ones in the house."

"Be great. I got time for one before I head back into town. The old lady doesn't come home from work until past seven. Works at the 7-11 in Bainsbridge, over by the tracks," Stan said as he followed John into the farmhouse. They took a seat at the table.

Stan looked over at Sarah who was engrossed in her shows.

"Hi, there missy. What's your name?"

"Sarah." She went back to her program.

"Not very friendly, is she?"

John frowned. "Pay her no mind. You know how moody teenagers are." He changed the subject quickly and they resumed talking about restoring vehicles.

A little past six, Barbara came home and the visitor took his leave.

****

Gradually the young woman became aware of her surroundings. Carefully she opened her eyes and glanced around. He was gone. Slowly she eased herself off the bed and went into the bathroom.

As she stared into the grimy mirror, over the filthy sink, she could see the results of the latest beating. Huge welts were forming around her throat and the bruising was starting. She shuddered as she thought about what caused these injuries. Her memory was the clearest right after a session and then it began to fade. She washed herself the best she could with the dirty washcloth and cold water from the single faucet.

Something caught her attention near the base of the toilet. She held on to the sink bending down cautiously to see what it was. It seemed to be a syringe with some clear fluid in the chamber. Her torturer must have dropped it. Snatching it up quickly, she froze listening for John's return. Hearing nothing, she made her way back to the cot. She placed the needle under the mattress close to the head of the small bed.

The next day, John returned to the shop earlier than usual. Not expecting him so soon the girl was dozing on the cot listening to the faint music coming from the shop radio. Suddenly he was there standing over her. The malevolent glint in his eyes told her exactly what was in store for her.

"Please, please no more," she begged. "Ahh," she screamed as he wrenched her head off the greasy pillow and stripped off her soiled sweatshirt and then her pants.

"Shut up you little whore," gasped John as he once again began to beat her.

She rapidly succumbed to the beating and seemed to pass out quickly as he choked her. She forced herself to lie still as he got up off the bed.

"Bitch that was hardly worth the effort" he growled and moved off into the bathroom. It was too late; he felt the needle plunge into his neck. The drugs did their work leaving him paralysed on the floor.

She yanked on her jeans and moved towards the shop door. Quietly, she slipped from her prison and into the woods. As she stumbled along barefooted through the dense bush, she heard the sounds of trucks moving along the highway. She made her way slowly to the side of the road. Lights came towards her and brakes screeched as the semi came to a halt.

****

What the hell?

He would never forget the sight of the half-naked girl kneeling in supplication beside the road. Her outstretched arms pleading for help. Jamming on the brakes, he skidded as he brought the rig to a stop several meters down the road. The flashers on his rig pulsated in the night, illuminating his frantic race back to the waif-like creature.

"Oh my God. What's wrong with you?"

She collapsed in a heap, her pale face showing no sign of intelligence. Scooping her up, the truck driver carried his light burden to his cab. Placing her as gently as he could in the bunk behind the driver's seat; he radioed dispatch to send for the police and an ambulance.

Later, as the police questioned her in her hospital room in Port Franklin, it became apparent that the victim had no memory of any recent events. In fact she had very little memory of anything that had happened to her. She knew her name was Mary Beth, but that was all.

With her long dark hair and dusky complexion, she looked as though she might be of Aboriginal descent. Traces of the drug Ketamine were found in her system and it was obvious she had been severely beaten, raped and starved. The local police sent a detailed report to the Fort Sumac detachment, attention Hunter Campbell.

Chapter Twenty-Nine

That night Maya's emotions flipped back and forth between frustration and hope. She tossed in her bunk as she remembered her frantic conversation with Hunter. At least someone knew she was Joe's prisoner. He hadn't confronted Joe and taken her to safety; he had abandoned her. She alternated between liking the ruggedly handsome man to despising him for leaving her to her own devices. In the end, optimism won and she decided she would have to trust that Hunter would be true to his word. He would come back in two days. He had to.

After a fitful night of tossing and turning in her cot, she finally drifted off to sleep, only to be woken by Joe shaking her shoulder.

"Christ, you're dead to the world this morning. Get yourself together. Past six-thirty and the boats are out for the day. Tim's gone to town for parts, but there'll still be two guides and four guests wanting supper tonight. You can do double bread so as to get ahead."

Maya mumbled, "Okay," and then waited for Joe to leave the tent before she got out of bed. Dressing quickly, she made her way out of the tent and into her chore-packed day.

"We're going to need more flour soon. When's the truck coming in—this Thursday or next?" she asked Joe.

"This. If we have to buy bread, we will. Save most of the flour for the cakes and pies."

The satellite phone buzzed. Maya automatically went to answer it.

Joe slapped her hand away. "You don't ever touch that phone, girl," he hissed.

"Hello, Joe here. Right, Mr. R. Right. Copy that. Pick up on Wednesday. The truck comes into camp on Thursday. It'll be a pretty quick turnaround… No, we can manage. Just have to. No big deal. Done it this quick before. Right. Joe out."

She watched as Joe replaced the receiver and reached for the radio mike.

"River Bend to *River Girl*, do you copy?"

"Roger, River Bend. Bob here. What's up Joe?"

"Overtime next two nights. Tell Jason, and I'll update Tim when he gets back from town. Real quick turnaround this time. Bringing in Dave and Mike to help handle the cargo."

"Okay. Got it. See you later. Bob out."

Maya pretended to concentrate on measuring the sugar for the rhubarb pies. She listened as Joe made some quick calls. He made sure the truck was on schedule, and then she heard him order several dozen loaves of bakery bread. After finishing up the pies, she asked Joe if she could make halibut soufflé for supper. She explained how she didn't need to be in the kitchen if he finished cooking it forty minutes before serving. The soufflé, crusty sourdough bread, and a huge tossed salad would make an excellent, easy meal.

"Sure, fine. Getting tired of the same old thing. Be nice to have a change. Defrost the halibut that Tim got last week." Hearing a truck pull in, Joe left to see if it was Tim returning from town.

Alone with her thoughts, Maya quickly came to the understanding that another drug transfer was in the works. Wednesday was tomorrow. If the truck was due this Thursday that meant the guides would be loading the truck late Thursday night. There was very little time for Hunter to get his team together. Hopefully, he had already contacted headquarters and requested backup. Still, Hunter was only expecting to free her; the police might not be prepared to intercept a drug transfer.

As much as she wanted to be free of Joe, now was the time to catch the gang in full operation. She hated what drugs did to those who became dependent on their next fix. Her best friend in high school had succumbed to the stranglehold of Meth. Several of Chad's acquaintances had also used and abused drugs. Their lives had been ruined by the constant need for one more high. Yes, she thought, Joe could go to jail for a very long time. That was the very least the low-life deserved.

After finishing up in the kitchen, she went to find him.

"It's all pretty easy. Just beat up the egg whites and fold them into the mixture in the steel bowl. Pour the works over the halibut and cook it for forty minutes at 425. Turns out great. I've never had it fail. Mind you don't open the oven door until it's time, or it'll go flat." With that, she turned and went up to the washhouse. It had been a very hot day and she longed for a cooling shower.

This evening, the eagles barely kept her interest. She startled at every little sound from the woods. Hunter was late and she was beginning to doubt that he would show. It had already turned seven. Forcing herself to stay calm, she watched as the male eagle returned to the nest with a small rodent clutched in his talons.

"I brought you something." Hunter had come quietly up behind her and dropped a chocolate bar into her lap.

"I thought you weren't coming. It got so late. There's so much I have to tell you!" blurted Maya as she burst into tears.

Hunter reached out gathered Maya into his strong arms.

"I said I'd try and come back, didn't I? No need for tears. You can count on me. Tell me, what's up?"

Maya relayed the latest information including the satellite phone call from a Mr. R.

"Hunter, I want to bury these guys. You have to catch them in the act. I know you'll only get the River Bend crew, but at least that will be something. Maybe they'll give up the rest of the people involved." Hunter could see her eyes shining with excitement. Finally, after weeks of being at the mercy of these thugs, she had a chance for revenge.

She watched as Hunter took in her words. Relief was written in his eyes.

He knew she wanted her freedom but she was willing to wait for it. She wanted justice more.

Maya could scarcely breathe. All the pain and suffering she had endured over the last few weeks would be worth nothing, if they didn't stop these drug runners.

Maya listened carefully as Hunter outlined his plan. It was quite straightforward and depended on the element of surprise.

"I'll gather the team in the woods outside the small campsite that's beside the lake on the dirt road. It's about six kilometres away. Once I've briefed everyone, we'll make our way through the bush to River Bend. We'll have to use darkness for cover, so you might have difficulty seeing us coming. If we are to nail these perps, we have to get as much evidence as possible. My guys will have to videotape the men handling the drugs and concealing them in the truck. No one will make a move until I signal the take down." Hunter paused to make sure she was listening.

"It's going to be up to you to ensure your own safety. You will have to escape from the immediate area, if you are to be safe from any possible gunfire."

"I can't go anywhere. I'll set off the collar," Maya reminded him. "But I could ask Joe if I should make sandwiches. I could tell him I was going up to the kitchen for sandwiches and coffee."

"Yah, that sounds natural enough. Good idea," he agreed. "I'll wait until you are on the way up the path and out of the line of fire, before I give the signal to attack. Hide in the bushes until it's safe to come out."

Maya felt his arms draw her into a quick hug and then loosen. Unwilling to give up the only comfort she had in months, she wrapped her arms around his waist. Standing in his solid embrace, she let herself relax. She felt his lips brush the top of her head, and then he was off moving silently through the undergrowth.

Chapter Thirty

It took several moments for John to clear his head as he regained consciousness on the gritty floor. Staggering to the girl's room, his gut twisted in fear. It was empty and she was gone. The shop door swung lazily on its hinges, in the afternoon sun.

Panicked, he punched Barb's work number into his shop phone.

"Stilman Vet Clinic. How may I help you?"

"Barb, it's me John. She's taken off. She's run off somewhere. For Christ sake get home quick."

Barbara hastily hung up the phone. This was the worst possible outcome. Never before had one of them ever escaped. They all died. Now, they would be in serious trouble if she couldn't find the little tramp. If the girl got to the cops all would be over. Sarah would certainly be put into foster care if anything happened to her or John. She had to move quickly. It would be next to impossible to locate her if she got deep into the bush that surrounded their place. If she got to the highway, they were truly screwed.

She knocked on the examining room door. Pushing open the door, she interrupted Dr. Stilman as he checked over a litter of kittens.

"Dr. Stilman, I have to go. There's a bit of an emergency at home. John's burnt himself with the welding torch. I'll see you tomorrow." She grabbed her purse and left quickly before he any chance to ask questions.

Gravel flew from her tires as she came to a jarring stop in front of the house.

"John, John, I'm here," she called as she jumped out of the car. "What in hell happened?"

John angrily explained; showing her the puncture mark on his neck. Still swaying drunkenly from the effects of the small amount of the drug, he sat down heavily on the front steps. He was in no shape to help. As usual, it would be up to her to fix the situation.

"Any idea which way she went?"

John shook his head in frustration. "I didn't see. I was out." He roughly grabbed her arm bringing her up hard against him.

"Get out there and don't come back until you get the little witch," he demanded throwing her against the car. "Find her or we're all fucked."

Barbara dashed into the shop and took a couple of syringes of Special K from John's stash. Then she climbed back into the Honda and began driving the roads.

****

Searching along the highway and the side roads yielded no results. Her last hope was the dirt road to River Bend. If she couldn't find her there, she'd have to start looking in the woods. It was well past eleven when she wearily veered right and began to bounce over the washboard towards Joe's place.

Chapter Thirty-One

Parking his unit in the far corner of the campsite away from the direct view of the dirt road, Hunter set up his headquarters. He had to contact his superiors and get a team in place. Hunter punched Captain Smythe's number on his cell phone.

"Hunter here, have some results, but I'm going to need a team here as soon as possible. Do you have any Emergency Response Team personnel in the vicinity?"

"Not really. Kyle's on holidays and Justin pulled a groin muscle and is on sick leave for a couple of weeks."

"Oh damn, I guess there is time to send the Fort Sumac guys if they leave right away."

Hunter then filled in Captain Smythe on the facts, as he knew them.

"Yes, it was a stroke of luck to find the girl. She is in pretty rough shape but she's more than willing to hold tight so we can bust these guys. This Joe fella has done a number on her. We can get him for rape, unlawful confinement and torture, as well as any drug-related charges we can make stick. Best send down a victim's service woman as well as the Emergency Response Team. She's going to need someone." Hunter paused as his boss fired questions at him.

"No, Captain Smythe, we have no idea on the identity of Mr. R. Perhaps Joe and the boys will give him up. We will be able to book most of the guides for trafficking and Joe, Bob and Tim for kidnapping. I'm hoping this all goes down without casualties. I'd sure like to see them pay big time."

"Oh, Hunter listen up," Smythe added. "We got a report for you from the Port Franklin unit. A trucker brought a badly beaten, half-starved female to the hospital last night. Docs say she's suffering from amnesia and had traces of a powerful tranquilizer in her system. Want to check it out later? The victim isn't going anywhere in a hurry. Social Services has been called but she is in too bad shape to be released yet."

****

A silent group of men stood beside the lake that Thursday morning. Hunter assessed the Emergency Response Team that had arrived shortly before midnight. Robert, the oldest and father of three boys, brought with him twenty years of experience in detective work. Hunter had worked closely with him on the missing girls' task force for several years now. Trusting in Robert's integrity, experience and skills; he made him his second in command.

Geordie was young but had phenomenal skills with surveillance equipment. He had seen action in both Ottawa and Victoria. His audio and videotapes had been instrumental in sealing the fate of several high government officials, with fraud charges, a few years ago.

Doug was relatively new on the force, but he came with high recommendations from the Toronto bureau. He was the smallest of the men, having just met the height requirements for joining the force. He compensated for his stature by being an avid gym rat. Between all of them, they had over thirty years of knowledge and training. Smythe had sent a strong, experienced team.

Drawing a map of the River Bend camp, Hunter went over the locations of the lodge, tents, washhouse, and docks. He then showed them two possible routes through the wooded area between this lakeside camp and the River Bend camp. Hunter meticulously detailed their plan of attack.

"We can't rush in too quickly. Geordie has to have time to video each one of them handling the drugs. That'll be key evidence when we get to trial. Then there's the girl, Maya. We have to give her time to get out of the way. She can't go too far without setting off an alarm. If she does, Joe shocks her into submission. Yeah, you heard that right. The sadist has a dog restraint collar on her. The perimeter stakes are run pretty tight around the main part of the camp and up into the woods to Joe's tent. Her plan is to hide in the bushes, so be careful if we have to fire off any rounds."

The men listened intently to Hunter as he outlined their individual assignments. They respected him as their leader and voiced their agreement with his simple but effective plan.

Hunter observed the team as they concentrated on checking and rechecking their equipment. After he had answered a few more questions and fine-tuned the attack plan, the group settled in to wait for dusk. Each man had his own method of preparing for the attack. Some dozed in the heat of the afternoon sun while others went for a brief jog down the unpaved road.

As the sun sank in the western sky, Hunter called his team together and led them into the woods. Moving quietly over the uneven terrain, the heavily armed men slowly began closing the gap between themselves and River Bend.

It was rough going through the scrubby bush in combat gear, but the team pushed on drawing on their years of experience and highly-honed skills.

Darkness fell as they approached the edge of the campsite. Hunter raised his hand and pointed to his night goggles. Each man silently switched on his night vision gear, and Geordie readied his camera equipment. Separating into pairs, the team moved in, taking up positions near the fuel dock. The long wait began.

Shortly after eleven, Hunter heard Joe tramping down the path to the fuel dock. He was talking to Bob and Tim. In one hand Joe was carrying a rifle which he carefully placed beside a tree at the edge of the pathway. Surprised, Hunter noted that both Bob and Tim were also packing weapons. Handguns were in holsters hanging from their belts. He wondered if the men were expecting trouble or if they were simply being cautious given the value of the cargo. He silently signalled to his men that the perpetrators were armed.

A low chugging sound drifted over the water. Two of the Boston Whalers were being moved slowly over from the boat dock. As each boat reached the fuel dock, it was securely tied to the dock's mooring rings. An engine started in the parking lot. Roy brought the van over to the waiting guides.

"It's gonna be a bloody long night with just us," Bob complained to Joe. "Why don't you go get that useless tit of a girl? She can at least help load the stuff. When are you gonna off her? She knows too much. That piece of tail will be the end of us if you're not careful."

"You mind who you're talking to," Joe said evenly. "*I* say what goes around here. The season's coming to an end soon, and so is she. You fetch her from the tent and tell her she's to help with packing the van."

Bob moved off into the woods, and the guides began transferring the drugs from the duffel bags in the small boats. Ripping open the duffel bags; they piled the off-white bricks on the wharf.

Hunter watched as Geordie made sure he recorded each of the guides and Roy handling the cargo. Joe was videotaped as he stood directing the operation. Roy opened up the van and began stripping out the panels and the floorboards. The high pitched whine of the power drill reverberated in the night air. Little conversation passed between the workers as they began packing the drugs into the compartments. Silently the policemen waited for Hunter's signal.

Chapter Thirty-Two

Maya was roughly shaken awake. Bob was standing over her cot. It was almost dark but she could see that he was in a foul mood.

"Get up you lazy cow. Joe wants you to help with the unloading and to rustle up some grub for us," he growled.

"Okay, okay. I'm getting up. Leave me alone for God's sake."

****

Joe glanced up as Bob returned pushing Maya in front of him.

"Here she is. Want the bitch to load or go make up some food?"

"She can load for a while," replied Joe.

Joe looked meaningfully towards the rifle. "Get your ass on that boat and pass the bricks up to Bob and Tim. Mike and Dave will show you what to do."

Maya climbed on board one of the whalers and looked at Dave. The short wiry man grunted and pointed to some plastic-wrapped packages in a duffel bag.

"Unpack those and hand them to me. Don't take all day. We have at least twenty more bags to do."

Recognizing the bags and their contents from the beach, Maya knew that this was it. The drug transfer had begun.

Unable to see from where she was on the boat, whether or not Hunter and his men were hidden in the bush, Maya began to panic. She waited for over an hour. As she emptied another bag she said, "Dave, I have to ask Joe about the coffee. I'll be back in a sec."

Maya slid past Dave, climbed up on deck and on to the wharf.

"Hey Joe. Should I go get some coffee started? Looks like it might be a good time. I can bring back some sandwiches too, if you want."

"You do that," Joe responded curtly.

As Maya sped quickly up the path towards the kitchen, she caught sight of a heavily armed man hiding behind the washhouse. When she was out of sight of the men unloading the boats, Maya doubled back and crouched down in the brush. She had a clear view of Joe and could see most of what was going on from where she was shielded by the shrubbery. Although prickly bushes scratched at her bare arms, she didn't dare move around. She steeled herself for what could be a long wait. Still, the police waited on Hunter's signal.

After making sure Maya had had enough time to make it out of range, Hunter spoke quietly into his radio.

"On my count of seven, go. One, two…" The team rapidly stood up, drew their guns, and charged towards the unsuspecting men.

"Christ! What the hell's going on?" Joe leapt towards the rifle that was leaning against the pine tree. Hunter, leading with his shoulder, tackled his target, knocking Joe to the dirt. As Joe fell, the transmitter on his belt dislodged and tumbled to the ground. Hunter simultaneously yanked Joe to his feet and brought his foot down, crushing the transmitter. The instrument of torture lay shattered in a dozen pieces.

Out of the corner of his eye, Hunter saw movement as Maya stood up from behind a bush, turn, and begin to run in the direction of the road. He quickly secured Joe's hands with handcuffs and let him fall to the ground once again.

"Stay there, you son of a bitch. You move and you're dead."

Joe stayed where he was, lying sprawled beside the fuel dock.

Mitzy began barking wildly. Roy glanced fearfully around, scooped his little dog up, and took off running into the bush. Doug fired one shot over Roy's head. Terrified, Roy fell heavily to the ground still clutching Mitzy in his arms.

As the Emergency Response Team approached with their guns drawn, Bob and Tim had raised their hands in surrender. In their surprise, neither guide had thought to go for their weapons. The team disarmed them and then advanced on the other two men in the boats.

Dave succeeded in starting the boat's engine only to discover the craft was still tied to the fuel dock. He raised his hands in defeat.

The sounds of a splash and then frantic flailing of arms carried in the night air as Mike attempted to flee in the river. As a spotlight illuminated him struggling in the water, he too saw that escape was futile.

Soon all the drug traffickers were subdued and forced to lie like driftwood on the ground. Only one shot had been fired.

Hunter yelled, "Maya! Maya, wait!" There was no response, just the sound of Roy moaning in fear and his dog whining anxiously while it licked its owner's face.

"Robert, take command here. Gotta go after the girl. She doesn't know where she's heading." With that sharp command to Robert and a quick check of the immediate scene, Hunter dashed in the direction Maya had gone.

"Maya! Maya!" he called as he charged headlong through the scrub. Bushes whipped at his face, and roots and holes in the ground threatened to trip him as he pounded through the woods. On and on he ran as the night suddenly turned cold. A steady rain began pelting down, drowning out the sound of his voice.

Chapter Thirty-Three

Rain started to pour down, soaking Maya's hair and clothes. Still she ran and ran, slipping and tumbling over the rough, wet terrain. Once, she thought she heard someone call her name, but the sound was lost in the heavy downpour.

Unsure of which way to go, she paused trying to get her bearings. Her hair fell in her eyes, and her clothes were now plastered to her body. The drenching rain was bone-chilling cold. She scanned the woods, panicking that she was lost. For all she knew, she could have turned around and was now running back in the direction of the camp. *Calm down,* she willed herself. *Calm down.*

Harsh, quick breaths escaped her lips as she fought for self-control. What if the raid had gone wrong? What if Hunter had been killed? She knew Joe would not be afraid to use that gun. She couldn't depend on anyone; it was up to her to get to safety. The last thing she needed was to be recaptured by Joe. He would kill her for sure.

Noise of someone crashing through rain-soaked bush suddenly reached her ears. *Run! Run!* These were the only thoughts coursing through her mind. So Maya ran.

She fled along the trail until her feet felt the hard-packed dirt road beneath her shoes. As she stood there in the rain, breathing in harsh ragged gasps, she saw a flickering light. A small car was bobbing and weaving its way up the rough road. Since she didn't recognize the car from camp, she jumped out onto the side of the road and frantically tried to flag the car down.

The car slowed but didn't stop. As it passed by, it hit one of the water filled potholes, sending up a spray of water soaking her jeans. Relief flooded through her veins as she saw it was a woman driving. She waved and waved to attract the woman's attention. The car braked and slowed as it reached the bend. Desperately, Maya began chasing after the vehicle.

Then the car came to a stop a short ways up the road; a blonde-haired lady got out.

"Help me, Help me!" Maya begged as she reached the car.

"What are you doing out here in this weather?" the woman asked kindly. Before Maya could answer, the woman said, "You know what? You don't have to tell me."

She went to the back of the car and opened the trunk. Dragging out a painter's drop cloth, she opened the passenger door and spread the cloth over the seat. "Come on, get in. Just sit on this plastic so all that mud doesn't ruin the seat, okay? Do you want me to take you to town?"

Maya simply nodded, and the blonde compassionately helped her into the car and closed the door.

The chilly rain and the overwhelming stress of this night's events made Maya weary. She leaned against the seat thankful to be out of the weather. The plastic crinkled under her and stuck to her wet hands.

As Maya sat on the cold plastic, shivering and exhausted, her intuition kicked in. Every nerve became taut and her gut told her something was dreadfully wrong.

The older woman climbed into the driver's side and looked at Maya. Their eyes met. Maya heard an ominous click as the driver locked the car doors. Fumbling with the handle, she managed to unlock the door and push it open. She fled, lurching up the road trying to get away from this strange woman. She slipped and slid as she tried to gain purchase on the muddy surface. Falling to her knees, she fought valiantly to regain her footing. It was no use. Maya had no more energy left. She was unable to fight or flee.

Hands grabbed her from behind. As Maya felt a sharp pain in her arm, she glimpsed Hunter coming out of the bush. Her screams rose into the night sky. Again and again she shrieked as she was dragged backwards by her hair. She seemed to be floating out of her body. Then she felt nothing, nothing at all.

Chapter Thirty-Four

Hunter emerged panting from the bush in time to hear Maya's panicked screams and see her struggling with a woman dressed in a light canvas jacket and blue jeans. The contest was a brief one, ending with Maya falling limply into the stranger's arms. Dragging Maya by her head and hair, the woman shoved her into the passenger seat of a small, dark blue car. The tall blonde slammed the door shut and then bolted around to the driver's side and clambered in. The car jerked and skidded as the accelerator was punched to the floor.

Instinct and training took over. Shooting from a kneeling position, Hunter took out both the front and back right tires. The car screeched along, dragging its rims. Sparks flew as metal rubbed on metal. As the car halted, the driver's door flew open and the woman fled into the night. He could hear crashing sounds growing fainter as she moved off through the timber.

Reaching the car, Hunter saw Maya slumped against the door. His eyes riveted to the drop cloth covering the seat. A chill shook the seasoned cop as he hauled her body out of the car and laid her beside it.

Hunter's fingers checked the side of Maya's neck and found a faint pulse. She was barely breathing. With Maya lying like a rag doll sprawled in the drenching rain, Hunter radioed to his men.

"I need back up and an ambulance here on the camp road about ten kilometres from the highway. I have the girl. She's alive, but barely. She could be drugged. There's a syringe here on the seat in the car. Some blonde woman took off running into the bush. Send the medics fast. I don't know how long this girl can last."

He then called the detachment in Port Franklin.

"Sgt. Baker please," he told the dispatcher. "This is Hunter Campbell. I need to speak to Sgt. Baker."

Sgt. Baker came on the line. "Hey Hunter, how can we help? Thought you were coming in tomorrow to interview the girl."

"Things are moving faster than I can handle. Took down a drug transfer tonight and I am waiting on an ambulance for an injured female. I'm out on the dirt road that leads to Joe's fish camp… you know River Bend. I need you to send some good trackers to this area. An unidentified female took off into the bush and I can't give chase. Have to stay with the victim until she is transported. She's hanging on by a thread."

"Not much point in trying to track in this weather. The perp will get cold in the wet bush tonight. She won't be able to make much headway. I've got a real good tracker by the name of Merv Wilcox. He's a cowboy out of Mason. Can get him there by morning. You need any help with the drug bust?"

"No. All good there. My team has it covered. Send a couple of men out here to secure the scene and to wait for your guy Merv. Not hard to find the location, there's a blue Honda with no right side rubber in the middle of the road. It isn't going anywhere. Can you meet me at the hospital? I'll catch a ride in the ambulance."

"Will do."

Sgt. Baker immediately dispatched officers to Hunter's locale. Soon the wail of the ambulance and the sirens of the police cars could be heard as they sped up the highway.

As Hunter held Maya in his arms, his thoughts raced. *What a strange and unexpected turn of events this was. Who would have suspected the Valley of Despair killer might be a woman? Women didn't fit the profile of a serial killer. Usually, a woman's motive was revenge or jealousy.* Then his thoughts jumped back to the present. *Had his men secured the camp scene? Would the ambulance find them in time?*

He checked her pulse again. It felt weaker and she was steadily losing body temperature. Wrapping his jacket securely around the slight girl, he clutched Maya tighter, gazing down at her matted hair, filthy face, and soggy clothes. After all she'd been through; this girl deserved a whole lot better than this.

Feeling a presence watching him, Hunter glanced upwards towards the trees. He could see an eagle perched on a spruce snag, sheltering from the downpour of frigid rain.

With a sharp call, the magnificent bird wearily stretched its wings and took off into the night sky. It circled once and called again. As the eagle disappeared over the treetops, Hunter felt Maya stir. The torch had been passed.

CPSIA information can be obtained at www.ICGtesting.com
Printed in the USA
LVOW11s0532240316

480552LV00001B/5/P